the black guy

Dedicated to: Foluke and Mahalia, daddy loves you.
The crew at 42: Jackie, Brian, Paul, Steven, Clive, Colin, Les,
Lorraine, Esther, Ian. I'm always looking forward with haste to
being with you guys.
Dad, Auntie and Uncle Vin. We couldn't have asked for better
role models.
The memories of Marlene Joyce Sailsman, Clostilda Salmon,
Hugh Henry Salmon, Sister Mabel Peddie, who dwell in eternal
peace.
My sister Pat – so far away but always in our hearts.
Caroline, forever true.
Malcom, you feel like Blood.

Credits and thanks

Cover Photography	Mike Williams
Cover Design	Andrew Evans (875 Design)
Editing	Caroline Grant
Production	Mike Taylor
Comments, assistance and encouragement	Elaine Anglin
	Caroline Grant
	Malcolm Hinds

the black guy

John Sailsman

TWIN FLAMES

Published by Twin Flames
Creative Development and Consulting, PO Box 2771, Reading RG30 2FU

Published in United Kingdom by:
Twin Flames. An imprint of Creative Development & Consulting
PO Box 2771, Reading RG30 2FU

ISBN 0 9533858 1 7

British Cataloguing in publication is available.

Printed by Antony Rowe Limited

Distributed in UK by Turnaround Distribution,
Unit 3, Olympia Trading Estate, Coburg Road, London N22 6TZ.
Tel: 0181 829 3000   Fax: 0181 881 5088

"Whether she be Black or white,
The enemy is not a woman that loves you."

Anonymous

prologue

Amanda Poulter wandered around Kensington with large bags of shopping in tow. She was nearing the car park where she had parked her Mercedes and was cursing under her breath for not having brought someone along to help her, because the bags were so heavy.

She had just finished doing most of the High Street shops and Harrods was to be her final call. As she approached the car park she wondered about what she should buy. She ended her ephemeral contemplation by deciding what she should have once she got in there. As she neared the Mercedes, she searched clumsily for the key. She had to drop the bags to find it. When she did, she released the automatic alarm and the central locking switches to allow herself in. She opened the big boot of the car and stuffed the shopping carefully to one side making space for the other set of bags that were to come. Then she slammed the door shut, applied the central locking and the alarm once again before zipping off to continue her spree.

Once back outside, her attention was drawn to a children's clothes shop that displayed what she considered to be the most beautiful array of clothing. She stopped and stared through the window at them as though transfixed. A smile appeared on her face as she imagined herself walking around busy streets hand in hand with a child adorned in some of the fashions that she was looking at. She became lost in thought. Her fantasy had taken her. When she snapped back into the land of the living, trickles of rain had begun to drop. They mingled with tears that she hadn't realised she had shed. She wiped them away, at the same time looking around to see if anyone had noticed her. Once satisfied with her appearance, she strolled hastily on to Harrods allowing the memory of her momentary lapse into fancy to subside.

one

The club was hot. The paled echo of misty red, yellow and blue lights only added to the feeling as they fell seductively onto the scantily clothed bodies that had crowded the dance floor. Thumping bass notes seared through the sweaty atmosphere as countless bodies writhed in a vain attempt to maintain its consistent rhythm. Some people were hardly concerned about looking good. Others, in fact most of them, looked silly and were proud of it.

'Crinkles' was a fascinating place. It was large and in the round. The revellers were able to stand on two floors. Those at the top occupied fancy couches, whilst others leaned over balconies that stretched right the way round the room watching the prancers jig unmajestically about the dance floor. Hundreds of people were milling about on the bottom deck. Most were not interested in watching the main dance area, but rather engaged in the type of socialising that was a typical pastime at this type of venue. Girls were flirting as the guys did the eyeing up, chatting up, shouting and propping up of the bars. The whole space accommodated over 5,000 people that were mainly white. The atmosphere was electric.

Ricky and Ingin were unimpressed. They stood watching the dancers, both with one hand in their pockets, and holding their respective glasses of lager. Ingin rocked his head slowly, hardly allowing his long dreadlocks to move, but sufficiently enough to suggest that he could possibly get into what was going on. Ricky was motionless as he watched the movement both before him and across the other side of the room.

They were two of possibly only about twenty black people in the whole club. They knew few people except for the odd old school friend, or some guy that they had played amateur football with at some point on some distant Sunday morning, or some woman that they might have worked with or knew from school. It was a Friday night and the two friends had fancied a change of scene from the Reggae dancehall vibes that they were used to. Ricky was more into 'swing' and 'R&B' music and was perhaps more used to going to nightclubs than Ingin was. But they both considered the music boring. They were used to hearing loads of bass in their music, but not so much of the BPM's or the shrill acoustic noises that made modern day house music so dramatic yet so poppy.

The experience was also an education. Not so much a new lesson but more a reaffirmation to them of the fact that white people simply can not dance. Well at least most of them. Of the few that could, only a couple of them showed natural ability. The others looked like they had been trained. Ricky would regularly shift his head back with a disgusted "tuh!" noise every time he noticed someone trying to dance but looking more like a chicken with elbows flapping monotonously from side to side. They clumsily stamped their feet as if they were doing a frenzied marching band type of movement. Ingin turned to Ricky slowly then walked off signalling him to follow, which he did in an instant. It was time to circle again. A steady walk around the club eyeing up the talent was now a necessity, and it was the type of thing that they did every time they got bored and needed a bit more excitement. Just to show how much they needed it, this was about their tenth circle for the night.

As they steadily breezed through the crowds, they would gain the attention of onlookers. Ingin, the older of the two, was conspicuous by his large muscular frame, his long dreads, beard and dark looks. Big round eyes peered from a hardened face that had seen much streetlife, much hardship and much weed. He easily housed a 44-inch chest and his strong arms, tucked inside a long silk grandfather shirt, the length of which he extended beyond the waist of his trousers, were clearly visible. He was pert and his waist was slightly tucked in, revealing a shapely bottom standing atop thick thighs that made his Herculean presentation complete. His sway was steady and confident and drew many admirers, mostly women who, even if engaged, would sneak either a quick glance or blatantly give a double take. He frightened male onlookers. If they were coming his way they would quickly make space for him to ease past or they wouldn't look at him at all. That was the white guys. Black guys were different. They would see him coming, slightly heave and then relax, all the time keeping their eyes on him. They knew his type. Intimidating but friendly.

Ricky was less intimidating. His boyish good looks, short straight brushed hair and evenly trim frame won him many female admirers. Women told him that he had dreamy, 'come to bed' eyes as they were narrow with heavily curled eyelashes. His nose was broad but finely sculptured. He had thick brown lips and dimples emerged in his cheeks when he smiled. He face was drawn, though not so as to make him appear tired. He had a finely honed facial bone structure. His neck was thick, though not overtly so, but it stood on a set of broad shoulders. His chest was muscular and its contours could be seen clearly, as he had put much work in at the gym. His frame was neither broad nor slight, but he had obviously perfected his look and the expressions on the women's faces as he walked passed suggested that he was 'to die for'. He was a stylish dresser too. A black Nehru jacket sat over a white silk grandfather shirt that, just like Ingin's, ran down past his waist, covering a pair of black matching slacks. A gold crucifix adorned his chest. He had a stud in one ear and a tiny cross hung from a gold ring in the other. A single gold ring on the middle finger of his right hand completed his modest array of jewellery. Unlike Ingin whose neck seemed weighed down with trinket-like gold things hanging from six seemingly long and heavy gold chains.

As they walked around, easing their way past the marauding human traffic, Ricky suddenly became transfixed. So much so that he stopped cold. He stared long and hard at the woman that had grabbed his attention then turned away in embarrassment. Once away from her glare he took a couple of steps forward and leaned against the balcony to watch what was happening on the dancefloor. He had been taken so much by surprise that he had forgotten that he was with company. He was soon reminded of that fact when Ingin approached him. He had with a slightly embarrassed look on his face.

"What happened to you guy?" he queried with a half-worried tone. "How come you just let me walk off on my own?"

Ricky was cautious.

"Listen man, don't let her see you," he said, "but look at the woman behind you. The one in the red. Tell me what you think."

Ricky should have known better than to ask Ingin to be subtle for it was not his forte. He turned quickly, locking his eyes directly onto the sultry looking thing that Ricky had drawn his attention to. She was white and stood at about five foot seven. She had blonde short-cropped curly hair, that someone had taken his or her time over sculpting. Her face was thin, slightly mature, but strangely full of a youthful innocence. She had big eyes that brought a cute quality to her countenance. A classic bone structure accentuated a complex facial configuration that a pair of thin well-painted lips merely added to. She was tanned, too well, Ingin thought, for she was positively brown. It was such a good tan that he reasoned it could not have come from spending hours on a sun bed, but rather, many, many hours under real sun. She was shapely too and as the big dread ran his eyeballs over her quite stunning frame, he could not control the slight raise of his eyebrows or the slight curl of his lips into a lecherous smile. She was quite busty. An obvious D cup on such a thin but shapely figure made her so well proportioned in that area that Ingin imagined them to be implants. But it was the large nipples at the end of her breasts that impressed him the most. They were big nipples, as they stood seemingly erect from beneath the red silk, slightly see-through blouse that she had on. What made the effect even more stunning for him was that she wore a bra. He knew nothing about bras but he instantly surmised that it was of high quality as it made those two heavenly globes seem simply awesome, not just in size, but also in shape. As he ran his eyes further down, he expected to see no stomach for even if she had one, the way that her boobs protruded, the blouse would simply cover it and he was right. A matching pair of trousers covered her well-shaped legs. They were slim, but strong.

The woman was almost perplexed by Ingin's overlong

survey of her, but she knew what he was thinking. She sent him a stare back, her eyebrows raised as if to ask him what the hell he was looking at. Ingin caught her drift and turned his attention to the woman standing next to her, who was pretty, but was hardly dressed for the occasion. She was a middle-aged woman, with long blonde hair and a long straight face, a good bone structure and lips that looked like they had been manufactured. They were too big for a white woman. She too, looked as though she worked regularly on her figure. Not that he could see much of it as it was hidden under a long black outfit, a trouser suit that revealed nothing but the air of a guarded woman - slightly afraid and slightly misplaced in a nightclub. To Ingin, this seemed like a paradox because the way she knocked back her gin and tonic and the way that she gleefully whispered to her friend, obviously hinting at Ingin's attentions, made her seem like a good-time girl.

By now the two had turned their heads away, but Ingin noticed that they had only turned their heads and not their bodies and the fact that they had stayed exactly where they were was a good sign to him.

"Nice," he concluded.

"So what you sayin'?" mused his friend. "Chat to it?"

"Whenever you're ready," replied Ingin. "I'll concentrate on the friend. She looks hungry."

Ricky chuckled to himself.

"Come, let's we see whether we can score tonight," he said as he moved confidently past his big friend and towards the women.

Ingin was slightly surprised by Ricky's confidence. He would usually dilly-dally in situations like this, but for some reason, he didn't this time. He reasoned that there must have been something very special about this woman to make him initially so tentative, then so confident. Still, he realised something about himself whenever he met a woman that he just could not let go without even at least trying for a phone number. In those situations he would find Dutch courage from somewhere and go for it regardless of the situation. Ricky had the air of man who had found himself in exactly the same position. He was bold, cool, calm and collected and was about to go for something that he just could not let him get away from him. The friend? She was OK. He'd trouble her.

Ricky stepped to the women with poise. The lady in red started when she noticed him approaching, staring sharply at her as he walked. She began to heave nervously and was angry with herself for doing so. Her friend took a stance that suggested that she was ready to do battle. But not with Ricky. He guided himself smoothly right into her friend's path. She noticed that before being startled herself by Ingin's big presence in front of her.

"Sod off Bob!" she said arrogantly and without remorse. "Go on, get lost. No-one wants to talk to you, you great big Rasta."

Ingin was surprised, not by her words, but by the sheer posh, upper class tone of her voice.

"My name's not Bob," he retorted.

"Yes you are. You're Bob Marley aren't you?" she replied.

Ingin giggled to himself.

"No woman, no cry," he said sarcastically to her.

"Har har, very funny," she responded. "Got a joint then Bob? You know some of the old blow, what do you call it? Spliff?" she asked.

"Might do. What's it to you?

"Want some."

"You can want all you want. Don't mean you're gonna get."

"If you've got a spliff, you better hand it over. Me gaggin' fa some ganja mon."

Ingin was unimpressed with the makeshift Jamaican accent. Ricky giggled.

"Really?" replied Ingin.

"Oh go on Bob, please. I'll do anything you want," she replied coyly.

"That so?" smiled Ingin.

"Except sleep with you of course. 'Cos I know that's what you want."

"And how do you know that?"

"Maybe it's that hungry puppy-dog look you have on your face, or maybe it's just the fact that I could almost see you walking with your fat prick in your hand as you came towards me. Whatever. Either way you're not bonking me tonight. But you will give me a spliff and I will give you what you want," she said as she passed a finger down the side of his face.

"Let's start with a drink. Come on Bob, the bar's this way."

Ingin was shocked. Nothing in any of his 34 years of experience had prepared him for this. As the woman took him by the hand, he could only shrug his shoulders at Ricky, who hadn't yet spoken to the other woman yet as they had been simply riveted by her friend's performance.

"Careful darling, watch these black men, they want us. Maintain a stiff upper lip darling and we'll get out of this one alive. I'll be back in a minute. I'm buying Bob Marley here a drink," she whispered to her friend whilst holding onto Ingin's arm for dear life.

As the two wandered off the woman turned back to look at her friend, pointing to Ingin's backside and following it up with a thumb in the air. Her friend smiled, then relaxed slightly. She had been a tad nervous, but was thankful for her friend's ability to completely break ice. Ricky smiled at her.

"She always like that?" he asked in friendly mood.

"What Amanda? Oh she's the life and soul of the party," came the reply.

Ricky was taken aback. She had a very posh accent and it had immediately caused him concern but he gathered his thoughts quickly. Black people were always adjusting their behaviour in these situations he thought, and he wasn't going to allow himself to do that now. He would be himself and if she didn't like it, well, it would be her loss.

"What's your name then?" he asked.

"Claire," she responded. "And yours?"

"Ricky."

"Pleasure to meet you Ricky," she said, extending her hand to shake his. "Come here often?"

"It's cliché time is it?"

"I don't do clichés. It's a perfectly normal question."

"Not really. You?"

"Darling, I wouldn't normally be seen dead in a place like this."

"But you are in a place like this. So how come?"

"It was Amanda's idea. She wanted to let her hair down. Every now and then she likes to party with the…" She stopped mid-sentence. Ricky eagerly awaited her next words, which were carefully chosen. "…Masses."

"Masses?" Ricky explored.

"Hmm," she responded dismissively. She was embarrassed. "Let me get you a drink. I think I've got some money here."

"You came out without money?"

"Money? I don't do money, sorry, it's too much trouble," she responded clumsily, searching a small handbag that was strapped to her shoulder. "I paid my way in with a credit card. Oh look, ten pounds, so that's what they look like," she giggled. "Come on."

They joined Ingin and Amanda at the bar. Amanda was busy chatting away and hadn't noticed the bartender try to serve her three times. Ingin looked at Ricky, raising his eyebrows slightly. Ricky did the same in return. Claire ordered a brandy and Coke for herself and asked Ricky what his preference was. He asked for a Malibu Spice so she ordered him a rum and Coke. Ricky watched her intently. In the few minutes that he had known her, she had made quite an impression on him. She was certainly sophisticated, but this was matched by an awkwardness that suggested a slight derangement in her character. It wasn't madness, but he concluded that she was out of place. She wasn't cool and the only mental steadiness that she portrayed stemmed from a type of pomposity that he could only equate with a certain degree of maturity and a certain degree of riches. She certainly looked like a woman that had money. She behaved like it too. Her obvious self-confidence would become arrogance, he thought, and soon she would become fatheaded. He'd seen her type before. She seemed to look down her nose at life. Still, he thought, she was beautiful and he felt an aura from her that made her compelling, even irresistible. He wasn't aware of any obvious feelings towards her as yet, but he could like her. Ingin grew tired of Amanda's gassing and ordered the drinks.

"Shall we find somewhere to sit down?" he suggested once they were in.

"Great idea Bob," replied Amanda. "I could do with having

to stop waving my arse around. Coming darlings?"

"There are tables upstairs," Claire replied.

She whipped out a cigarette and held it to Ricky's face for a light. Without a word he whipped out his lighter and lit it for her and one for himself too. He noticed that she hadn't offered him one and actually hadn't even bothered to find out whether he smoked or not. She just seemed to assume that he did. As they climbed the stairs, Ingin and Amanda first, Ingin turned to Ricky, jerking his head towards the dance floor.

"See dat Black ting on the dance floor?" he asked.

Ricky turned to look.

"What the big ting?" Ricky returned.

"Yep. Sharon Ferguson. Used to trouble dat. Love a white man."

Ricky eyed the girl intently as he climbed the stairs. He beheld a voluptuous looking Black girl with enormous breasts, hardly dancing, but rather merely shaking herself and shoving her gigantic assets about for everyone to see.

"Tart!" said Claire with venom.

"I wish I had some," joined in Amanda, holding one of her small breasts and giving it a slight squeeze.

Claire joined Amanda as they climbed the stairs. Ingin took a step back and put his hand on Ricky's shoulder.

"That bitch! She love use dem tings to get man attention," he said angrily.

"She'll get anybody's attention with them things man!" observed Ricky.

"Listen man. For the longest time she been trying to use them things to catch a rich man. You watch. She'll walk out of here with the ugliest redneck in the place, trust me. Makes me sick how some of these bitches like to use their body to get money!"

Ricky said nothing. He looked at Ingin wondering if he could see the irony in his statement. Clearly he didn't. Claire and Amanda had made their way to the seating area. It was plush and Ricky could see the satisfaction on Claire's face as she took a seat. Amanda held out a hand to invite Ingin to sit next to her, which he did with pleasure. Ricky took his seat next to Claire. The dance floor was still visible from where he was and he couldn't resist another look at the girl with the big breasts and how she was getting on in her manhunt. He could feel the white boys' nervousness as they swooned around her all hoping to hang on to a sumptuous black thing for the night. She loved the attention and the two friends that she was with, both white girls, were doing their best to enjoy themselves too, even though their glory had been stolen.

"Can't take your eyes off them things can you?" snarled Claire politely. "You obviously like your women big."

"Not quite," corrected Ricky. "I'm just interested in seeing how she gets on, that's all."

Amanda wasn't buying it.

"Looks like we've got a head between the breasts job here Claire. It's a good job you can hold your own in that department," she said.

Ingin laughed. Claire stayed silent, as did Ricky. Amanda put her hand on Ingin's knee.

"This chap here reckons he's got a plonker nine inches long. Is that true … erm, what's your name?"

"Ricky. Yes it's true, I've seen it. You should enjoy playing with that."

"Who says I want to play with it? I'm not a tart you know."

"Oh come on Amanda, you're the biggest slut out," intercepted Claire "You'd screw the back off Archie if you thought he could show you a good time!"

"Archie?" queried Ingin.

"Her dog, he's a Doberman."

"What? You fuck your dog?" inquired Ingin.

"No! Don't be so bloody stupid!" Amanda pleaded.

"Thank God for that," said Ingin in a relieved tone.

"He's got a bloody long tongue that hound," Amanda mused aloud.

There was quiet. Ingin and Ricky eyed each other. Their expressions spoke volumes. Amanda broke in again.

"Let's dance," she said, sipping her drink.

"We just got up here, now you want to go back down again?" complained Claire.

"Oh it's just because you can't dance! Come on Bob!"

"I told you, the name's Ingin."

"Well why do you flipping well call yourself Ingin anyway?"

"I told you. Engines go on and on and on. Just like me!"

"Is that true? Erm … what's your name?"

"I told you it's Ricky. Yes, it's true!"

"What, you've slept with him?" asked Claire sarcastically.

"Don't even go there please," dismissed Ricky.

"What's wrong with sleeping with your own sex?" wondered Claire.

"Yes, what's wrong with fucking the shit out of your own sex?" Amanda joined.

"What? You fuck her?" asked Ingin.

"Hardly, but we fucked the same man once," replied Amanda.

"Amanda please," begged Claire.

"Her husband."

Claire held her head in her hands, then raised her eyes to the ceiling in embarrassment.

"Well, her ex-husband. It was a long time ago."

"A very long time ago," reinforced Claire.

There was silence again. Ricky and Ingin eyed each other one more time. Claire broke in.

"Oh shit, here she comes, the Hottentot Venus!" she alerted.

All eyes shot round to view the voluptuous black girl. Her make up had been smudged by the sweat that had dropped profusely down her face. She was walking their way. Claire and Amanda averted their eyes as she stepped closer. They didn't want to give her the attention that they knew she craved. Ingin and Ricky didn't give a hoot. Those two huge breasts looked twice as big as they bobbed their way towards them. The short navy blue one-piece number, with a split round the bust area did absolutely nothing to understate the sheer hedonism contained within her figure. She was braless too and that just made things worse. She stepped boldly, holding the hand of a short balding little white man with a slight beer gut who looked proud and very contented with himself. He was well dressed and looked as if he had money. You could tell by the sheer casualness of his dress sense, the confident air, the suntan and the Rolex. They glided slowly past the foursome, engaging in what appeared to be meaningless conversation that was probably put on as a refuge from the immense amount of attention that they were getting, not least from Ingin and Ricky. As they walked the man eyed Claire intently. She threw him a quick glance sensing his attention. They both wondered where they had seen each other before. As the lady elegantly strode past, she eyed Ricky. He eyed her bouncing boobs earnestly in return. She then eyed Ingin and gave him a quick hello upon realising who he was.

"Yaaright?" was his very self-conscious response.

Once out of the way and out of earshot, he leaned over to Ricky, his eyes screwed up in pain.

"I told you man! Bitch out for just one ting! Bare fuckri."

"Boy it's each to their own you know," replied Ricky calmly.

"Each to wha?" Ingin was becoming animated. "Boy! I could barely go over there and arx de bitch what she playin' at!"

Claire zeroed in on Ingin's frustration; she was slightly surprised at it but challenged it all the same.

"So what is it motor…"

"Ingin!"

"Sorry, Ingin. Is it the fact that he's white or the fact that he's got money? Or is it both?"

Ingin straightened up in shock. He was a man not used to being taken to task. Particularly by a woman and most particularly by a white woman.

"None of 'em!" he replied sharply. "It's none of 'em!"

"So what? You own her?"

"I don't own nobody! She's free to do what she wants."

"Is it the fact then that she used probably her only enduring assets to snare herself a man?" persevered Claire. Ricky was impressed by her guts.

"Yeah! That's what it is! Why she got to do that?"

"Suppose she did that to you?"

"She did."

"What did you do?"

"I fucked the shit out of her."

"That's probably what he'll do."

"So she's an old flame?" Amanda pursued.

Ingin turned his attention to Ricky, with a slightly less hostile tone.

"Boy, I remember at school we used to line up to drill that thing! She used to tek all tree man one time!"

"You gang banged her?" asked Amanda in pleasant shock.

Ricky held his hands up.

"Not me. We went to different schools, in different years. He's older than me," he joked.

"Woman's a slut man!" Ingin declared.

"I have no doubts," interjected Claire. "But probably she does what she does because she needs to."

"Better get she a pimp then ennit? She could get paid too," replied Ingin coldly.

Claire released a gust of defeated breath.

"So I guess you won't be screwing anybody tonight then? Because you don't believe in, well, what she's doing? I mean you're not a slut are you?"

"Yeah but she's a wo... anyway, never mind." Ingin closed, realising that he had dug a hole for himself. Amanda sought to save him.

"Come on Bob let's get that dance," she said holding his hand.

"The name's Ingin for fuck sake!"

"Whatever you say darling. Come."

Amanda led Ingin away by the hand winking at Claire as she left. Once out of view, Claire turned her attention eagerly to Ricky.

"Bit touchy, your friend," she began.

"That's my man Ingin."

"Why do you hang around with him? You're such different people."

"Are we? How do you work that out?"

"Well, you're more poised, more thoughtful, less aggressive..."

" You mean I ain't your typical Black man?"

"Does race have to come into everything with you people?"

"Yes, because you need to know what you're saying."

"Ok, I suppose he does fit the stereotype. He's big, black, misogynistic, got a short fuse, smokes weed and has a big dick. Hey, come on. What do I know? I merely read..."

"Bullshit."

Claire was stunned into silence. She hadn't expected such an aggressive onslaught from Ricky. She noted keenly the way that he defended Ingin's indiscretions. It wasn't about his friend. It was something deeper. She too, was unused to being challenged, but she liked Ricky, for he knew where he stood.

"You kind of gave him a hard time," Ricky continued in a relatively serious tone, even though he was enjoying the debate.

Claire splayed her arms out and shrugged her shoulders with a cheeky smile.

"Hey, come on, I'm a woman," she said. "Why have I got to sit here and listen to his self-righteous, testosterone-laden, misogynistic half-arsed sexist crap? OK, so the girls got big boobs…"

"Big boobs," smiled Ricky

"…But hey, they're hers," she continued, ignoring his jest. "'My name's Ingin because I go on and on and on'. Please. What are we living here, fantasies? The man's a dog. I really think that you can get better friends than that. I mean, what?" her voice lowered, allowing her tone to get serious. "Does he come with the territory?"

Ricky smiled a wry smile.

"Love me love my dog," he said calmly.

There was an uneasy silence. Ricky broke it.

"So what were you doing in the seventies?" he asked, trying to lighten the mood once again. "Sounds like you were beating the women's lib drum loud and proud."

"No. Actually I was doing adult magazines."

"No shit."

"It's true. I was young; I didn't know any better. I was studying at the time. Needed to pay the bills. You know how it is."

"No I don't. I mean, dirty magazines?"

Claire threw him a look of disgust. Ricky corrected himself.

"To use the layman's term. What? Deep pussy shots and shit like that?"

"Oh God no, they were clean. Just boobs, bottom and beaver. No holes."

"You obviously went through quite a dramatic psychological reconstruction. You know, I mean from sex siren to Miss Feminist?"

Claire lowered her head and began to play nervously with the ring on her finger. She held the uncomfortable silence. Ricky sensed that the comment had sent her on a jarring memory trek. He was right. When she eventually looked up at him, her face was red.

"I guess it comes from twenty-five years of being married to a no-good, lying, sexist pig whose only function in life was to fuck every woman that you ever called a friend and to tell every guy that you considered close, how good or bad your blowjob was. Who would embarrass you at dinner parties by grabbing your crotch and proclaiming you as his personal orifice before handing you over to some fat greasy slob at wife swapping parties that I had no idea we were going to. While some bitch would suck his dick, another would lick his balls then want to make polite conversation with me afterwards. A pig-headed, lying, self-indulgent sonofabitch who would make me persuade my friends into threesomes with him because he was no longer satisfied with fucking just me alone."

"Hence Amanda?"

"Hence Amanda. Hmm, that kind of experience is either going to make a woman of you or a slave. I chose woman."

"Did he see you in the mags?"

"That's how we met. He was a friend of one of the photographers."

"Well I don't suppose he married you for your hoovering skills right?"

"Didn't marry me for my brain either. He just wanted a good little wifey that he could spend his money on and expect her to be grateful. Someone whom he would allow a certain degree of self gratification just so long as she didn't complain when he shagged the town black and blue."

"No kids?"

"He didn't want any. He convinced me to have my tubes tied the minute my G.P. felt that I was psychologically able to cope with making such an almost irreversible decision. He didn't like children. Said they cost too much money and hence weren't a sound financial investment."

"He sounds like one heavy guy."

"Indeed. But hey, he laid the groundwork for my life's mission."

"And what's that?"

Claire stared at him deeply, the determination of her thoughts visible in her eyes.

"Liberation."

The force with which Claire delivered that single assertion threw Ricky somewhat. It unnerved him slightly. But he recovered and headed back to the subject at hand, albeit slightly more wary. He realised that he was dealing with someone who was more than just a grieving housewife.

"He's now your ex-husband right?"

"It's not official. The divorce comes through in three months. He's an architect. He's now worth over fifteen million. I get another three million on top of the two I'm living off now."

"You're wealthy."

"Why don't you state the obvious?"

"What's it like?"

"It's nice."

"So nice you don't have to give a shit?"

"You've lost me."

"Rich people don't give a shit do they? Don't give a fuck about anyone or anything but themselves."

"Oh I wouldn't say that's necessarily true."

Ricky became animated.

"Let me tell you a story. It happened to me last week. I'm walking up this long road. It's a busy road heading out of town and there's a lot of traffic. Out in front there's a wealthy looking woman in a Shogun and she has three kids in the back all wearing football strips and jumping up and down like little fuckin' jack rabbits. She stops the Shogun, just before the traffic lights, because they're on green and she doesn't want to go. She wants to get the attention of the person in the car behind, which just happens to be another wealthy looking woman. This one's driving a seven series BMW. She stops the car and peers out of her window trying to get this woman's' attention. All the time the traffic is building up behind them. The lights are on green. She can go but she decides to carry on trying to get this woman's attention. The traffic's building up even more and they're starting to wonder what the hell is causing the delay. Finally the woman in the BMW realises that she's trying to speak to her, so she winds her window down and sticks her head out. When she realises she's got her attention, the woman in the Shogun shouts, 'Janice, Jamie's lost a sock, have you got it?' I mean that's what being rich is about isn't it? Not having to give a single solitary fuck about anyone or anything but your own insignificant concerns."

"You're being a bit general don't you think? Princes Diana was rich."

"Yeah but she never gave a shit about the money. I mean, she was more concerned about the people that didn't have any."

"What about Richard Branson?"

"OK. Find two rich do-gooders to try and contradict what I'm saying. You know what I'm on about. I mean what about all these fat cat so-called 'captains of industry' giving themselves fat pay rises, whilst they send people like me summonses, court judgements and bailiffs even though I can't even find two pennies to put a biscuit in my mouth? Fucking politicians, who talk about helping the poor, but don't ever do anything because they've never been poor themselves. They're so fucking rich they don't know what being poor is like. So they give you forty fuckin' quid a week to live on. Or they expect you to take some £4.50 an hour bullshit job and expect you to fucking well cope."

Claire was surprised by the passion with which Ricky spoke, but she hung in there all the same. He continued.

"I got taken to a casino once when I was on the dole and this guy lost five grand on one bet and didn't even think about it and I remember thinking shit, that was more than my dole money for a whole year."

"What did you want him to do? Give you a hand out?"

"No, I wanted him to lose."

"You sound bitter."

"I think have a right to. Let me ask you something. Do you know what it's like waking up in the morning, wondering where the hell you're going to get your next meal? Then on that same morning, you find out that the council is taking court action against you for unpaid poll tax? And the electricity board want to cut you off because you're overdue. Do you know what it's like having to make a choice with the little money that you have between eating or paying bills? Ever driven a car without tax and insurance because you had no choice. Praying all the time that the police don't stop you, because if they do, you won't be able to take your daughter to the nursery, who themselves are threatening to kick her out because you can't keep up with the payments? Ever decided not to run for a bus, because the little money you had was going to buy you a drink and a bar of chocolate because you knew you were going to have to be out all day and not going to get a chance to eat? Ever had to worry about any of those things?"

"No."

"Do you even give a fuck about people who have to go through these things?"

"I care about people."

"Only as much as you need to. You see, at some point, society will give you a reason and a justification for not having to care about anyone else. You could spend two hundred and fifty pounds on a handbag and not even consider that someone somewhere could do with that money to feed his family and please, spare me the Conservative Party option about the scroungers and the lazy so-and-so's who don't want to work, we...."

"I take it you don't like me then?"

Claire had heard enough. It was clear where Ricky's politics lay, but like Ingin she thought he had gotten carried away, almost forgetting where he was. She lightened up to get onto more important matters.

"Yeah I like you," smiled Ricky. "You're OK for a snob."

"Thank you," smiled Claire.

"So," continued Ricky, "does Amanda come with the territory?"

"Love me, love my alcoholic."

"She's an alcoholic?" queried Ricky with surprise.

"Yes," replied Claire solemnly. "I love her to bits, she's my best friend. She's had such a hard time of it and I have to stick by her."

"Why does she need to turn to drink?" inquired Ricky.

"She can't have kids. Well at least she doesn't think so. It's not been confirmed by her G.P. or anything, but after so many years of trying, she's convinced herself that it's something that she can't do."

"She's married then?" Ricky asked, thinking of Ingin.

"Yes. Not that it will make any difference, your friend will fuck her tonight. He's away. He's always away, on business. That's part of her frustration I suppose. No, once every now and then, and it's become more recent over the last couple of months, she drags me out to some dosshole like this and picks someone up. Then it's back to my place. I'll shower and go to bed, she'll fuck the night away with some stranger, who she'll tell blatantly not to come back, once they've finished."

"Do they always comply?" inquired Ricky, once again with Ingin's interests at heart.

"The one about her husband having a gun and knowing mobsters hasn't failed her yet. Tonight will be the first night she's had a black man though."

Ricky thought for a second. He knew of Ingin's reputation. Tonight Amanda was going to get the fuck of her life. The thought made him smile inside.

"Well I suppose it's getting late," said Claire, glancing at her gold watch, "I suspect once they make their way back here, it won't be long before you're following us in your car. Back to my place. You have got a car haven't you?"

"Yes," replied Ricky. "Why do you allow her to do this?" he asked thoughtfully.

"She's my friend. She's like a sister to me. What can I do? I love her so much and she's been so unhappy over the last few years, I just want her to be … free, I guess."

Claire was cut off by the immediate appearance of Amanda and Ingin. She was beaming from ear to ear and so was he.

"Bob's coming back for coffee," she announced proudly.

"Sure," was Claire's knowing response.

There was silence as both Claire and Ricky rose up out of their seats to leave. Ricky looked at Ingin who threw him a quick wink. As they left, he turned his head to get a last look at how the girl with the big boobs was getting on. She was sitting a couple of tables opposite and was engrossed in a conversation with her 'pick up'. She noticed Ricky's glance and gently raised her eyes to meet his. She smiled at him and he smiled back. Claire looked at the man that she was with. He looked so very familiar. He had been racking his brains as to where he knew her from. He wondered at one point if he should say something to her, but he chose not to. He was too engrossed in his newfound friend. He touched her hand, she touched his, and they kissed.

two

"These bitches got money," Ingin declared.

"I know," Ricky replied thoughtfully.

"I'm about to put a hot one in this Amanda bitch tonight boy! Mek she dish out the finances."

"Hmm."

Ricky was pensive. This was one of the things that he disliked about his friend. He was the kind of Black man that thought all he had to do was sex his way into money. Tonight was an opportunity that Ingin had craved for a good deal of his adult life. Outside of this all he did was play dominoes and live off the state. He reasoned that this was an unfortunate plight, but perhaps a scenario that too many Black men were forced to play out. His little B reg. XR2 ticked over nervously as he followed the Mercedes 150 SEL down the dark country lane leading to Claire's house. It was exactly the type of area that he had imagined Claire lived in. Dark, woody and out of the way. It was clear that Ingin was excited about the experience. But he just took it in his stride. There were few things that surprised Ricky and he had already put his expectations of what was going to happen tonight in check.

"So you and that Claire gonna get together?" asked Ingin, thrilled.

"Dunno," Ricky replied. "Let's wait and see."

"Give her a good fuck man, then mek she pay you for it. Anyway it look like she likes you. What the fuck? You need to make sure you go to your bed with ten grand in your pocket," Ingin asserted with nauseating capriciousness.

"We'll see what happens yeah?" was Ricky's nonchalant reply.

Amanda was unsteady as she pushed her Mercedes recklessly

along the dark country road. She was the worst driver in the world and on top of that she was merry.

"Careful, tree," warned Claire in an accustomed mood.

"Thank you darling, didn't see that for a second," replied Amanda with a smile.

"So I guess it's the same as usual tonight then?" Claire inquired.

"Don't worry darling," Amanda said softly "I'll make it quick."

"And you'll wash the sheets later."

Amanda rolled her eyes to the sky.

"Yes darling, I'll wash the sheets," she replied in 'you've told me a million times' fashion.

"Wrong lane darling," Claire warned.

"Tuh! Silly me." Amanda got serious. "So what about this Ricky? He's really quite nice," she brooded.

"And..?" replied Claire, keen to hear what she had to say.

"C'mon Claire, lighten up darling," thrust Amanda. "That last guy you were seeing, the fucking mystic…"

"Clairvoyant dear."

"Yes him, the weird one. I mean, really darling, I know you could have done much better than that. I mean, was he strange or was he simply … strange?"

"So what are you saying? I should get together with Ricky?"

"Why not? He's nice."

"And the fact that he's black?" queried Claire, almost seeking approval.

"What's wrong with having a black guy for a boyfriend? This isn't nineteen forty whatever, after the blitz you know, it's the nineties darling. Black is in."

"I should see the guy because his colour is in?"

"No darling, because you haven't been shagged anyone for ages. Because you're lonely. You never spend any money. You never go out. Because you spend endless nights alone in front of pointless fucking videos, and because you like him." Claire was quiet. "You like him, don't you?" Amanda persevered.

"We'll see," Claire dismissed. "Fox, darling," she closed here eyes.

"Oh sorry! Couldn't get out of the way in time."

The two cars drove steadily down a short country lane before turning into a long drive that was a few yards along. The end of the drive revealed a massive country house illuminated by a hefty array of security lights when the two cars entered. Amanda pulled up with a jerk into a gravel area just by the back door and Ricky pulled up next to her. He jumped out of the car first, motioning to his friend to lock the door as he came out. A tape of original music produced by Ricky on his portable studio at home had been playing in the car. Ingin took it out of the tape deck and shoved in into his back pocket. He then jumped out curiously to see if the ladies were OK, mentioning that Amanda had driven like a maniac and how courageous Claire had been to have even contemplated sitting next to her. Ricky was keen to simply find out just where in God's name they were and how the hell he was ever going to find his way back to civilisation. Claire relaxed him by promising to go over a road map with him later on.

Once inside the house, Ricky and Ingin were gobsmacked. As the ladies disappeared to fix drinks they discussed quietly how in the hell anyone could live in a house so big. The living room was littered with antiques that sat well with the expensive Victorian style decoration that adorned the space. Beautifully crafted Wedgwood furniture seemed too precious a place to rest their drinks on when they finally did arrive. Both Ricky and Ingin held theirs in their hands as they all sat and talked, whilst sinking in the large soft cushioned single settees that they were in. It was small-talk time and realising that it was going nowhere, Amanda took the initiative and found an excuse to escort Ingin out of the room and up to one of the six bedrooms upstairs. Ingin rubbed his crotch as he made his way out of the door as if to make sure his goods were in working order, whilst Amanda made eyes at Claire in Ricky's direction, soliciting her to get on with whatever she thought they should be getting on with. Claire was the first to speak once they were out of the room.

"You won't be fucking me tonight," she said matter-of-factly.

"I know," smiled Ricky.

"I just don't do that," she excused.

"S'fine," said Ricky waving away the notion.

"Not that I wouldn't want to…" she began under her breath.

"What?"

"Oh nothing."

Ricky smiled to himself.

"So tell me some more about yourself," asked Claire gingerly.

"Well," Ricky began. "That £4.50 an hour bullshit job I mentioned earlier? I do one of those."

"Oh. How quaint. What do you do?" probed Claire patronisingly.

"Warehouse work. I pack bottles of wine."

"Sounds like a job I could do."

"We can't drink the stuff."

"Oh well, maybe not then. Tell me more."

"Well, I have a daughter. I'm no longer with her baby mother…" Ricky continued.

"Names please. Not titles. Especially not crude and sexist ones," interrupted Claire viciously.

"God, you sound like a black woman."

"Good for black women. Does she have a name?" she emphasised.

"Shaniqua."

"That's a lovely name. What does it mean?"

"Fuck all."

"What's your daughters name?"

"Tanika."

"What does that mean?"

"Fuck all." Ricky felt the need to explain. "I don't know…" he began, shrugging his shoulders. "There's a generation of Black women that just plucked all these fancy names out of thin air for their kids, they mean fuck all. Tanika's three anyway, she's a lovely girl."

Ricky pulled a picture of her out of his wallet and showed it to her.

"Why did you and Shaniqua split up?"

"I'm twenty-nine, she's twenty-two. Generation gap, I guess."

"That's your story and you're sticking to it right?"

"If you say so," replied Ricky arrogantly.

"How long were you together?" probed Claire.

"What's this, the third degree?"

"Just trying to make conversation, don't get defensive."

Claire backed off. She realised quickly that this was a place where Ricky did not want to go. She had already made an impression on him. Realising the strength of her argument and her acute ability to decipher all things sexist he put blocks up. Just like his friend he would get angry or agitated at the first sign of challenge. Those similarities with Ingin disturbed her. She took a deep breath in the ensuing silence and wondered where to go from here. She chose sincerity.

"We seem to get confrontational with each other quite easily," she observed.

"Isn't that how you get when you meet a challenge?" asked Ricky with an understated wisdom that his tender years could hardly justify.

Claire was unable to respond as their musings were interrupted by an almighty shriek of what seemed like pain from upstairs. She jumped to her feet, instantly recognising that the scream came from Amanda. With agitation and concern written all over her face she ran to the door. Ricky though, was cool.

"My God, what's he doing to her?" she cried in disbelief.

"Screwing her probably," was Ricky's calm reply.

"I don't think so!" Claire concluded, whisking out of the room and up the stairs. Wearily Ricky let out of gust of air and followed, albeit a tad calmer.

"I knew this was a bad idea," he heard her say as she sprinted ahead of him. "Are you OK darling?" was her distraught cry as she rushed up the stairs.

There was no answer. Claire stopped at the door to the bedroom and listened intently, her body shaking with nerves. Ricky stood opposite her and cocked an ear to the door. It was bedlam inside.

"Fuck me! Oh fuck me! You great big Rastaman from Zion! Ooohhh! Ooohhh!" cried Amanda from behind the door.

It took Claire a second to decipher what was going on and when she did, she relaxed with a giggle.

"Told you," whispered Ricky.

"My God, she's never made that much noise before!" whispered Claire in absolute and total amazement.

"She's never been fucked by Ingin before," concluded Ricky.

Amanda's cries rose to a crescendo and they soon became mingled with the screeching of the bedsprings and the violently consistent banging of the bed-head against the wall.

"Oh fuck me you great big lummox! You great fat black ox! Ooh yes! Yes! You fucking great big horse! Get deeper, deeper ohhh ohhh! More! More!" cried Amanda.

Claire stared at the floor, eyes wide, listening intently whilst nervously twirling the gold chain that hung from her neck.

"He's killing her," she declared in amazement.

"I don't even think he's got started yet," said Ricky, amused.

"Just listen to that bed! My god he'll ruin every spring - and my wallpaper!"

Claire had reason to fear as the hullabaloo of raw intercourse began to fill not only the room but also the whole corner of the house. Amanda was ecstatic. Her screams increased in volume with every thrust of Ingin's mighty nature between her soaking legs. She held onto him for dear life, it was all she could do. Never in her life, or even in her wildest dreams had she ever received such a salacious walloping. She could only lay, legs splayed as wide as possible to allow Ingin all the space in her gaping vagina that he needed to work her and where there was no space, he created it. His constant banging soon became serpentine before destroying her once again with vicious propulsion.

"Aaarrghh! Aaarrghh!" Bawled Amanda with painful rapture. "Ooh ooh stab me, kill me! Murder me! Ooh fuck me! Fuck me with that great big black cock of yours, you fucking great big black stud! Ooh, you fucking charcoal monster! You fucking Jamaican yeti! You fucking great big black baboon!

Ingin stopped working her. "Leave it tha' fuck out!" He warned before re-commencing his ride.

"I love it so much ooh, ooh," cried Amanda, ignoring him.

The bed rocked furiously, as did the two joined bodies. As Amanda experienced her orgasm it was like the heavens had opened as thunderous noises of passion escaped from her mouth. Her whole body trembled with uncontrolled disorder. When it was all over, she lay, with Ingin on top of her, heaving ferociously.

"Faaacking hell!" she screamed.

At the sign of the end of the intercourse, Claire and Ricky quickly tiptoed down the stairs, both in a fit of suppressed laughter. Once back in the living room, they made themselves comfortable, waiting patiently for their friend's appearance, which wasn't long in coming. Amanda was adorned in a dressing gown, her hair seriously ruffled and partly covering her face. She would send it back across her head, but it would only stand up for a second before falling back over her face again. She walked over to the coffee table where she had earlier placed her cigarettes and lit one. Then she turned to Claire.

"I think a trip to the Caribbean might not go amiss this year darling," she announced.

Claire could not hold her laughter and neither could Ricky. Ingin tried to see the joke, but failed. There was polite banter before Ricky announced that it was time for them to part company. Amanda kissed Ingin on the cheek and told him that he would call her. Ingin reminded her that she didn't have his phone number so she feigned ignorance and reluctantly scribbled it on a piece of paper. Then she escorted him to the door, leaving Claire and Ricky alone.

"So?" asked Claire coyly.

"So?" replied Ricky with the same amount of shyness.

"Maybe I'll see you around," she said.

"Sure," replied Ricky, emotionless. He headed for the door.

"Or maybe you could ring me, erm, sometime."

Ricky whizzed round. A smile appeared on his face as he beheld her holding out a crumpled piece of paper. He took it from her knowing that her phone number had been scratched on it.

"I wrote it down whilst you were watching the Hottentot Venus" she said with a cunning smile.

"The real Hottentot Venus had a big fat bottom," Ricky said coolly.

"So have you," she said tapping his and ushering him towards the door. As Ricky stepped outside, she and Amanda watched them leave. Amanda turned back inside after giving Ingin a slight and obviously erroneous wave goodbye.

"I gave him a false number," she whispered to Claire before walking off.

"Bitch," whispered Claire back. She called to Ricky. "I like facing challenges," she shouted.

"So do I," he called back. "Sit by your phone."

Ricky entered the car and switched the engine on. He expected a tune from his home produced tape to click in, but all he heard was the radio. He pressed the eject button confused. There was no tape in the deck. He turned to Ingin.

"What happened to the tape that was in here?" he asked.

"I dunno," replied Ingin. "Are you sure there was one in?"

"'Course there was!" Ricky said irately.

"I thought it was the radio. Was it one of your own?"

"Yep."

"You got a copy?"

"Yeah."

"So what you worrying about? Come man let we go home. It late."

Ricky echoed the notion. He stopped worrying about the tape, pledging to search the car for it tomorrow. In a second he was off, but to where, he hadn't a clue. He had forgotten to search the map and get directions back home.

"Arm tellin' you man, all they're good for is suckin' dick and spennin' maney thas ool." Shaniqua was in full flight as she sat in the garden of her new housing association dwelling. Her heavy South London accent tumultuously gracing the warm ether on this pleasant Sunday afternoon. She was a dashing young woman. The commonness of her accent betrayed the sensuality of her look, which was fair and sophisticated. Her hair was cut short and styled in a wavy bob that charmed her. Her eyes were moody and her nose relatively straight. She had thick lips that were evenly shaped. Her complexion was copper-toned and well nursed. As she sat cross-legged, she oozed style, expressing herself sharply with chic hand movements.

"They use everyfink dey can to snare black men an' them suckers fall for it every tarm! Arm tellin' you it's nothin' but disrespek."

Her three closest friends had joined her in the garden. Tamika was a tall, dark, sultry looking thing with big lips, sullen eyes and a tight, fit body. She wore her long hair tied at the back and wore a lot of make up. She had big cheeks, which made her big smile appear even bigger, causing her face to literally light up when she was happy. She lit a cigarette and held it between two long fingers, the nails of which were perfectly manicured and painted a bright red. At twenty-two years old she had two kids; De-vante, a boy who was six and Mercedes, a girl who was four.

Then there was Chantelle, a short stubby young lady who wore make up all the time as if to compensate for her heavy appearance. She was a pretty girl and really needn't have bothered, as her complexion was soft and immaculate. She was pretty with big lips with a short curled nose that was rounded at the end. She, like Tamika, had her hair pressed. She wore short skirts and long boots that covered her knees. She tucked graciously into the few sandwiches and cake that Shaniqua had prepared for them. At twenty-three, she had one child, a four-year-old girl by the name of Tamela.

Finally there was 'T', an abbreviation for Theresa, a name she hated because it was too ordinary. At nineteen years old, she was the youngest of the posse and had two children, two girls Chelsea, five and Karima four. She was a short pretty girl, shapely and with a refined look. 'T' loved jewellery and was adorned in gold. Each of her ears had been pierced four times and gold rings hung from all of them. Her nose was pierced too and a stud lay in it that made her look cute. Around her neck hung a series of necklaces that had a number of small trinkets attached to them, ranging from boxing gloves to ganja leaves and at least one, inevitably, was the letter 'T'. All the girls including Shaniqua had a ragamuffin style and they all dressed their kids in the same way. They were playing at the bottom end of the garden and like their parents were loud.

"No but is de man dem fault," entered Tamika into the discussion. "Black man nowadays, is like they're juss arfta one fing."

"Thas right, are totally agree wiv ya," joined Chantelle. "They fine a piece a skirt, get undaneef it and then…" she snapped her fingers in the air "…onto the nex' one. An' it don't matta what colour they are, what nationality, nafink. To dem all cratchiz is for grinin'!"

"Yeah but can you blame dem doh?" inquired T. "Vese fackin' little white wimin, I mean, I agree with Shaniqua. They buy our man dem. We black wimin ain't got the maney like they have so they use it to vere advarntage."

"An' when we do have de maney…" Shaniqua dived in, "…we ain't givin' it to dem anyway, cos we as black wimin don't want no man livin' off us. Cos arm tellin' ya, wiv dese black men nowadays it's all about the Benjamin's believe."

"All about the what?" Inquired T, clueless.

"The Benjamin's." Repeated Shaniqua "Ain't you heard Puff Daddy sing abaaht dem. It means wonga." She stretched out a hand and started to rub her four fingers against her thumb. "Capitoo, bucks, collateral, pesos, corn, queens head, dollars, bread, dough, lira, filffy likka, maney!"

"Are fink dat's filffy lucre lav," T responded.

"Thas what are said filffy likka," replied Shaniqua, at which the other girls laughed.

"Anyway, speakin' of maney," inquired Chantelle. "How's your baby farva doin'? Is he givin' you any maney for Tanika doh?"

"He gives me what he can, but he does a lot for her you know, so are don't pressure him ool dat match." Shaniqua replied.

"Arm sorry, are don't care what he does, mah baby farva gotta supply dat maney on a regla too else are'll get the law on him," replied Chantelle.

"Thas right," replied Tamika shaking her head and waving a fist in the air, "long live de Charl Suppoot Agency mate."

"How do you apply to them anyway, cos my baby farva's bin goin' on a bit stink with the finances lately an' arm soon ready to shop his arse!" said T.

Tamika and Chantelle, in tandem and with zeal, began to explain but were quickly cut off by the piercing sound of Shaniqua's telephone. She ran through the patio doors to her living room and quickly placed the receiver to her ear.

"Hello?" she enquired.

A dark husky voice spoke from the other end of the phone. It was Bones, her boyfriend.

"W'happen? Cool?" he asked.

"Yeah so-so, got the girls raaned, we're avin' a little chat."

"Me need a money you know," he stated.

Shaniqua raised her eyes to the ceiling.

"Bones, are gave you some maney yesterdee. Are gave you andred quid yesterdee. Wat you dan wiv it?"

"Had to len' me sista. She had a few tings to buy from chemist true she sick an' ting."

"Was wrong wiv 'er nar den?"

"Bladda business, she a pee-pee a funny colour, Docta give har ninety pown wort a description."

"Prescription."

"Seen. Look man I will get it back to you nex' week man."

"Bones, you don't even need to go dere, cos are know are ain't seein' nafink."

"Truss me baby, nex' week seen."

Shaniqua bowed her head and thought, she liked Bones even though he was a roach. She knew herself too. She was the kind of person that tried hard in relationships and despite her boisterous nature, which really was just a show to her friends, she wanted to do all she could to make her relationships work, even if it meant a small degree of dishonesty.

"How match?"

"Fifty pown."

"Jesus fackin' Christ! Look, I'll call you back in a minute." She said. "You on your mobile?"

"Yeah," was Bone's sceptical reply.

Shaniqua replaced the receiver and picked it up again immediately. She stabbed a few digits and put it to her ear. Ricky answered the phone.

"Are need some maney for Tanika, she needs new shoes."

"I gave you money last week, what have you done with it?" replied Ricky, clearly displeased by the request.

"I've got to feed her as well you know! Bladdy 'ell!" Shaniqua replied angrily.

"How much?"

"Andred."

"So where the hell are you buying the girl shoes for a hundred quid, Harrods?"

Shaniqua fidgeted for a second.

"Well are fought are could get 'er a coat as well, 'sgettin' colder nowadays y'know."

Ricky went silent on the other end of the phone. Then spoke up again.

"Look," He said aggressively "I hope you ain't taking none of this money to give to Bones you know? That skinny fucka's always runnin' up at the mouth 'bout how his woman gives him money! And I hope he ain't feeding you that bullshit about his sister either, Tanya's fit as a fiddle."

"Please." Replied Shaniqua with the appearance of one distraught by the suggestion "Give me some fackin' credit please. Ar've got no maney and Tanika needs shoes, This is your doota we're on abaaht!"

Ricky went quiet again.

"When?" he asked.

"Can you bring it over later tonight abaaht eight?"

"Sure, see you later," Ricky replaced the receiver with disgust.

Shaniqua replaced her handset and stuck it back in her ear. She punched out a few more numbers and waited.

"Yo," replied Bones.

"Check me arfta nine," she said. "You bess 'ave summum good waitin' for me too," she said.

"Every time baby, everytime. Layta y'hear," replied Bones with a smile.

Shaniqua replaced the receiver, she felt satisfied, albeit slightly guilty. She walked back out into the garden, to behold Tamika put a slap under De-vante's bottom.

"What you mean you're ganna cut her up, if she does that again?" she shouted. "You're gonna start spendin' a lot less time wiv your farva, young man!"

three

Ricky was in his bedroom sitting by his music system that was a bit more than the average. A sampler was rigged from his set that housed a DAT machine to a computer. Ricky regularly sampled music in his room and, despite regular complaints from his neighbours, it was something that he persevered at. Five thousand pounds worth of exclusive music equipment packed out his tiny bedroom. He had collected it all over the course of a couple of years and they represented his only real valued possessions. He had a mini studio and he loved to sit in there and make music. He fancied himself as a rapper and a music producer. Whilst he didn't plan to try and make a career out of it, it was his peace. He had written down the lyrics to his latest number, which was called 'Talk To Me'. As he ignited the studio into action he neatly placed the paper with the words in front to him, pulled the Shure Prologue microphone to his face and prepared himself. He moved the mouse for the computer from side to side selecting the required beat from the computer screen. As it clicked in, a jumpy, bassy mid-tempo groove issued forth from the four large Bang and Olufsun speakers that were placed the four corners of the room. He nodded his head rhythmically waiting for his cue.

"Lord save me, the world is going crazy
This life that we're living ain't worth it if we're just killing
Every opportunity that's here for you and me
To make the world a better place and achieve the state of grace
That we be hoping for, praying for, crying for and bleeding for
So Lord help me, every day I'm on my knees
Begging father please to just give us a squeeze
Because the babies have their needs and the mothers don't have the means
To make their lifestyles fruitful, meaningful and beautiful.

I can't take it, just need to make it in this life
Without the trouble and strife
And put an end to all the misery, because it's getting' to me.
I'll light a spliff and hope it takes away the pain
But instead of sunshine all I see is rain
When all of my people
Are livin' only for gain.
Talk to me.

Ricky bobbed his head to maintain his rhythm and cue him in for the hook, which he sang under his breath.

Talk to me people; tell me your plight
All I know is that brothers got to get up and fight
To maintain their own sanity, hindered by vanity
It's all crazy, getting lazy
But one-day maybe, we'll think about the babies.

It was going well, Ricky was pleased. His constant head bouncing helped him maintain a rhythm consistent with the beat. Without hesitation he jumped into the second verse.

Life in a closed community, should bring about some unity
But my passions make me rage, we need to turn another page
Lost in a culture that we never really knew
The only thing that makes you live is what you know of you.

Ricky's rap was cut short. For in the distance he heard the high tones of his telephone ringing. He lowered the volume and shifted the wheeled chair that he sat on steadily to his left to reach for the receiver.

"Yo, Ricky," he opened.

"Ingin boy, what you up to?" came the reply.

"Chillin'," Ricky shot back.

"Hey yo, you call that bitch yet?" inquired Ingin.

"Who?"

"The bitches from last night guy, was 'appened to you? You forget already? Hey yo, I'm looking to fuck that Amanda bitch again. The number she gave me belonged to some blasted chemical factory. She was probably so fucked up last night she couldn't think straight. So you need to get me that number guy," replied Ingin in greasy tones.

"Yeah sure, I'll do it and call you back later."

"Frigg that. You need to do it now boy, I'm itchin' to hit that pussy again. Make sure of that payday know what I'm saying? The bitch is taxable. I'm sure she gonna wanna pay for the dicky. Shit man. You should'a heard that bitch screamin' last night, she ain't never had no fuck like that in the whole of her life."

Ricky tired easily of Ingin's bravado, he'd already had an ear full of it during the drive back from Claire's house. He wondered just why the hell Ingin couldn't get a life.

"Hey man, I didn't tell you did I? I split the sock whilst I was up that pussy," Ingin continued.

"What?" replied Ricky slightly worried.

"The bag burst out on me man!" shot back Ingin. "Boy, I fucked that pussy so hard the rubber burst out on me. Shot all up in the bitch and everything."

Ricky remembered Amanda's problem with having children and thus paid it little mind. Ingin, obviously though, had been thinking about it.

"Boy if that bitch breed, I'm in the money!" exclaimed Ingin.

"What about the child?" asked Ricky disgusted.

"He'll be in the money too, so will all my kids, all nine a dem. An all dem baby moddas, they'll be safe!"

"Sure, well you better hope she breeds then," replied Ricky dryly.

"Hey yo! Talk to the bitch man. Call me back in five," closed Ingin.

Ricky replaced the receiver once Ingin signed off. He rubbed his face and wondered what to do. He figured that Claire was probably due a call anyway, so he walked over to the jacket that he had worn to the club and pulled out the piece of paper that she had handed to him. He pressed the numbers and waited. Claire's voice greeted him on the other end of the phone.

"Hi, it's me," he opened.

"Oh hi." Claire greeted him with joy. "I was wondering whether you got back safely this morning, I forgot to go over the map with you," she said.

"We got lost a couple of times, but we made it. Didn't get to bed till four."

"Oh gosh. I hit the sack straight away, I was bushed," replied

Claire. "I'm glad you called, I was wondering if you were going to bother or not."

"I was going to bother. Guess I was waiting till the right time. How's Amanda?"

"She's fine, she left not twenty minutes ago."

"Ingin wants her number, the one she gave him was wrong."

Claire brooded and replied nervously.

"Is he angry?" she asked cautiously.

"No. He doesn't even think she did it on purpose. That's what she did right?"

"We talked about it this morning, I'm afraid Ingin won't be seeing her again. What shall we do?"

"Dunno."

"Can you stall him, maybe he'll forget."

Ricky became slightly angry. He didn't want to get caught up in the middle of Amanda's mess. He really didn't see why he should.

"Why couldn't she just tell him?" he asked, in a fed up way.

"You're right, maybe she should. Does he have a number?"

"Good idea, it's a mobile 04123 6689451. I'll tell him to expect a call from her. You busy today?"

"Yes, I've got to go to a meal with Paul, my ex-husband. We have these very close friends Rosy and Colin. They used to invite us round for dinner and they were upset when we split up. They made us promise that despite our separation we would continue to eat with them so, we figured we'd do it you know, for them. I'm free tomorrow evening though."

"So am I, where shall we meet?"

"Brown's in Covent Garden, about seven."

"That's some fancy restaurant right?"

"Don't worry, it's on me."

"Sure, I'll see you there then."

Ricky replaced the receiver; thought for a second then dialled Ingin who was satisfied with his explanation. He felt slightly guilty at the way he had betrayed his friend, particularly in favour of some one whom he knew little of. But he reasoned all the same that Ingin probably deserved the brush off that was about to come. He settled back into his chair and engaged the computer once again. His beat cranked to life and he commenced to finish his rap.

"I'm burdened, heavy laden", he began
For too many, crack is the only haven
From the misery of this existence
But I'm a soldier, putting up resistance
Gaugin' my A.K, to shoot my way out of the fray
Let Christians pray and let players play
Let wisdom help me through the rain
And let my enemies feel the pain
Let goodness and mercies follow me the days of my life
Let purposeful intentions take me through the strife
I can't take it no more my only choice is to fight
It's the only way we ever gon' see light.
He bought in the hook for the last time.
Talk to me people; tell me your plight
All I know is that brothers got to get up and fight
To maintain their own sanity, hindered by vanity
It's all crazy, 'cos we're getting lazy
But one day maybe, we'll think about the babies."

It was an impossible drive for Claire and Paul to Rosy and Colin's place. They had been silent for the majority of the journey as they basically had nothing to say to each other. They had talked many times on the telephone but it was the first time since splitting up that they had shared the same space, never mind going out together.

As it was, Rosy and Colin had insisted on their presence together. Present partners, if they had any, were not allowed. They had asserted that come what may, they would only entertain them together. They both took a deep breath as Paul slowed up his Lexus in the driveway and parked it next to a Mercedes that belonged to Emma and Peter, the other guests. Rosy met them at the door to her very large and expensive house, She was a skinny little woman, whose face was a collection of wrinkles that sat beneath a heavy dose of badly applied make-up. She had a blonde hairstyle that belonged to the sixties but looked elegant all the same in her long black Lurex dress with a v-neck front. She kissed them both and took their coats before ushering them into the living room. Claire took a second to admire her former lover. Paul stood tall at six foot and though he was balding the years had not changed his handsome appearance. He jogged every morning and took regular saunas. He was a healthy man and didn't it show. Regardless of their separation Claire had always been astounded by his look. He was an elegant man that even the emerging wrinkles and the grey hair could not disguise.

Both Emma and Peter greeted them with kisses. Claire shied away from Peter. She disliked him intensely. He had sucked her toes and eaten out her pussy a few years ago at an orgy and he still fancied his chances of going the whole hog with her. To him, news of her separation with Paul was the best news he had received in years and he had been secretly calling her in an effort to entice her into bed.

Colin stood by the Victorian corbel fireplace that occupied the very centre of the far wall sipping a glass of dry white chardonnay. He greeted no-one. They all had to come to him. He was a tall man approaching fifty with a commanding presence and a very serious expression on his fat piggish face. His gut hung dangerously over his trousers and it seemed as though the bow tie that he had on was strangling him for the sheer size of his neck. Claire and Paul advanced towards him. She had to stand on her toes to kiss his cheek. He refused to bend down. Paul shook his hand and greeted him with a nervous hello. His little wife approached them, took a pathetically awkward stance placing one hand over the other and asked them timidly what they wanted to drink. She disappeared instantly and returned with a bottle of white sauvignon and glasses, which she handed to them and poured. She appeared conscious of her over-bearing husband all the time, well aware that at any point he could erupt and embarrass her if she ever put a foot wrong.

"Dinner will be ready in a jiffy," she said shuffling her little body back into the kitchen.

"Well hurry up about it woman, for Christ's sake," ordered Colin in his gruff voice. "It'll be the second coming before we eat tonight."

Rosy stopped in the middle of the living room, flicked back

her head and issued an imbecilic chuckle to hide her discomfiture, before shifting with much more pace, back into the kitchen. Peter stepped across the room and gave Paul a hearty slap on the back, which made him choke slightly on his drink. Claire slipped away quickly to join Emma, before she too came over to them.

"How's the divorce going?" Peter slyly asked of Paul.

"It's costing me a bloody packet," he replied, knowing that Claire was just a stone's throw away. "I've got to pay my solicitor and hers too. And these bastards don't half like to drag things out. Claire and I have agreed terms and all we want them to do is to get on with it."

"You didn't declare your full earnings and assets to them did you? They'll take you to the bloody cleaners you know," warned Colin, also aware of Claire's presence.

"No way," replied Paul. "She had a go at me for not including the fillies and the Porsche, but I explained to her that they were more liabilities than assets, no bloody horsepower in either of them. On top of that I earn two hundred and fifty grand a year."

"Ooh you scheming little sod," interrupted Peter, "you mean you're going to do her out of all that lovely money?"

"Oh come on old man, do you think she would really let me get away with that? We've agreed her five million privately," replied Paul

"Good for you," said Peter, turning to admire Claire with a devious smile.

"So, Colin," asked Paul, "how's toilet paper?"

"Full of shit," Colin joked, his rotund face beaming. "We're about to move into East Africa. A lot of call for bog roll out there recently."

"What? Thousands of war torn refugees crapping themselves?" inferred Peter almost crapping himself with laughter.

"Cruel!" concluded Colin in Peter's direction.

Rosy popped her head into the living room, nervously trying to get her husband's attention. She was edgy and had wondered if she was doing the best thing by openly soliciting his interest. He noticed her, mumbled angrily and excused himself, wondering what the hell she wanted him for. Peter turned to Paul. A slippery look etched on his face.

"You're going to see this divorce thing through then?" he asked slyly.

"What do you mean?" asked Paul.

"Well, I mean, look at her," Peter replied, inclining his head in Claire's direction. "She's such a beautiful thing, you may not realise what you're actually letting go of, old man. Until it's too late of course."

"Well I think I'll have to suffer the consequences and just get on with it I suppose," replied Paul with honest resignation.

"Such a lovely little thing," said Peter almost in his own world. "Such lovely long blonde hair, gorgeous tanned skin, ripe full bloodied breasts." Peter was now in his own world. "A round shapely bottom that could make even gay men swoon. Strong tanned legs, delicious ankles, and smooth manicured fingernails. You know, I vividly remember that evening when you let me..."

"You're not developing a fixation for my wife are you!?" interrupted Paul enraged.

Peter jumped. The ferocity of Paul's question bought him back instantly to the land of the living.

"My God no." He said meekly. "I was just merely commenting on..."

Before he could finish what would have been a feeble explanation, the room was awash with the thunderous sound of Colin's irate voice from the kitchen.

"What the hell do you mean you forgot the lemons!!?" he roared. "How the hell do you expect to eat a good Moroccan dish without the bloody lemons!!? Are you totally incapable woman!!? My God, do I have to do everything myself around here!!?"

Everyone in the room went silent. The only noise eventually emerged from the kitchen. Colin, like he always did, allowed his voice to mellow out into a grumble, complaining under his breath whilst searching the kitchen cupboards and slamming them violently after scanning them and realising for himself, that there was no lemon. Rosy could be heard softly and ever so pitifully sobbing.

"Poor Rosy," said Claire cautiously under her breath to

Emma, "Colin can be a real bastard sometimes."

"He wouldn't be the only one around here with a sad bastard for a husband," said Emma.

Claire noted the distress in her voice. She liked Emma. She was a soft and very gentle person that didn't have it in her to hurt even a fly. She was a short thin middle aged woman with wide eyes. Her hair was black and cut short in a bob. She was a picture of quiet elegance as she stood in her long navy crepe dress with chiffon panels. Her drink held in one hand with the other hand covering it and her head slightly bowed. Claire knew immediately the source of her dolour wanting to coax an explanation out of her, knowing that it would ease her pain somewhat.

"That bastard Peter's screwing around again," she said.

Claire feigned surprise.

"Not again," she said. "Any idea who?"

"Some fucking American bitch that pretends to be his P.A."

"The blonde bimbo, big jugs, not an ounce of grey matter in sight thing?" asked Claire. "The one that came to Michael's little soirée in Paris?"

"The same," replied Emma nonchalantly. She changed her tone dramatically and looked deep into Claire's eyes." I do so admire you for what you're doing. I only wish I had the guts to do the same."

Claire rubbed Emma's exposed arm. She didn't have the nerve to tell her that Peter had been making phone calls to her. She figured that their marriage at some point would have to come to an end but she didn't want to be responsible for it happening. At least not in that way.

"After a while it wasn't such a difficult choice for me to make," she said with compassion.

"Oh, Just bloody well serve it!! We'll be here all bloody night!!" thundered Colin from the kitchen.

"You know," said Emma almost whispering but with grit. "You know sometimes I fantasise about having the complete arse fucked off me by a six foot Rasta with dreadlocks down to his bottom and a dick as long as…"

She stopped holding aloft the two forefingers of each hand slightly apart. She checked and moved them further apart.

"…that," she concluded giggling.

Claire was humbled by the consonance.

"Be careful what you wish for darling," she said winking.

"Whatever do you mean?" asked Emma inquisitively.

Claire pouted to shush her up as Rosy scurried back into the living room wearing oven gloves and carrying a giant pot. You wouldn't have been able to tell that she had just been crying.

"Dinner's ready," she said with an upbeat tone as she placed the pot on the table before dashing back into the kitchen. Colin arrived in the living room. His tall obese frame showered with dignity and uprightness. He implored them all to take their seats as Rosy dashed in and out of the room with food, which she carefully laid on the table.

When all was ready and all were seated Colin invited everyone to tuck in. The sauvignon flowed, as did the chardonnay. Eagerly the diners tucked into the well-prepared dishes of couscous, lamb and prunes, chicken and raisins, fried aubergines dressed in garlic and parsley, cannellini beans with cucumber and a grated cucumber salad with caraway and pieces of dried fish.

"Get this recipe when you went Marrakech?" inquired Peter. "It's delicious."

"Yes," replied Rosy proudly.

"With a little help from a book of Moroccan cuisine," added Colin. "She left out the bloody lemons though!" he squirmed. "Preserved lemons – they give a distinctive flavour to all Moroccan dishes," he added.

"Forgot the lemons," repeated Rosy.

She poured another glass of wine for herself and whipped it around her teeth to remove the pieces of chicken that had got stuck up in there. Then she rested her elbows on the table and rested her chin on fingers that were clasped together. She emitted a new aura and took charge of herself by slipping into motherly mode.

"I'm so glad we're doing this again. Claire, Paul. We should never stop eating together, no matter what happens to you both. Now promise me, we won't stop eating together."

Everyone was embarrassed except Colin who echoed the notion by nodding whilst ineptly stuffing large amounts of chicken into his mouth.

"We'll always eat together, Rosy," declared Paul, more interested in the food than in carrying on this particular line of conversation, "come what may. Right Claire?"

"Of course!" she retorted, paying the conversation little mind.

"So how is it going in the, you know, the sort of area of new partners then?" asked Peter tensely but with the cunningness of the sly fox that he was. "Any new loves for either of you on the old horizon?"

"Reprobate," whispered Claire under her breath.

"I'm sorry?" asked Peter in a high pitched tone

Paul threw him a dirty look.

"Marinate," responded Claire. "The chicken, it's beautifully marinat....ed!" she squirmed.

"Oh what a question to ask!" declared Rosy in disgust, throwing her napkin on the table.

"Shut up woman!" blasted Colin, chicken sauce dribbling down the side of his mouth and spraying all over the table as he spoke. "A perfectly normal question to ask. We're all grown ups here aren't we? Paul you first. What have you been up to? Keep it clean."

Paul reluctantly wiped the corners of his mouth with his napkin. He didn't want to speak but he didn't dare to disobey Colin.

"Well I met someone, a couple of weeks back," he began nervously. Claire took a keen interest. "Nice little thing," he added.

The air went quiet.

"That all?" probed Peter.

Paul threw him another dirty look.

"Well," he continued, nearly stuttering. "She's a nice young lady. What more can I say?"

"Damn it man you're avoiding the issue!" bellowed Colin with palms open. "How old is she? What does she do for a living? Has she got big tits? What are her blowjobs like? What? Information man damn it! Keep it clean."

"Is she married?" probed Peter staring hard at Paul with a slight but obvious raise of his left eyebrow.

Paul stuttered slightly. Peter was beginning to irritate him.

He was becoming more and more aware of the competition that was developing between them but rather than seek to avoid it any longer he met it head on. He stopped eating and rested back in his chair. Claire eyed him intently awaiting his next words with relish.

"Yes, she is actually," he submitted finally.

"Har! Har!" shouted Peter, victoriously waving his forefinger in Paul's direction. "You old dog you!"

Claire was still. She said nothing.

"She's married to some old fart that's terminally ill. Got a couple of year's left. She'll take his estate, all thirty million of it," Paul declared, no longer concerned at how anyone felt.

Claire was now shaking her head and staring at him through slitted eyes.

"I suppose you'll recoup your settlement then won't you?" she asked with controlled venom.

"Guess I will darling," replied Paul defensively. "What about you then?" He asked nervously flicking his fingers in her direction and easing forward to rest his elbows on the table. He tucked in his eyebrows, clasped his hands together and rested his chin on them scrutinising her incessantly. It had no longer remained a conversation but was becoming a battle of wits between Claire and Paul. The crowd was enticed and listened eagerly for Claire's response. Peter enjoyed the moment for all it was worth, Rosy was slightly embarrassed but wanted to hear more. Emma was worried for Claire and Colin gobbled his food quicker. His eyes were not watching the food but nearly popping out of his head for the sheer excitement. Claire composed herself and daintily cut the thin pieces of fish that were on her plate. Then spoke calmly and with indifference.

"Actually I met some one last night," she said popping a small piece of fish into her mouth. "He's twenty–nine."

"Ooh a young stud!" declared Peter with excitement.

"He's from Peckham."

"An artist!" announced Colin.

They all eyed him with bewilderment written all over their faces.

"Well they live in the poorest areas don't they?" was Colin's retort.

"And he's black," Claire proclaimed.

There was silence for a split second as the shock sank in. Peter immediately choked on his chicken and coughed profusely. His face red with the struggle. Emma dropped both her knife and fork and gazed at Claire in total admiration. Colin and Paul dressed back in their chairs and rested their hands on their stomachs in tandem to absorb the impact. Rosy shook violently then mumbling something under her breath left the table.

"Black?" asked Paul in a deliberately unimpressed tone of voice.

"As the ace of spades," replied Claire coolly, raising another piece of fish to her mouth.

Peter was downing copious amounts of wine to relieve the cough in his throat and Colin commenced slapping him viciously on the back. Emma spoke.

"Why I think that's wonderful darling, I'm pleased for you," she said.

"Thank you," replied Claire sweetly. "It's not quite off the ground yet but I'm sure it will be after tomorrow night."

"What is it you like about him?" asked Peter, in between broken but steadier coughs.

"Well he's intelligent. Got a good head on his shoulders. He seems like a sensitive sort of chap. His good looks..."

"His big dick!" interrupted Paul with angst.

"I don't know about that darling I haven't seen it yet," Claire replied with disgust.

"Oh but you've probably felt it," Paul accused, his tone getting louder.

"What in my hand, my mouth or up my snatch, darling? Which one?" Claire retorted. "Don't worry sweetheart, when I do get to find out what it feels like I'll be sure and let you know!" she said sarcastically.

"Oh yes, do!" jumped in Emma, forgetting herself.

Peter threw her a dirty look. She dug her face back into her food and ate quickly.

"You bitch!" replied Paul.

"Well if it wasn't for the years of sleeping around on your

part, I may not have to resort to seeing someone else now would I?" Claire replied with vexation.

"And years of boring me to the point of distraction wouldn't have led me up another cunt now would it?" responded Paul.

Claire shot up, flinging her napkin on the table, as did Paul. They began shouting at one another over the table, insults and accusations flying around with bane. Both gave as good as they got. Emma and Peter joined in to calm them down. Colin quietly ate more chicken chuckling and muttering to himself as he did so. Soon, the air was ablaze with angry screaming voices, Claire's being the most prominent. Then it all stopped suddenly as a mightier voice detonated from the kitchen.

"Claire! In here now!" It was Rosy, her voice had risen quite a few octaves from the squirming little housewife that met them at the door when they arrived. Now she was like a volcano and in this sort of mood, she bore more of a likeness to her husband than anyone else. Claire left the table with finger firmly pointed in Paul's direction.

"I'm not done with you, you bastard!" she said as she left.

"Go get 'em my little tigress," said Peter watching her in admiration as she left the room.

Paul threw him another dirty look.

Claire stepped into the kitchen, raging. Her anger was matched by Rosy's, who, leaning against the cooker, looked like a starved Rottweiler.

"What the hell do you think you're doing!" she pounced. "What are you now? A whore?"

"You have no right to judge me, Rosy," defended Claire.

"What the hell are you doing with a black guy? What can he offer you?"

"I don't know!" yelled Claire in desperation. "I only met him yesterday for Christ's sake! What the hell is everybody so ate up for anyway? Just because the guy's black!"

Rosy slowed down and dropped her tone also. She tried to reason.

"Claire, I'm the last person that anyone call a racist. Barbados is a lovely place," she began.

Claire folded her arms, stared hard at her and kinked her head sideways slightly, hardly impressed.

"You've always been like a sister to me and sometimes like a daughter, I only want the best for you, I don't want some pimp hustling you out of your money," she said.

"He's not a pimp. He's very a very nice young man, actually!"

Rosy raged again. Her voice hitting earth shattering proportions this time. She stabbed herself furiously with her finger. Her hair flew everywhere and her face a blood red.

"I remember Profumo!" she said with vehemence. "Christine Keeler! It all started with those blacks in Notting Hill. Nothing but pimps they were!"

"Oh get back to reality please!" begged Claire.

Rosy lowered her voice again. This time adopting a threatening tone that made her sound like Yoda the Jedi knight.

"I'm as real as you'll ever get my dear. But let me tell you one thing, he'll not put a single foot in my house do you hear me? Never!"

"That's fine," announced Claire placidly, a tear rolling down her face. "And as long as you keep up this attitude, neither will I!"

Claire turned from the kitchen furiously and beheld Paul with his coat on standing in the hallway ready to go. He eyed her poisonously.

"You won't take five million pounds off me and give it to some reggae boy!" he said coldly.

Claire was enthused and put a slap onto his cheek so hard it turned red.

"You'll give me my five million and you won't give a fuck about what I do with it, you bastard!" she said.

Paul approached the front door, opened it then stepped out.

"We'll see about that," he said calmly.

Claire walked over to where her coat hung, put it on, then called a cab from the phone that was in the hall. She sat down on the chair and waited. Rosy walked past her saying nothing, as did Colin a couple of times. She was moved and had to work hard to stop more tears from falling. She could hear the distasteful conversation that had developed from the living room. It moved her more. She wondered where she was and what time frame she was in. Was this really the back end of the nineteen nineties, just about to approach the Millennium? Were people still so stuck in their ways, that they still were unable to see and appreciate the condition of one's heart and see this as no reflection whatsoever by the colour of their skin? She cried. She could do nothing else. But she cried, not for herself, but for them. Emma strolled up and knelt before her. She took her hand kissed it and rubbed it against the side of her face.

"I've always admired you," she said. "For your sheer courage and strength of character. Sometimes I wonder if you were meant to be here, I mean with us. You're a different breed, unlike us. All we know to do is to bitch, squabble and boast about all the money we have or all the money we're going to make before we rip one another to pieces with our cutting comments and our self deflating ego trips. My God, we think we're so important that we don't have to give a shit about the way we make even our so-called friends feel. This decadence is death. We should be ashamed."

Emma rose to her feet and kissed Claire's cheek, which by now was soaked with her tears.

"Date who you like my queen, for a queen is what you are. Enjoy every moment of it and cherish ever second that you spend with him. If he is to be your dark handsome prince, make him your king and if he does love you, love him back ten fold. Take his head and gently rest it between your breasts to give him comfort and make him feel secure. Let him feel your devotion and let him feel your love my queen for a queen is simply what you are."

Claire looked up at her through watery eyes. She leaned forward and wrapped her arms around her waist and cried some more.

Emma gripped her tightly and spoke again.

"I'll never forsake you. Never," she said softly.

Amanda was sitting alone in the dark. She had drowned a bottle of Sangre de Toro and was halfway through the merlot. She had cocked up her feet on the footstool and was staring blankly at the television. She had been back to Harrods and the ten thousand pounds worth of shoes and handbags that she had bought were still in their carrier bags and scattered across the settee. She was out of her mind. Depression had set in. The doctor had given her a course of tablets, which she had neglected to take. They were no fucking good anyway, she had concluded, because they did nothing to ease her pain or brighten up her spirits. She raised up her waist from the chair, slightly, to let out a loud fart. Then she eased back and carried on blankly watching the TV screen. She had hardly noticed the sound of a key twisting in the lock of the front door or the;

"Darling? Darling? Hi, I'm home!" That came from her husband Alan as he struggled through the door with his suitcases. He was a thin man whose grey hair was balding at the front. He had a thin slightly wrinkled face and a sun tan. He lived in suits. The one he had on this evening was pinstriped. He dropped his bags in the hall and picked up a small bundle of unopened letters from the small table in the hall. He proceeded through to the living room expecting to find no one around. Once through the door he laid surprised eyes on his inebriated wife and said nothing. Amanda turned her head to him, her eyes half closed.

"You're back, I see," she said in insouciant fashion.

"Yes, but only until Thursday, then it's Taiwan for three days," he announced.

"Hmm," was Amanda's tired response.

Alan walked over to where she sat and eyed the bottles that she had been drinking from. He noticed the empty bottle then picked up the merlot, examined how much of it had gone and put it down again.

"You really must do something about this drinking habit you have you know," he said.

Amanda said nothing but stared fixedly at the TV. He walked over to the settee and picked up a Harrods bag. He pulled out the pair of shoes that were inside and threw Amanda a look. He investigated another bag to behold a leather handbag.

"Been shopping then?" he asked in an effort to become jovial, but again Amanda gave him no response. He dropped onto the settee and began to open up the letters. They were fairly unimportant but he stopped at the third one once he had opened it.

"Oh for Christ's sake!" he exclaimed.

It was his credit card bill and statement. He was not impressed that Amanda, over the last month, had spent seventy thousand pounds on nothing that she needed. He scanned the itemised statement again, just to check that he believed his eyes. He read through endless purchases of shoes, handbags, clothes, make-up and perfume. He knew that Amanda shopped regularly, but never before had she run up a bill the likes of which he was looking at.

"You've spent a lot over the last month," he exclaimed.

Amanda turned to him and smiled an intoxicated smile.

"Have I darling?" she asked. "Oooh."

"You spent over seventy thousand fuckin' quid! What do you mean, oooh?" Alan snapped.

"Oooh!" smiled Amanda.

Alan was flabberghasted. He hardly knew what to say.

"This has got to stop!" he said to no-one in particular, shaking his head angrily.

Amanda rose out of her seat and rocked slightly from side to side as she folded her arms to confront her husband.

"What's got to stop darling?" she asked, ready for combat. "What's got to stop? Me spending all your hard earned cash? Going on shopping trips at least every other day because I have fuck bloody all else to do with my time? Because my beloved husband is forever away jet-setting around the world going to business meeting after fucking business meeting without me his lovely wife to keep him company at nights?"

She was in full fettle. Her arms waved and her hair jumped around as she went hell for leather for him. Alan said nothing but stared at the ground. She lowered her tone slightly.

"I think it's quite a nice trade-off myself," she continued thrusting a thumb out behind her head. "You fuck off to Paris, Germany, America and Tai-fucking-wan and I'll spend your money! How's that? Let's make an arrangement out of it. You piss off when you like, I'll spend like a bitch! Either that or…" she pretended to think by placing a finger against her mouth. "…I know! We'll do a Claire and Paul! Yes, that's it! Divorce! We'll get divorced and you give me half of everything! Every fucking thing. How's that?"

"You're bloody sick!" retorted Alan.

"You're the sick one!" Amanda broke into tears. "You can't even give me a fucking child to keep me company when you're gone!"

Alan jumped up raising his arms to the sky.

"Oh we're not back to this again are we?" he pleaded.

"Yes we fucking well are!" screamed Amanda. "It never went away, it never goes away! I have it with me all the fucking time!"

"Look, I'm not getting into this again. If you're infertile…"

"How do you know I'm infertile!?" bawled Amanda with increasingly obvious frustration. "You've never suggested that we seek advice on this! You're too afraid of discovering that your manhood has withered. Or that your sperm count is too low!"

"…We'll adopt!" concluded Alan

Amanda was now at the height of her frustration. Her voice raised high enough to be heard outside.

"I don't want to adopt! I've told you already! I want my own blood, my own flesh and blood! Is that too much too ask? You get back from these business trips and the first thing you do is slip that greasy wrinkly little thing inside of me, go to sleep and the next morning you're off to get a fucking plane," she howled. "It wouldn't be so bad if you could produce a fucking child!" She changed her tone and mused aloud. "Maybe I ought to find someone who can give me a child. Find some young stud somewhere!"

The suggestion enraged Alan. He shot out of the settee and grabbed her by the throat.

"If you ever do that, or if I ever find out that you did that, I'll sue first then cut you off without a penny!" he shook her head violently. "Do you hear me!"

Amanda swung her arms erratically and wrested herself from his grip. She stood, back arched, rubbing her neck and pointing a finger at him.

"Don't you ever, ever, put your hands on me like that again!" she warned. She staggered past him in tears and left the room, slamming the door behind her. He jumped as a Venetian vase that was situated in the hall went crashing onto the marble tiled floor. Instantly the air was filled with the sound of Amanda's crying mingled with the hefty stamp of her feet as she ran upstairs. Alan felt the agitation, which released itself with a wholesome kick against the side of the settee and a loud "Fuck!" Which echoed from his mouth.

Amanda shot into her bedroom, slamming the door behind her and immediately plunged onto the bed. Her cries formed a sorrowful crescendo of noise. Her tears came from many things. It was the sheer arrogance and the sheer ineptitude of the man that she called a husband, in the way that he so callously treated her. She was expected to be a good subservient housewife to him. Not that she ever had to cook for him or clean up after him. He allowed her the privileges of staff to take care of the menial tasks. But it was the way in which she was expected to simply accept his lifestyle and the expectation that he had of her. The fact that she was not allowed to share it. It was also the way in which he saw her as a tool. In the early days of their marriage they made love for the pleasure of one another's company. Now he simply fucked her and quickly too, whenever he felt like it. Which was usually right after he came home. She knew that on his trips away he would treat himself to the delights of the local whorehouses and strip joints. She knew that he wasn't a faithful husband.

It was the way in which he refused to condemn their relationship as a sham. He would not divorce her, for he had made it clear that if it ever came down to it he may not be too disappointed to see the back of her. However, if it meant sacrificing that money it would never happen. She hadn't the guts or the nerve to fight him for he was too powerful. She had no evidence to base divorce proceedings on and in any case she would probably lose. On top of it all, the prenuptial agreement that she innocently signed on the day of their wedding had sealed her fate. They had no children and she didn't want to be cut off without a penny. She had grown too accustomed to the lavish lifestyle that he had bought her into. She didn't want to lose it. But most of all, her tears were about the children - or lack of them. It disgusted her that neither of them was able to find the courage to deal with the situation head on and answer the question of which one of them was unable to bear fruit. They were both too frightened to accept their possible failing in this area. His possible impotence and her possible barrenness. On top of this they didn't trust each other enough to keep it a secret from their friends. Neither of them wished to be considered a laughing stock in circles where people had many children and raised large families. To adopt would possibly reveal too much but it wasn't just that fact that upset her the most. As she had mentioned, she wanted her own offspring, her own children, her own flesh and blood. She was an only child and throughout her childhood she had wished for a brother or a sister. Now that she was older, the lack of a relative with whom she could share her thoughts was cutting her to the bone.

Her tears rained, soaking the bedspread as they flooded out. Her gut ached. Her spirit was broken. In the midst of what was considered life, there was no life. There was only desolation and loneliness. Her solitude had become unbearable. The world seemed to weigh on her shoulders. There were lots of things that she could be doing, particularly with the amount of money that she had. To Amanda it was all worthless and pointless, because the very thing that seemed to make life for her, was the very thing she could not have. Her tears poured out and as they did so, there was a slight and very timid knock on the door. She didn't answer so Alan entered the room anyway.

"Darling?" he said softly. "I'm sorry."

Again she said nothing. He walked over to the bed and lay over her, his arms extending his body from the bed and her body, which was still lying face down. He lowered himself to lie on top of her. She remained unmoved.

"I'm so sorry, darling, I really didn't mean to upset you," he said, and slowly began to kiss the back of her neck. He moved from there slowly and began nibbling her ear.

"I'm so sorry sweetheart," he said between nibbles. "I didn't want to hurt you. You spend as much money as you like."

She knew what was to come and sure enough in seconds it did. He began to steadily press his lower half against hers in circular motions, positioning his penis between her buttocks. She still remained motionless, conscious of what was going on all the time. Once he had received his erection he began to undo his belt. She let him do so with little regard for what he was about to do. She simply didn't care. Taking her stillness as a sign to continue, he dropped his trousers and his pants in one movement to reveal his bare bottom and a stiffish prick lying between her covered behind. Whilst still writhing his lower body, he lifted her skirt. Again she did nothing to stop him. In a swift movement he pulled her pants down, but because she didn't move he couldn't bring them fully down to expose her naked bottom so her ripped them off. He realised that she had decided not to move and was not going to risk a struggle by asking her to. She had not opened her legs to allow him into her vagina. He was not going beg or struggle with her to do so. So he held his cock in his hands, parted her buttocks and crudely and without remorse jabbed it into the nearest available crevice.

four

Browns was busy. Claire and Ricky had queued for a long time before they were able to get a seat. Once they did, they decided that they would stay for as long as they wanted to irrespective of whom or how many people were waiting. The food wasn't long in coming and it was tasty. Claire revelled in the fact that Ricky was unaccustomed not only to the food, but the atmosphere of the place and was enjoying it.

"So," she asked, staring hard at him. "How do you feel?"

"OK," he said quietly, not looking into her eyes, but rather eyeing the people around him.

Claire wanted to speak to him about the dinner party at Rosy's, but she declined, not wanting to upset him. She was also cautious wondering whether the news might put him off the possibility of their having a relationship. But she stayed on the subject all the same, curious to discover not only his feelings but also his intentions towards her.

"Have you ever been out with a white woman?" she asked timidly.

"Yes," he replied, "but nothing major. I guess I never took those relationships seriously."

"In what sense?" she probed.

Ricky tucked into a piece of meat.

"I fucked them, took their money, that sort of thing."

Claire was not surprised but somewhat angered by the brutality of his honesty.

"Really?" she replied in a half-disgusted tone. "How long ago are we talking about here?" she continued. Ricky sensed her agitation.

"Ten, twelve years ago," he said. "I was a kid then, you

know? Guess I never really took anything seriously," he stuck piece of a fried potato in his mouth. Ricky thought for a second, then looked at Claire. She knew from the look that there was more brutal honesty to come. "But I'll tell you one thing though." He stopped chewing. "Young or old, then or now, white women's attitudes to black men haven't changed."

"And what are those attitudes?" inquired Claire, eager for the debate.

"You see something in us that you feel you have to pay for. You give us a lot of devotion and a lot of dedication. You make sacrifices for us that even our own women wouldn't make. You'd give us your last penny, if we asked for it. That's how white women treat black men." Ricky dumped another piece of meat in his mouth.

"It sounds like love to me," replied Claire.

"Black women love us too. But in the main they won't go to half the lengths that white women do. I don't think it's wrong or warped. But it's a fact."

"Perhaps it's because we're more tolerant of you than black women are," reasoned Claire.

"That's a fact. The question is why?" queried Ricky.

"Maybe we have a different perception of what love is, compared to most black women. But the truth is, we won't allow ourselves to be trampled on, just like black women."

"I think you will. At least for longer than black women will," shot back Ricky. "The truth is that you are more tolerant of us, even our bad ways, but we still haven't found out why."

Claire thought further. "Maybe it's not about love so much then, but more about the reasons why we love," she suggested.

"I've always been of the opinion, that if you love someone for anything else other than their personality, you either don't love them or you love them for the wrong reasons," intoned Ricky, sipping his orange juice.

"So what are you saying? White women love black men for the wrong reasons?" asked Claire.

"You all love that tough, strong black man image don't you?" said Ricky. "It's exotic, sexy, fun, dangerous, exiting and different. You white people certainly love things that are different. To a point."

Claire thought hard. She couldn't connect with his reasoning, she strove to present another view.

"So what's wrong with that?" she quizzed.

"Those things are all cosmetic, if they're not stereotypes. It should be about making a spiritual connection with your partner. Black and white spirits are different; we belong to different cultures and have different heritages and thus we are constructed from different spiritual forces. It's difficult to connect with a spiritual force that isn't the same," he motioned.

Claire was disappointed by his view. In her opinion he had left no room for the obvious and most immediate factor. Freedom of choice. Freedom to love, to be impressed with whatever you wanted to be impressed with. It sounded to her as if Ricky disliked or distrusted the idea of being in a mixed relationship. She reasoned that if these were really his views their relationship would end as quickly as it had begun. This worried her, for she liked him and he was growing on her all the time. He had come out with a lot of points but none that explained any attraction that he might have felt towards her. She decided to seek further for it concluding that if it did not emerge they would leave the restaurant as they had entered it. Single. Her approach this time was more direct, almost to the point of desperate.

"So I don't have a chance with you?" she asked. "Because I could never love you for the right reasons? We can never hope to make a spiritual connection?"

Ricky was honest in his appraisal.

"I've never held out much hope for relationships between black people and white. I've always been sceptical about them. They are relationships that are forced to work. They aren't relationships that work naturally. Someone has to make a sacrifice that is above and beyond the call of duty. It's called self denial."

Claire dropped her head. She concluded in an instant that it wasn't going to happen between them.

"However," continued Ricky, "I have faith in human nature. If everything I was told by my parents is true, then love should conquer all barriers. I'd expect couples to find something, something real, that they can both cling on to and allow to flourish."

Claire smiled, her faith had been re-energised.

"And you think that could happen with us," she asked expectantly.

"I've never run from a challenge," Ricky replied. "And I do like you," he said.

She touched his hand. "I like you too," she said. "So shall we give it a try?"

"Sure," Ricky replied nonchalantly. "What have we got to lose?"

Claire smiled again, looking deep into his eyes. She wanted to savour the moment as a streak of happiness shot through her stomach. But she couldn't.

"Oh shit! I don't believe this!" she said, turning her head sideways. "It's her again, the Hottentot Venus!"

Ricky turned his head to behold the woman with the big breasts that had been in the nightclub when they met. Ricky laughed.

"Of all the joints in all the world...." he began.

"Don't even go there please!" ordered Claire. "I wouldn't be surprised if she followed us here! I reckon she's got the hots for you."

"Oh be quiet." Ricky said laughing.

The girl was with her beau from the nightclub. She was dressed a bit more conservatively this time although her large frontal area was still evident underneath the black polo neck jumper that she wore which housed a large gold chain around her neck. She had a blue jacket and a black skirt that covered her legs, which were very well kept. She had a pretty face and long relaxed hair. Her eyes were large, her nose flat and her lips big. She was dark and dangerously voluptuous. They were ushered to a table by a young waiter who addressed only the man, clearly desperate to avoid giving even the impression of admiring her. Her boyfriend pulled out a chair, inviting her to sit down which she did with grace. He sat down opposite to her with his back facing Claire and Ricky. As they peered at their menus her next glance up was straight into Ricky's face. A smile greeted him as she watched him over her boyfriend's shoulder. She noticed Claire's unhappiness. Ricky noticed it as well.

"You find her threatening don't you?" he asked her.

"I don't," was Claire's defensive response, "But I've noticed the way that she looks at you. She likes you."

"How can you tell?"

"Black or white, trust me darling. It's a woman thing." Claire said. "I just can't help feeling that I've met her boyfriend before though," she said thoughtfully.

"You sure?" asked Ricky.

"I just have this nagging feeling ... oh, never mind," she said, waving the notion away.

Ricky put his reasoning hat on again.

"Black guys that I've known who go out with white women always complain about their women being possessive," he said, inviting her in to another debate.

"So I'm possessive now am I?" asked Claire, stunned. "Well thank you. I've been seeing you for two minutes and I'm possessive!" she joked.

Ricky's ploy hadn't worked so he tried another route.

"So how do you find my views on mixed relationships then?" he wondered aloud.

"Difficult," she said after a slight pause for thought. "I feel as though, if I spend money on you, call you regularly or suck your dick, then you'll only see that as me conforming to a stereotype that you have of white women."

"But if I have a big dick, have a short fuse or smoke weed then I could feel the same way," Ricky argued.

"Look Ricky," she said calmly. "You're giving me as many stereotypical images as I could give to you. I've heard talk about white women dating black men as some kind of throwback to slavery..."

"Oh? Where did you hear that then?" asked Ricky, quite alarmed that Claire had even delved into some aspect black culture.

"A book," she said, laughing slightly to hide her embarrassment that this knowledge had not been imparted to her face to face. "I've read about those things. You know, about how the lady of the house rewarded the slave for secret services rendered and all that. About black men that sleep with white women to pay them back for all the grief that black people suffered through slavery. I've read all of that. But it's all crap to me. The truth is, how do you know what we're like? How do you know that white women don't treat their white husbands or their partners in the same way that we treat black men? What? Do we automatically adopt a more submissive stance when we start to deal with you? I don't think so."

Ricky was quiet for a second. He became thoughtful, almost as if humbled by what she said. But he soon gathered his thoughts and struck back.

"The question for me is, what do you like about me and what do I like about you? All we know about each other is what the media, society, whatever tells us. Where do we find the common ground to base our honesty and integrity in a mixed relationship, without losing essentially the things that make us what we are?"

"Then maybe all we like about each other are our respective stereotypical images," smiled Claire, rubbing the back of his hand. "But at least that's a start."

The thought made both Ricky and Claire stop and think. Once she'd realised the implications of what she had said. In the ensuing silence they both thought the same thing. It was something that they would have to be careful to note. Ricky wasn't about to go there with this relationship, or at least he concluded that he would try not to. Claire told herself the same, though she was confident of her position. She liked Ricky. She liked the fact that he talked and had views. He stimulated her mentally and she told herself that this was what she had always wanted from a relationship. As educated as Paul was, he never affected her in that way. Ricky was a challenge to her and she suspected that she had the same effect on Ricky. She was satisfied that they had both been adult about it and had chosen to deal with it rather than to run from it. She looked forward to finding out how their newfound relationship would go. But a thought disturbed her and she couldn't let it slip.

"What about my money?" she asked.

"What about it?" he replied, sipping his drink.

"I've got lots of it, you don't have much."

"So?"

"You don't see it as a problem?"

Ricky was pensive. He thought for a second, took another sip of his drink then looked into her eyes.

"I won't be asking you for any of it," he said matter-of-factly. "If you choose to spend it on me, that'll be up to you. You can pay for meals, cinema tickets whatever, when I've got no cash. I'll pay for my own and possibly yours when I do have cash. If you buy me things like clothes, that's your choice. I'll not refuse anything you buy for me, but I won't ask for it, not unless I'm really in dire straits. Then I might consider asking you for a loan. I have no interest in what you do with your money or what you spend it on. It's yours and I will never consider it mine."

Claire was dumbstruck. She admired not only his forthrightness but his uprightness also. She rested her chin on the lower part of her palm and stared at him through loving eyes. She shook her head in admiration as Ricky continued.

"I know a lot of guys that have had white girlfriends and for them it's just been about the money. I'm not like that, I never will be. Going out with a millionaire doesn't mean all that much to me. What I am concerned about is me and you and whether this could work for all the right reasons," he said.

"Do you think you could settle down with me then? Would you? I mean, if things worked out?" Claire asked.

"Steady on! We've only been seeing each other five minutes and you want me to settle down!" Ricky asserted jokingly.

"Sorry!" Claire said. "Guess I asked for that."

The thought gave Ricky cause for more musing, even though he had made light of it. He heard the voice of Ingin and most of his other friends going on about how they would fuck white women but would never settle down with one. How they loved their rice and peas too much and how they couldn't come home to chips every night. He remembered echoing those same views, even though he now considered himself a bit maturer in his outlook. The thought of settling down with a white woman disturbed him. He knew within himself that he was strong enough to be seen to be going out with her. There were enough mixed relationships going on in London without him having to worry about the stigma that some black people attached to it.

But settling down though. That was a whole different kettle of fish. This had implications for his commitment. But he let the thought rest there, hoping that Claire wouldn't cotton on to what he was thinking. For Claire the issue was cut and dried. She knew that she would receive the same sort of treatment that she had received from Colin, Rosy and Paul, but she was unfazed by the prospect. For her, Ricky's colour or culture was simply not an issue. She would settle down with any man that she loved strongly enough and who loved her the same. She figured that some black people might have a problem with it, but she reasoned that if Ricky was behind her, she wouldn't allow it to bother her.

The rest of the evening passed off smoothly. They left Browns with full stomachs. Claire noticed the Hottentot Venus give them both a glancing look as they walked out. She didn't notice Ricky eyeing her intently. They walked down Shaftsbury Avenue and into Soho, stopping occasionally at the windows of dirty bookshops and making jokes about the sorts of sexual things they could do to each other. Ricky went into Tower Records and bought a couple of CDs before walking Claire back to her car. She invited him back to her place but he declined, citing tiredness and the need for an early start for work in the morning. They made arrangements to meet again. Ricky kissed her on the cheek as she left. She felt insulted and ordered him to kiss her properly. He refused, asking why white people liked to kiss in public and that it was a thing that black people never did. He implored her to wait until they were alone. She complied. As she sped off in her BMW Z3 she kissed her fingers and blew the kiss at him. He waved and headed for his car. It was a whole tube ride away on a side street in Earls Court, but he figured it would be an enjoyable journey.

Ricky pulled up his car suddenly outside of the King Centre and shot out. He was late. He had an appointment with Shaniqua and Tanika and he was late. Ricky knew what Shaniqua was like in these kinds of situations. She was not going to be pleased. It was a Saturday afternoon and most people used the centre as a stop off before they went shopping. Most guys would meet their baby mothers in there, but those women would regularly end up having to sit down and wait for them. They would usually pass through and interrupt a game of dominoes or cards that the guys had been playing. Ricky walked through the main hall where endless games of dominoes were happening. Ingin was involved in one of them.

"Yo, Ricky!" he called as he spotted him. "Wanna talk to you guy! Don't bodda fling till we chat!"

Another friend of theirs, Mattik, was playing with them.

"W'happen rich boy?" he called to Ricky. "Man got a rich woman you know!" he said to Four Star and Buzzard the other guys who were involved in the game.

Ricky ignored them and walked straight through, angered at the fact that Ingin had been telling everyone about Claire. Their relationship was now a week old and already too many people knew about it. He walked through the main hall to the back room, which doubled as a restaurant. It was Bruce's place. Bruce was a tall, thin, Jamaican dread who had franchised with the centre owners to sell Caribbean food from the back room. It had proven to be a goldmine as the place was used regularly. As Ricky entered the room, his immediately caught sight of Shaniqua sitting at a table with Tanika in her lap, engrossed in what appeared to be a difficult conversation with Bones. The room was packed and there was a lot of loud talking. Every table was occupied with people eating and there was a queue at the counter as other people waited for food. There was the odd white face in the room. They were mainly women, who had either black baby fathers or boyfriends. They seemed very comfortable, but were careful to avoid the admiring glances that they got from the black men in the place, because they knew how possessive their guys were.

"W'happen Ricky?" called Bruce from behind the counter. "Ya eat?"

"No man. Ain't stoppin'," Ricky replied.

The call alerted Shaniqua to Ricky's presence. She turned her head to the door and stuck a finger up in the air. He acknowledged her request and immediately dropped his head and waited. Bones gave him a sharp look that spelled worry on his face. Ricky couldn't help thinking that he had seen tears in Shaniqua's eyes and he wanted to find out more. From her body posture he could tell that she was trying her best to conceal their conversation. Bones was speaking to her in what appeared to be an aggressive manner albeit under his breath. They were situated at a table by the counter, so Ricky decided to use it to his advantage. He approached the counter, just by the table. Tanika noticed him instantly and her face lit up. She raised her arms to the air and shouted.

"Daddy!"

Ricky blew her a kiss and waved.

"See you in a minute darling," he said.

As Ricky looked at his daughter's beautiful face, he noticed instantly that her mother's lovely face was pained. She turned her face away from him in an effort to hide her distress. It was confirmed. She had been crying. Ricky raged instantly. Bones had upset her. He didn't have a problem with that so much because Shaniqua had made her own adult choice about whom she chose for a boyfriend, but when his daughter was involved it was a different matter. Bruce approached him.

"Wha ya seh?" he asked, wiping his hands on his apron.

"Cool y'know" replied Ricky. "Gimme a Caribbean Punch no?" he asked.

"Gimme fifty-pence," said Bruce dumping a large polystyrene cup in front of him filled with a red liquid.

Ricky counted his small change and handed him a fifty. Bruce tilted his head to where Shaniqua sat, leaned forward and spoke softly.

"Bones a stress oat yuh baby Madda again," he said.

"I know," said Ricky.

"Fuckin' eedyat a smoke too much crack!" exclaimed Bruce.

"For real?" asked Ricky, surprised.

"Everybady know boat Bones! Look pan him face how it draah! Every minute him a look money! Listen cool oat seen me a work!"

Bruce clenched his fist and pushed it towards Ricky who obliged by meeting Bruce's fist with his own, which was clenched too.

"Wha ya seh?" asked Bruce of another customer.

Ricky waved at Tanika.

"See you in a bit," he said, walking out of the room but not before throwing Shaniqua a dirty look.

Once out in the main hall, Ricky drew up a seat and sat at the table at which Ingin and Mattik were playing their game.

"W'happen star?" asked Four Star in his heavy Bajan accent.

"Easy," Ricky replied.

He said nothing to Buzzard and Buzzard said nothing to him. He was a friend of Bones's and for that reason Ricky disliked him.

"So w'happen?" asked Ingin, holding his seven dominoes up to his face. "Dis Amanda ain't called me yet."

"No?" asking Ricky feigning surprise.

"No!" replied Ingin. "Looks like de bitch used me for a whore!"

"That's what you are ain't you?" asked Mattik, slamming down the opening domino.

"Suck it, alright mate," replied Ingin in a fake East End cockney accent. He turned to Ricky. "Fuck de bitch anyway, dat pussy couldn't keep me satisfied."

Ricky was relieved at his resignation.

"But look guy," continued Ingin. "I'm looking for you to set me up you know Star. Tell that Claire bitch to hook me up wid some of her friend's man. Dem rich bitches want the black dickey boy, serious! I'm lookin' to make my fortune!"

Buzzard stared hard at Ricky, who avoided his gaze.

"We'll see what happens yeah?" he replied.

"When you meeting her again?" asked Ingin.

"Next week," said Ricky, "Said she wants to go to the Reading Rock Festival."

Mattik smiled.

"You must be fuckin' crazy, you won't catch me at them fuckin' places," he said, placing another domino.

"Shut the fuck up idiot!" jumped In Ingin "He's doing the right thing man! You got to be prepared to make them sacrifices for the money. Know what I'm saying? Never mind the rock festival, I'll be the first nigger in the opera, if she wanted me to, wha' you mean?"

"Yeah but it's the camping and shit doh innit?" returned Mattik.

"Yeah Roight! The rasshole camping and olla dat shit." entered Four star.

"I ain't got to worry about that, we're staying in a hotel man," Ricky declared.

"Wicked!" shouted Ingin, "Now that's what I'm talking about, "Five star hotel and shit innit Four star?"

"You know that boy!" he replied.

"Hey listen. You know how this boy got his name?" said Ingin turning to Ricky excitedly.

"No," replied Ricky, curious.

"Dyam arse tek himself to Amsterdam right. You know the red light district? Fool seh him warn buy pussy. He picks up dis ting and carry it back to a four star hotel!" Ingin emphasised the last three words by shouting at the top of his voice. "Him ready fi go down in the pussy right." Ingin started to laugh, "Him fine oat seh is a man!"

"No?" replied Ricky, wide eyed.

"Beat the livin' fuck out of him," continued Ingin. "Put the homo in hospital for days man!"

Four Star banged a domino hard on the table, making Ricky jump.

"Hole dat inna you rass! Fuckin' key card!" he shouted.

"Why you don't watch de fuckin' game?" asked Mattik, disgusted with the way his partner had just sacrificed it. His face lit up suddenly. "You imbeciles want to hear a joke?" he asked shuffling the dominoes.

"Oh no!" cried Ingin with a laugh. "He comin' wid his foolishness!"

"Oi en warr hear nuttun," said Four Star defiantly.

"Well you gonna hear it. Come on man! Lighten up you soul!"

"Lighten up you rasshole!"

"Go on then," said Ingin smiling. "I could use a laugh."

Mattik rubbed his hands.

"Right, so we're in Jamaica…" he began.

"Not no rasshole Jamaican joke?" complained Four Star.

"How oi supposed to understand no rasshole Jamaican joke?"

"You didn't want to hear it anyway!" Ingin reminded him.

"So oi can't have a laugh too? Oi outcast now?"

"Tell the rahtid joke," ordered Ingin of Mattik.

"So we're in Jamaica," Mattik continued. "This guy an' his wife just about to have sex. But he can't get … you know … his … thing up."

"His dick?" asked Ingin.

"I forgot, but I knew I could rely on a starving reprobate sex maniac like you to remind me," said Mattik with a cheeky smile.

"Live boi the dick, doi boi the dick. Thas all oi I know boat he," said Four Star.

Ingin raised a middle finger in his direction.

"Let the man finish the joke nuh?" asked Ricky impatiently.

"He can't get it up," continued Mattik. "So his wife says…" Mattik raised the pitch of his voice to sound feminine. "…'Come arn no man! Full time no man! Is aboat time yuh sart oat yuh prablem'. So she rings the local Obeah man. After speaking to him she turns to her husband and says 'arright it sart oat. Guh see de Obeah man mek 'im sart you oat. Come back an' I'll be ready for you! So he goes by the Obeah man and the Obeah man says. 'Yes man five hundred dalla, I gwine mek you grine like yuh neva grine before. My man's excited now, so he pays the money -his life savings - and the Obeah man works a spell on his … you know … thing. After a while he says 'it ready no man. You gwine give you wife sex like she neva get it before. All you have to do is say pip, an' it gwine rise to massive proporshan. Jus' seh pip pip an' it will go down again. But you only 'ave tree chance.' The man was so excited he says 'I want to try it oat now'. The Obeah man says 'well if you do you only 'ave two chance leff.' So the man says pip, 'an his thing starts to grow. Five inches, six inches, eight inches, twelve inches, rock solid. He says pip pip and it went down again."

The three listeners were in absolute stitches.

"He's excited now so he rings his wife," continued Mattik. "'Aright darlin' I comin' fe you. Get ready fi me. Me a de punnanny murdara! De pum pum killa! De champian cratchiz serva! Numba one pussy batara!"

"OK!" ordered Ingin.

"So he gets in his car and drives as fast as he can to get home," Mattik continued. "But he has to stop at the traffic lights. While he's waiting for the lights to go green. A friend pulls up in his car and notices him. Pip on the horn. The man starts to break out of his trousers again, six inches, ten inches, twelve inches, rock solid. Pip pip on the horn and it goes down again. Now he's starting to fret. He's only got one chance left and he hasn't got any money to pay the Obeah man for another dose. So he comes off the road and drives like mad to his house, over hill and gully, mountain and field. Eventually he arrives. He skids the car at the door. Jumps out and runs into the house. His wife is upstairs and she hears him come in. 'Yes man, tank Gard man! Me ready fi you man! Mi a tek arff me clothes! Come gimme me suppa! Gimmie me breakfuss! Gimme me dinna! Gimme me puddin'!'"

"OK, for Christ's sake!" cried Ingin.

"The man runs up the stairs to her," Mattik went on. "Meanwhile, he's taking of his shoes, his socks, his trousers his brief, his jacket, his shirt and he stands outside the bedroom naked. The wife's inside and she shouts 'yes-man! Come man! Me ready fi you no man!' He's excited and he shouts pip. Six inches, ten inches, twelve inches. Rock solid. The wife's inside, she's confused so she shouts, "hey a wha you a do oat deh so long stop de pip pip an' come!'"

The room erupted with laughter, Ingin covered his eyes to stop the tears from falling. Mattik was calm as he smiled and shuffled dominoes, Ricky and Four Star held their stomachs in mad laughter.

"Alright, alright it wasn't that funny," said Mattik, seeking to start a new game. No good. The laughter went on and on.

Eventually the excitement subsided and as the players gathered the dominoes for another game, Shaniqua joined them. Ricky got up and said his goodbyes by either touching fists or bouncing them off someone else's. He felt no vibe to give Buzzard one who had said nothing the whole time and who even now was staring hard at him. Ricky noticed Shaniqua give him a worried glance before striding of with him to the shopping centre. Outside Ricky pushed Tanika's buggy and spoke.

"Wanna tell me what that was all about?" he asked of Shaniqua.

"No," she said calmly, brushing him off.

"You were crying," he pursued.

Shaniqua became inflamed and without regard for the fact that they were in a public place, she let rip at the top of her voice.

"Listen it's nan of you're fackin' bizniz alright! Just Fackin' well leave it aaht!" she screamed.

Ricky didn't need to be told twice but he took exception to the language in front to his daughter, for which Shaniqua apologised.

"Did you know he's a dopefiend?" asked Ricky.

Shaniqua was calmer in her response this time. She threw him a sharp look and said.

"I fought are tode you to leave it aaht?"

Ricky obliged. The short walk to Mothercare was done in silence. Once inside, Shaniqua proceeded to choose clothes for Tanika. After half an hour of picking, choosing and checking items up for size by holding them against her daughter she gave up in disgust.

"Are don't lark de fings in eyah," she said. "Let's go to Adams."

The air was lighter between them now and Shaniqua was relaxed enough to engage Ricky in some conversation.

"So wasappnin' man ain't you got yourself a woman yet?" she asked.

Ricky flinched. This was the one question he hoped she wouldn't ask because he knew what her reaction would be. He concluded within himself however, that he couldn't lie.

"Yeah, I met a woman last week," he began.

"A woman eh?" Shaniqua pointed out. "Not a girl, a woman?"

"That's right," Ricky replied sternly.

"How ode is she den?" asked Shaniqua.

"In her forties," Ricky replied. "And she's white."

Shaniqua stared at him, eyes agape as they walked.

"Fack off?" she asked.

"Straight up, she's white," he stated.

Shaniqua could hardly believe her ears.

"Whatchoo want wiv a crinkly arse, don't cream their body, can't wash dere foot, leave dere baggy all over de place stinkin' white woman for then? She rich or samink?" she asked.

Ricky said nothing.

"Are don't fackin' well believe this!"

"Shaniqua please, Tanika!"

"Are don't fackin' believe this!" said Tanika in her baby voice.

"You see!" said Ricky, enraged.

Shaniqua stopped walking, signalled Ricky to stop and bent down to admonish Shaniqua that even though she had heard mummy use it, she was never to use that kind of language again. Then got up and turned on Ricky once more.

"C'mon, lover boy, talk to me," she said. "What you doin' wiv 'er den? You some toy boy or samink?"

"I like her."

"You like 'er? Nah mate. You're off your rocka, you gotta be. I mean just because you see everyone else doin' it, don't mean you gotta do it too! Whatchoo want a white women for when you can get a narss black goo, big booty, lavly skin everyfink, steada some wrinkly ole suppum that don't even wash good. Wassamatta wiv ya?"

"She's not like that, OK?"

"Toppa dat, she's not just some white bitch, she's some old white bitch! Are can't believe it. Never in mah born daze! Are'll tell you sammink doh, She won't be avin' Tanika. No way! Whenever you take 'er, you betta tell me where you're takin' 'er cos are don't want no greasy ole white fing puttin' 'er 'ands on 'er no way."

"Aren't you jumpin' the gun a bit?" Ricky asked hardly able to keep up with her.

"Jampin' de gan? Are ain't leff de graand yet mat! She better not come wiv no fanny bizniz when are see 'er neeva. Dey're all the same! When they ketch a black geezer, thas it mate, vey fink dere it."

"Oh please!"

"Nah is true an' you know it! Are was aahtside Sainsburys just the ovva day an' this black goo got inta some bovva with a white goo. 'Fore you know it, 'er big straptin' gorilla lookin' black boyfriend's beatin' the crap aaht the black goo!"

Ricky laughed.

"So you bess tell 'er, don't cam the miss fing wiv me mate or are'll knock 'er aaht."

Ricky remained silent. He knew all the angst that many black women had when faced with the subject of black men dating white women. They saw it as disrespectful. He could see with the point that Shaniqua made also about white women's attitudes changing once they got a black man. But he saw this as a defence mechanism. White women reacting to the angst that black women had, before they were confronted by it. But yes, he had made that observation many a time. Still he concluded that for the best, it would be a long time before Shaniqua met Claire.

Shaniqua was confused. As she strode through the High Street, she struggled to understand just what had gotten into Ricky. For most of the time that she knew him, he had abhorred the idea of having a white woman for a partner. They reasoned many times about slavery and the difficult social plight that black people were faced with in Britain. They had squarely concluded that white people were the cause of their problems. To her, white women dating black men was the ultimate exploitation and a blatant disregard of the needs of black women. In her eyes black men weren't dated, they were poached and bought. The lure of sex, money and obedience was too much for some black men and usually the kind of black men that couldn't handle a black woman. She was disappointed in him. But this came from another place also. Ricky was different, not like most of the guys that she knew. She had really wanted to make their relationship work and when Tanika came along, she really felt that she had made it, particularly with the man of her dreams. He wasn't violent, he was thoughtful and caring and despite his lowly financial status had a lot more going for him than his present occupation suggested. He was good looking, charming and witty too, but he was often led astray and she pictured Ingin immediately when this thought sprang to mind. She couldn't disguise the fact to herself that she still loved him and even though he had walked out on her, if he said the word she would take him back immediately. His dating this woman wouldn't diminish her love for him. In fact it made her yearn for him even more. She longed to show him what he would be missing.

Claire sat at home watching *Titanic* for about the fifth time. Her video recorder had been playing up and she had thought about getting a new one but she hadn't gotten around to it. As white lines appeared all over the screen she cursed. Her feet were curled up, tucked under her bottom as she drank red sauvignon and hoped for the distortion to disappear. It did. As she paid even closer attention to the movie she was interrupted by the phone. She felt for the remote, eyes still glued to the TV, and when she found it paused the film. She stretched her arm over, barely moving a muscle to pick up the receiver. Her 'Hello' was filled with expectation. She hoped it was Ricky. She was disappointed. Very disappointed.

"Hellooo," came Peter's greasy tones from the other end of the phone.

"Peter," she said with obvious frustration. "How's Emma?" she asked in an effort to show no interest in him at all.

"Staying with friends," he said happily. "I'm not home either, actually I'm in Devon at the moment, but I could easily get over to you."

"My, whatever for?" Claire asked in mock surprise.

"Whatever takes your fancy," the turd replied.

"There's nothing that takes my fancy dear. Nothing that you have to offer me anyway," Claire stated calmly.

"Oh I don't know. A bit of toe sucking, perhaps or a good…"

"Don't even bother!" said Claire raising her tone. "I don't want to know! I told you last week and I'm telling you now, I don't want to know!"

"Really? How disappointing. And I always figured you for a good time girl! I mean, the way you reacted that night when I had my mouth between those fine legs of yours, eating that snatch! Ooooh! It tasted just like an orange!"

"You disgust me."

"And you disgust me Claire, but in a nice way!"

"Suppose I told Emma about these little calls?"

"Oh you spoil sport!"

"That's what I'll do if you don't fucking well leave it out! Now piss off!"

"How's your little black boy? Keeping you busy is he?"

"Peter fuck off. Just fuck right off!"

"He could never treat you the way I..."

Claire replaced the receiver. The conversation was ended. She was incensed. As she fumed she simply wanted to pick up the phone and tell him a few things about himself. He saw her as nothing but a toy, a fixation that he could get off on. She thought of Emma and pitied her for having such a bastard for a husband. She turned a pale red as her body temperature heated up. Then she acted. She picked up the phone and dialled Emma's number. The answer machine kicked in.

"Emma darling it's Claire," she opened. "I'm sorry you're not in. I'll be going to Reading tomorrow for three days, call me when I'm back, we need to talk."

She replaced the handset, then picked it up again and called Ricky.

"Hi darling, how are you?"

"OK. You?" was his response.

"Just a quick one sweetheart. How's Ingin?"

"He was OK last time I saw him."

"Guess he's still smarting from what Amanda did to him."

"I think he might just be over that now."

"I've got a little job for him."

"Oh shit."

"Yes. Her name's Emma."

"I'm sure he'll be pleased."

"I'm hoping she will be too. We'll discuss it in Reading. Bags packed?"

"Nearly there. Just a few more shirts to go."

"Good. Can't wait to see you tomorrow darling."

"Same here."

"Bye for now."

"Bye."

Claire laid the handset back down. She sipped her wine and

pushed the remote in the direction of the TV and carried on with her film.

Ricky found Reading difficult. It was a small town on what he considered to be the edge of nowhere. His minuscule London mind imagined it to be the sort of place that had one milkman, one postman and one policeman. It wasn't even north of the gap, it was sort of to the left a little. The Rock Festival was the only place that had put Reading on the map in his opinion. He hadn't even heard of one single player in their football team. He was pleasantly surprised to find though, that it was quite a large and active town and there were enough black people around for him to feel relatively comfortable. Whenever he went to a new town, he always assessed how much of an influence the black community had made on it.

They stopped at a petrol station to fill up because Claire had not done so before leaving home and even though they had hit Reading, she was running dangerously low. Ricky checked the way he was greeted by the attendant when he went in and bought himself a local paper and a packet of Softmints. If white people disrespected you, it meant that the black community wasn't making it's presence felt. However, if they respected you, it meant that they were alive and kicking. Manchester and Birmingham were places where white people behaved themselves, showing no or few signs of racism. In fact, in those places he found them to be quite scared of black people. He satisfied himself that the blacks in Reading were alive. He heard that they had a Carnival, always a good sign of influence and pledged himself to check it out one day. It had been a long drive, particularly after coming off the M4. The festivalgoers were arriving en masse. He had a slight headache and knew that if he didn't get something to eat soon, it would get worse.

Claire knew the town and drove her Z3 straight to the hotel that they were staying in with no problems. The Renaissance Hotel was a big building and luxurious to look at. It was the most expensive in the town. They were greeted in the foyer by the sound of live piano playing. They dumped the bags that they were carrying at the main counter and checked in. A Middle Eastern looking lady who was pretty and well dressed dealt with them. She eyed them both and threw Claire a wry smile before handing the room keys to her and telling her to enjoy her stay in Reading.

"I'm sure I will," Claire responded, throwing the lady a cute smile.

The couple took their bags to their room via a lift. Ricky had rejected the advances of the porter even though Claire was keen for him to carry them. Once into their room, Claire brushed back her hair and felt at home.

"I hate hotels," she said. "But I can do this." She surveyed the room, sitting on the bed, bouncing slightly as if to check it's springiness. The room was adorable, Ricky was unused to it and felt strangely uncomfortable. He eyed the shower room and raised his eyebrows as if impressed. There was a large double bed situated at the head of the large room and a small portable TV adjacent to it. The lighting was soft and big windows over looked the main through road that ran through the town.

"Let's check out the gym and sauna," said Ricky excitedly.

"Hold on a minute," said Claire springing from the bed. "This is the first time we've really been alone," she said throwing her arms around the back of his neck and pushing her face into his. "Is a snog out of the question?"

"Guess not," Ricky replied.

He pushed his face into hers and met her lips gently with his. They kissed for a minute. Claire was becoming more passionate with every stroke of her lips. She caressed the back of his head slowly and Ricky, enjoying the moment, grabbed the back of her head, allowing her hair between his fingers to drop over them. Then he stopped.

"More of that later," he said. "The gym!"

He took Claire by the hand and picked up the keys to lock the door. Claire was sullen. She wanted to stay and relax but she gave in to her lover's eagerness. The gym was small and busy. There were rowing machines and multigyms. Ricky walked through eyeing the equipment. He moved through to a small section that housed a steam room and a sun bed.

"Impressive," he said.

"Hmm," replied Claire with relative disinterest.

The entrance from the gym led them to some stairs, which brought them out to the swimming pool area, which had a Jacuzzi at the end of it.

"I'll have some of this," he mentioned.

"When are you going to have some of this?" asked Claire under her breath.

Ricky heard the comment but said nothing. He was going to enjoy his two days in Reading and that didn't just mean fucking Claire, even though he looked forward to their first session together.

As they walked hand in hand to the leisure complex that housed the outdoor festival Claire mused aloud.

"I've been coming here now for years," she opened. "And I rarely see great numbers of black people."

Ricky smiled to himself.

"How many black artists do you see here?" he asked.

"Not that many I suppose," said Claire.

"It's all black music," continued Ricky. "But it's so far removed from it's Blues roots that we don't recognise it anymore."

"Is it true that black people were the first people on the planet?" she asked. "I read that in a book."

Ricky was happy to give her a lesson in black history and even more pleased that she had bothered to ask.

"It's true. The first recorded human remains were found in Africa. It's the home of mankind and certainly the home of the first civilisation."

"Egypt?"

"Yep. They don't teach us in schools that black people were responsible for science art, architecture, agriculture, and mathematics in fact every damn thing that makes society function. It was Alexander the Great and people like Napoleon that made sure that the world never knew these things," replied Ricky.

"Is that why people are racist towards black people, because they don't know these things?" Claire probed.

"I suppose so," replied Ricky.

"Paul went nuts when I told him about you," she said. "So did a few more of my friends."

Ricky looked at her with a raised eyebrow.

"Good for them. Fuck 'em. Truth is they probably wish they were in your position and frankly if they don't it's because they don't know," he replied.

"Is this a demonstration of black pride that I'm being hit with?" she asked smiling.

"Damn right," he said. "Come on Claire, I mean, how can people begrudge us for acting this way when we have to deal with that sort of bullshit on a daily basis. Although, I have to confess Shaniqua went spare when I told her about you."

"Reverse racism," Claire stated.

"Hell no. Racism is about power, we don't have any which means we can't act on our prejudices. But I can't deny that it is prejudice," replied Ricky. "There are many black people that harbour bad feelings towards white, but the truth is, you've given us cause to."

"So black people hate us?" she asked.

"That's the problem. We should do but we don't. If the situation were reversed and we held the power in this society. We would treat you differently. For us it's not about skin colour. It's about the colour of your heart and really only two colours count. Good or bad."

"So what do we need to do to change the situation?" she asked.

"Treat us like human beings that's all."

"Things are getting better though?" Claire asked.

Ricky looked at her with a grin.

"I suppose they are. But you know what? I think night clubs have done more to advance the cause of good race relations than any piece of legislation."

Claire laughed, held his hand tighter and kissed his cheek.

The festival was packed. Over ten thousand revellers were jammed onto the huge field that was equipped with beer tents, sound stages and food stalls. It was wild. The music was loud, the bars were full and everyone was having a good time. Ricky enjoyed the atmosphere. He felt able to, as few people seemed to make an issue of the fact that he was with a white woman. They got many looks. Some were envious others admiring. Claire drew a lot of attention from both men and women as she had worn an almost see-through T-shirt that allowed her braless breasts to show through. Each time a guy would admire her, he would hold her hand tighter, she would squeeze his too. There was no doubt that they enjoyed one another's company despite not only their racial differences but their social ones too. Claire wondered how long it would last. She hoped forever. Ricky for his part enjoyed the moment. Claire did something for him, he was sure about that, but what it was, as yet, he had no idea. He simply liked being around her and he left it at that.

He had cause for slight dismay later on in the evening when a black woman, perhaps showing Ricky too much attention, upset her. They were at the bar, a marquee erected by the main sound stage. As the black woman glided past them, Claire eased backwards into her path knocking her drink to the floor. Her beer saturating her ripped jeans as it fell. Claire apologised profusely, but didn't bother to offer to buy her another drink. Ricky eyed Claire suspiciously after that. He remembered what Shaniqua had said to him and he wondered if the disrespect of black women by white women that had a black man went further than just the business of stealing him. It was about how they physically reacted and behaved towards black women too. He had reasoned within himself, that he would look for the evidence that suggested any form of wicked or evil intent on Claire's part. He didn't want to judge, but, hey, she was rich. He believed his philosophy about rich people being selfish, mean and uncaring and he had concluded that if Claire showed any of that sort of behaviour, he would stamp on it. This was perhaps the first piece of evidence that there was perhaps another side to her that he needed to know about. He would keep his eyes open.

Claire too was bugged by Ricky's other nature. She felt that he had paid the woman too much attention and she hoped that she was wrong. She thought deeply about Ricky. She liked the man and wanted a meaningful and long-lasting relationship with him but she had to be careful. She didn't know a lot about black people and she admitted to herself that her thoughts might have been guided by stereotypes. But she wanted Ricky to display none of them. For whilst she had mentioned to him that maybe those stereotypes had bought them together, they could easily rip them apart.

The first evening of the festival ended late for the couple. At 2.30 in the morning they were walking back to the hotel enjoying the cool breeze. Groups of people were leaving a nearby nightclub and they stopped to observe a brawl between a group of women which was taking place outside of it. Ricky laughed, calling Reading a mad little town. Claire herself was scathing of the women, one of whom she saw swing a bottle across another girl's face. The behaviour disgusted her and she gave thanks that didn't belong to that sort of crowd.

The hotel lobby was dark. A few late night drinkers were still at the bar, though still engaged in what sounded like intelligent conversation. They threw Ricky and Claire a hello, hoping perhaps that they would join them, but they were having none of it. Once into their room, they fumbled about nervously, both wondering how they were going to get a point when they were going to hit the sack. Claire excused herself and went to the bathroom taking a couple of small items of clothing with her. Ricky lay on the bed and flicked on the TV with the remote that was lying on the small table next to it. He had barely gotten into the late film that was showing when Claire emerged from the bathroom. She looked stunning. She had bought a red sheer negligée and decided to put it on. For her, they had gotten to a point where there were simply no more questions to be asked and none to be answered. It was simply time for sex and sod what he had to say about it.

This was a moment that Claire had dreamt about for a long time. Since they had met, Ricky had showed himself to be not rushed in that respect, but from the day that she had met him she had wanted to make love to him. Ricky smiled after grabbing an eyeful of the siren that stood before him. She had brushed her hair and had even applied a touch of lipstick for him. Her long slender legs and her large breasts were the most eye-catching and she had positioned them both to be so. She moved over to him slowly and sat next to him on the bed. She said nothing and neither did he. She kissed him. He kissed her back and as they did so she began undoing the buttons to his shirt. They lay back on the bed once Ricky's shirt had made its way onto the carpet. Then she lay on top of him, kissing him fiercely whilst, at the same time, rubbing his crotch to make him erect. She eased off him a bit to undo the buttons on his trousers, which didn't take a minute and before long she was playing with his dick, gently massaging it and stroking his testicles too. Ricky was becoming ecstatic as she worked him. She was good and she pleased him to the point of distraction as she concentrated her efforts more on masturbating him. Ricky's groans became louder, his erection now at its peak. Claire worked him expertly but didn't stop there. She moved her face away from him and pulled his trousers and his pants off and without further ado dropped her mouth on his cock. Ricky moaned again. He was always surprised at the way white women loved to give blowjobs, even sometimes regardless of what state of hygiene the cock was in. But he soon kicked the thought into touch. Why the hell was he complaining? The shit was good.

Claire worked him like a hungry dog and he could have sworn she was enjoying it as much as he was. He tried a token gesture by sticking a finger up her pussy but she wasn't having it. She pushed his hand away as a "uh-uh" issued its way from a mouth full of cock. Ricky soon realised that Claire didn't need to be turned on, she needed no stimulation. For her, the very thought of being with him was all the stimulation that she needed. He wondered if making love to a black man had been something that she may have fantasised about in the past and whether this, for her, was now the fulfilment of that fantasy - or did she always make love like this? She left his penis and moved up to his face to kiss him, he turned his face away. Claire instantly knew the reason for this and didn't push it. She knew that they weren't going to kiss again for the whole night.

Eagerly he pulled her shoulder straps down to expose her breasts before laying her down and lying on top of her. Without any further thought, Ricky dug his head into them, squeezing them tightly whilst frantically sucking and licking her nipples. This was more for his pleasure than for hers, but her frenzied moans of pleasure and the increasingly reckless movement of her waistline told him what he needed to know. There was little left for him to do now but to do the business. He was no Ingin but he knew that he could hold his own in the fucking department and by the way things were going so far, Claire had already revealed her key card. His key card lay between his legs. It wasn't massive but he knew what do with it. On top of that, he had good stamina. So when Claire raised her legs to allow him into her pussy, the groan of sweet ecstasy that issued from her mouth, was the first of many for the night.

The second day of the lovers' visit to Reading began with a hearty breakfast. Claire had expressed a wish to do some shopping, so before long they were admiring the recently erected shopping complex in the town centre. It was an impressive retail compound. It was so big, Ricky had likened it to a futuristic city calling it Mega City–One. He had observed Claire's wide-eyed expression as she waded through a myriad of shops. He lost count of the times that she had whipped out her credit card and certainly had lost count of all the money that she had spent. She offered to buy Ricky some clothing, but the sorts of clothes that she wanted to see him in just didn't appeal to him. The issue came to head, when Ricky went looking in a sports shop. Claire had taken out a tracksuit and invited him to try it on offering to purchase it for him if he liked it. He told her that he didn't like it and Claire offered nothing else. He wasn't going to ask her to buy him something, but he soon realised that she was not going to spend money on him on something that he liked. She would only buy what she wanted to see him in. He was not amused and cursed her inwardly for her pomposity.

The same thing happened again in another shop in the High Street. But this time Ricky could not contain his frustration. Saying nothing, he marched over to an Abbey National Building Society and withdrew a hundred pounds from the hole in the wall. He then proceeded back into the shop and purchased the sweatshirt that he had preferred. Claire said nothing of what had transpired and was keen not to address the issue. Ricky remembered the way, in the night club, that she, without asking, had stuck a cigarette in his face expecting him to light it and when he had expected her to offer him one, she didn't. He mused. He had noticed what was possibly a very self-centred streak in Claire and he felt uncomfortable with it. He also wondered if she was keen on turning him into something. He considered that possibility, concluding that perhaps she hadn't taken him on as her partner for the things that he was, but rather what she figured she could turn him into. He remembered his point about self–denial before laying the issue to rest. He paid the issue no more mind, but pledged himself to keep his eyes open.

Claire herself was becoming more wary of Ricky's personality. She saw his pride and his ignorance. She couldn't help seeing a rebellious child whenever she looked at him. She mused over what his motivation might be, asking herself if she was disappointed at the way that he showed no form of dependency upon her whatsoever. She concluded that she was. Her next thought was to decide whether it made sense to try and create for him a dependency on her. She knew that she could, but wondered at the purpose. Using her money to snare man was not her style and anyway, if she did, she would have only conformed to the stereotype. She pondered the issue no more but pledged to keep the matter on hold. Claire concluded that she liked him and wanted to keep him. If necessary, she would do whatever she needed in order to keep him so long as it was honest and full of integrity.

It was a pleasant evening. As they sat in the field with the massive crowd waiting for another act to come on stage Claire felt a surge to dig deeper into Ricky. She remembered his reaction when she asked him about his and Shaniqua's separation but she decided to pursue the issue again. Once she dropped the question Ricky was slightly upset, more by her persistence than by the actual query. Now that they were an item, he had no excuse to keep information from her, so he dived in, though somewhat nervously.

" I felt that she was sleeping around," he said, avoiding her glances.

"Was she?" asked Claire.

Ricky gave the question a second thought before he answered. When his answer came it happened in tandem with the dropping of his head.

"I guess not," he said, almost ashamed.

"So why'd you leave her?" pursued Claire.

Ricky was silent. He was clearly pained. Claire remained silent also. She wanted to hear what he had to say so she prepared herself to match him action for action, quiet for quiet in a bid to allow him no escape route. Ricky didn't seek one.

"I didn't leave her. Well, yes I did," he replied.

"Make up your mind," she said sarcastically.

Ricky became thoughtful and when the words eventually issued from him, he was pointedly more anguished.

"She got pregnant," said Ricky almost whispering. "I didn't believe that Tanika was mine, so I left her."

Claire was not only surprised, but slightly angered. Ricky could see her slipping thoughtfully into 'feminist woman' mode.

"You didn't?" she asked with more of an accusation in her voice than anything else.

"I didn't intend to leave her for good though. I only left until I was sure that the child was mine," Ricky stated in a quieter voice.

Claire could feel his regret, but she pursued him all the same.

"You made her carry that child alone for nine months? Did you have any real evidence that she was sleeping around?" she asked, her voice becoming more distanced and more hostile towards him.

"None," replied Ricky. "It was just an excuse, I guess. I just couldn't handle the thought of being a father."

"Oh for Christ sake!" Claire bellowed, her face a picture of ire. She was raging. "Do you think for one second that she could bear the thought of being a mother for the first time? Especially without her man at her side?"

"Suppose not," said Ricky, almost apologetically.

"What made you accept the child? I suppose you insisted on a blood test?" Claire wondered in a disgusted tone of voice.

"Didn't have to," he said. "I only had to look into Tanika's eyes." Ricky took in a deep breath of air. Then let it out again. "That was the first time I saw her, three days after she came out of the hospital."

"You weren't even man enough to help her through the birth," noted Claire.

"Guess not," he replied. "On that same day Shaniqua asked me if I was ready to be a father. I told her yes. She told me that that was good. But that I would have to do it from a distance, because she wasn't having me back."

Claire's body shook. "Good for her," she stated. Ricky said nothing.

"Talk about a strong black woman," he said eventually. "I couldn't believe it. She was just a kid. We've not been back together since. Tanika's three."

Claire felt more than a sense of injustice. The first time that they had discussed the issue she had for some reason felt that his relationship with Shaniqua had only recently ended. She pushed one more question out.

"How many relationships have you had, since Shaniqua?" she asked.

"Not a single one," said Ricky, looking away.

They both went quiet. The next band was about start, but they ignored it. Claire thought for a while then turned to Ricky with the air of someone who had received a revelation.

"Black women will put up with a lot less than what a white woman would. I guess black men know that. I suppose that there are a lot of black men who are with white women for just that very reason," she turned to Ricky and looked deep into his eyes. "Are you one of them?" she asked coldly.

Ricky turned to her. A tear had welled up in his eye.

"I don't know," he said softly. The tear ran down his face as the other eye swelled up with water. "I don't know," he repeated. Claire dropped her head and as she did so Ricky rose to his feet. He dropped his head in to his hand to conceal his tears as he slowly wandered off. Claire felt his sorrow, concluding that he needed to be alone and find peace with himself. No matter how long it would take, she would let him have his space. She would see him back at the hotel. She turned around to grab a glimpse of him just to see where he would go. She caught his back just as it disappeared deep into the crowd.

It was four o'clock in the morning when Ricky quietly opened the door to the hotel room. He needn't have worried about disturbing Claire's sleep because she was still awake. She was watching yet another old movie, but from the look on her face he could tell that she probably hadn't been paying too much attention to it.

"Where have you been?" she asked, careful not to sound too intimidating.

"Black people got a club here … The Central Club or

something. They had a reggae dance on, I went to check it out," he replied, hardly prepared to give an explanation for his whereabouts. Claire sensed this, but had to get the issue off her chest anyway.

"Why?" she asked.

Ricky eyed her as if to tell her not to ask him any more questions.

"You wouldn't understand," he said, unconcerned about how she felt about it.

Claire took a deep breath and watched as he undressed and jumped into the bed. Once under the sheets she turned to him and rubbed his hand underneath the blanket.

"Are we still an item?" she asked in a concerned tone of voice.

Ricky turned to her, looked her deep in the eyes and leant over to kiss her cheek.

"Yes," he said defiantly.

Claire and Ricky spent most of the final day of the festival in bed. It was two o'clock in the afternoon before Claire woke up and even then she was still bushed. They weren't supposed to check out of the hotel until the next day so they were able to have a lie in. Claire arose and fixed herself a coffee she sat up in the bed watching the TV whilst Ricky slept. The noise of the TV woke him up and his first action was to take her coffee from her and place it on the table next to the bed. He pulled her back gently and lay on top of her. Before long the moans and groans of sexual delight were heard as Ricky rode her for all he was worth. Claire had been ecstatic and was out of breath when he orgasmed. She had come three times. She held Ricky tightly around his shoulders and spoke softly.

"I love you," she said.

Ricky was surprised by this comment and expressed his disappointment in her by saying sarcastically.

"That's nice."

Claire wondered why he had greeted those words with such apparent disdain but she didn't question it, for his response made her feel slightly embarrassed that she had said it. Ricky's thoughts were clear. That comment didn't create a great deal of hope in him that Claire was any different from the white women he had known or from what he had felt he knew about them. He almost heard Ingin saying to him "Take the money" or "They'll pay for the dickey boy." He had credited Claire with a great deal more grey matter than that. To allow herself, only two weeks into a relationship, to feel that she loved him just because he gave her good sex. Wasn't this the basic fascination that white women had for black men? Wasn't this the very reason why they showed so much devotion? Wasn't this exactly what Ingin was getting at, with his derogatory attitude towards them? Wasn't this purely what they wanted black men for? A good fuck? He looked at her whilst she dressed herself after taking a shower and wondered just how long it would be before the novelty wore off. She had exposed herself to him and he was disgusted by it. His distaste reached a new level when, in an attempt to lighten what was becoming an increasingly heavy atmosphere she turned to him and stroked the top of his head and said

"Why don't you grow dreadlocks?"

Ricky was stunned into silence. Claire could see anger etched on his face and didn't know why. She became coy, knowing that Ricky was about to verbally lay into her.

"Why don't you get real?" he asked with bane. "Didn't you hear anything I've told you? Haven't you thought about any of the things that we discussed?"

Claire opened her arms out wide, a look of confusion written all over her face.

"What have I done?" she asked.

Ricky was now in her face.

"I don't want you telling me you love me, because I fuck you so well it makes you come. I'm not a fucking sex machine and even if you think I am, I don't want you loving me for it. Secondly I'm not going to adopt some fucking image for you. You whiteys love dreadlocks. If you want a dread, fucking well go and find one. It ain't about image for me, have you got that?"

Claire was stunned, she wanted to argue the toss but she realised discretion to be the better part of valour.

"Is that what you think I'm about?" she asked calmly.

"Christ, you really take things to heart don't you?" she said, hoping Ricky had said his piece, but her words just made him explode.

"I've never met a white woman yet that didn't conform to the fucking stereotype. What the fuck? Do you think we black guys are stupid? Don't you think we know what's going on? You can talk about love untill the fucking cows come home, but we will always understand just what it is you love about us. Fuck it, I'm not about to go back to slavery again!" he shot.

"Oh please!" argued Claire.

"Fuck you!" Ricky was now shouting. "Your shit is just as racist as the fucking KKK. What do you want? A trendy little black boy to show off and keep you satisfied at nights is that it? You all think you're so smart. What am I? Something that you're going to pay for services rendered? Your own little fuck machine, that can fulfil everyone of your dirty little sexual fantasies. If that's the case, you keep your fucking love I don't want it. You learn to fucking well understand who I am and what I am and love that. Anything else is just a nasty little fantasy that you have patrolling your sick racist little mind! Have I made myself clear? You all don't know a fucking thing about black people, but trust me, we know everything there is to know about you! You bombard us with your bullshit everyday, whilst you can't even be bothered to find out what we're like, just what the fuck we're about. You would sooner hear all those fuckin' stereotypes and expect me to conform to them. When I do conform to them, you tell me that you love me and when I don't, you ask me to. What kind of bullshit is that? Well let me tell you something. Black people are about something infinitely higher and greater than the things that you cherish us for. And I will not belittle myself with the likes of you. Not whilst you see me as a little plaything, some little fucking toy for you to indulge your fantasies with, have I made myself clear?"

Claire was silent.

"Have I made myself clear?" shouted Ricky at the top of his voice.

Claire turned to him, with watered eyes and tears streaming down her face.

"Yes!" she shouted before falling onto the bed crying loudly.

Ricky stepped to the bathroom.

"You fucking well check yourself!" he warned.

Ricky took a shower. Even through the sound of the water gushing from the shower, he could hear Claire crying. He realised that he had upset her but he hoped her tears were not about the cursing that he had just given her, but the fact that she had learnt a lesson and was confronting her own individual problem. He hadn't noticed her stop crying and so was surprised to find her, once he finished his shower, sitting up in the bed, with more than an air of dignity about her. She had resolved the issues within herself, he thought. So he prepared himself for an argument thinking that with Claire's strong character this was to be their only recourse. It never came. When Claire broke the silence she did so with grace and a voice that was tender.

"I feel an overwhelming sense of endearment towards you," she said, not looking at him. "It's true that I've hardly sensed why it is or indeed where it has come from. In normal situations I guess I probably wouldn't and I guess, few people really do, when they find themselves here. They just enjoy the moment. But I guess this isn't a normal situation. In getting together and becoming an item I suppose we're challenging many of society's norms and prejudices. For you to tell me that in fact what I'm doing is simply conforming to them, hurts. But it tells me that this whole thing really requires a bit more thought and a bit more honesty in order to make it work. I feel that you're the sort of person, who, irrespective of colour, class or whatever wants to make his relationships work and I respect you for that. I respect you for reminding me of what I am and for reminding me of the disgustingly brutal, carnal, pretentious and conceited culture from which I have emanated. I respect your highly evolved sense of racial pride for not allowing me to plague your life with it. I have no other guide through this maze but you and I trust that your sincerity in these matters, of which I am most ignorant, will remain consistent. Forgive me. My intention was not to upset you and was certainly not designed to make you revile me. It was in fact the opposite. I said I loved you and I meant it. I love you more now. Please forgive me."

Ricky was floored. He hardly knew what to say so he didn't even bother to try.

five

Monday, early evening. Claire was shattered. She had taken Ricky back to Peckham and had made it home in no quick time. She had been stuck in rush hour traffic and had smoked herself to death after being in the jam for the best part of an hour. She wanted a drink, a shower, food and a video, in that order. She had made up her mind that whatever was going to happen this night, it would be quiet. As she dumped her bags in the hall, she moved into the living room. She went over to the telephone to check the messages. This was always her first action after having been away and today she wasn't surprised to find out that people had been trying to get a hold of her. There were three messages waiting for her and she pressed the button to retrieve them. She sat eagerly in the chair next to the phone. Her elbows resting on her knees and her chin resting on her palms ready to hear them. The machine clicked in. The robotic digital voice informed her of the date and time that the messages had been received. She heard the final tone before Amanda's voice clicked in. She sounded agitated, as if she had been crying.

"Claire ... It's me, Amanda. I mean ... if you can get that Jamaican out of your snatch for just ten minutes... perhaps you can give me a call."

Her voice sounded abrupt and angry. Claire figured that it was probably for the want of having to have made a few calls to her without success. Amanda despised answer machines and she would only ever leave a message if things were either urgent or if she felt that she had no alternative. By the sound of the distress in her voice, this was obviously one of those moments. The digital woman clicked in again before Paul spoke:

"I think we'd better have a talk. don't you? Give me a call."

He sounded bitter and fed up. She looked forward to speaking to him with no relish. Emma was the last person to speak. Her sweet little voice echoed daintily through the quiet evening.

"Claire, hi. It's lovely to hear from you. I got your message. I've been away too as you know. I had a great time. I'll tell you all about it. Hope you enjoyed Reading. How's your boyfriend? I hope everything's OK. Look, remember Allison? She's having a little get together. It's for girls only at her place on Wednesday evening. She said she wants to see you there so why don't you come along? They'll all be glad to see you again and we can possibly talk then. Call me anyway. Bye for now!"

Claire was enthused by the message. Allison's soirees were great fun. She was a great laugh. A very independent woman who had made her fortune by selling natural beauty products. She had no man in her life and when she had her little 'get togethers' she would insist that there were no men. She would accept no apologies and if husbands refused to baby-sit or whatever in order to let their wives out, she would talk to them herself, so she rarely received apologies. They were small get togethers of no more than seven or eight women and Claire counted herself privileged to be invited. So great was her excitement that she quickly forgot about Amanda's distressed message and made Emma her first call.

Emma picked up the phone and answered excitely. Claire had almost forgotten the reason why she had called Emma. She had wanted to tell her about Peter's harassment of her. She was frightened slightly by the happiness in Emma's voice, worrying whether she ought to tell her and obviously distress her. She bit her tongue, concluding that she was going to have to come clean to her at some point. So she prepared herself mentally to do so. After a couple of minutes of greetings and small talk, particularly about Allison's forthcoming do, Claire got serious.

"Darling I have to tell you something," she said.

Emma felt the businesslike tone and composed herself into seriousness.

"Go on darling," she said.

Claire hesitated, fumbled for a second then spoke.

"It's about Peter."

"Yes?" replied Emma.

"He's been calling me."

Claire was cut to the heart. She had not wanted to upset Emma, whose marriage she knew, was on the rocks. She was a woman that was easily upset and she grieved inside that she would be the cause of pain for a friend whom she cherished dearly. She was stunned however, not just by Emma's upbeat tone of voice, but also her response.

"I know," she said.

Claire froze.

"I'm sorry?" she asked, alarmed.

"I know," replied Emma. "I'll bet the bastard's been trying to seduce you."

"Well yes," responded Claire, nonplussed.

"It's been going on for quite a while now hasn't it?" Emma said. "I have a house to keep and I keep a tight reign on my bills. What else is a good housewife supposed to do? I have to check my itemised phone bills! He's been calling you for the last couple of years, every since that little get together at Michael's"

"Well yes," said Claire, embarrassed.

"Yes," continued Emma. "Don't worry darling, I'm about as ashamed of that little episode as you are. But I guess we're older and a lot wiser now. It's just a shame that that poor sod of a husband of mine isn't. Yes, I've known for a long time. I used to think that he was calling Paul, but when he left the house and the calls continued. It didn't take me long to figure out what was going on. I know he's always liked you."

"You don't think that I..." started Claire.

"Oh come on darling!" interrupted Emma. "I've always credited you with more sense than that! You can find better people to have an affair with. I trust you implicitly. You're my friend, so good and so gentle. So honest. I know, and I've always known within my heart of hearts that this has been as painful for you as it has been for me."

Claire was moved and it showed in her voice.

"Emma, I'm so sorry…" Emma interrupted her again.

"For what dear? For not fucking my husband? Give me a break. I know You've wanted to tell me for a long time. I've seen it in your eyes. Even at Colin and Rosy's the other day. I just wanted to see how long you would be able to hold out. Thank you my dear, for protecting me and for the consideration that you've shown for me over this. But you can rest assured Claire darling. I've dealt with it."

Emma remained silent as Claire sniffled and wept. Then, through the last of her tears, she spoke again, managing a slight laugh through it all.

"Remember at Colin and Rosy's, you told me that you had a fantasy?"

"Yes darling?" said Emma, half in question and half in response.

Claire remained silent for a second and waited for the penny to drop. It didn't take Emma long.

"Ooh!" she said sheepishly.

"I can set it up for you," said Claire, the sadness in her voice now replaced with guile.

Emma was stunned, she didn't know what to say. When she did speak, again she was sheepish.

"I… I've never done anything like that before," she said.

Claire knew that Emma was an innocent thing and she hardly wanted to preside over her moral deterioration. But she reasoned that Emma's state of mind was such that made her a doormat for Peter to walk all over. She needed to get something back. Some sense of pride for herself. Hell, if she wasn't going to leave the guy, why not do the same as he had been doing to her for so many years?

"I think it would help," Claire said matter of factly. Emma thought for another second. then with outgoing breath said.

"Sure, why not eh? Why fucking not?"

"I'll try to set it up for Wednesday," closed Claire as she signed off, with more than an excited air about her.

Her next call was to Paul. She wanted to get him out of the way as soon as possible, because she knew that this was going to be difficult. As the answer machine in his flat kicked in. She replaced the receiver and tried his mobile. The distant noises told her that he was in traffic as he answered the phone. The depression in his voice evident as he realised to whom he was speaking. He spoke clearly and with venom.

"I've been doing a lot of thinking," he said coldly. "My solicitors are now working on my behalf. I'm going to make sure that you get nothing out of me. I'm contesting the divorce settlement."

Claire raged.

"What the fuck do you mean, you're contesting!"

"Just what I said dear. Like I said at the party. You're not taking my money to give to some fucking pimp. We've had no children, so technically I may not have to give you anything. If you're seen to be at fault with the break up of this marriage, I don't have to give you anything, is that clear?"

"Clear as day! You've not heard the last of this!"

Claire hung up the phone. She would have cried again but her anger wouldn't allow her to. Paul was still the selfish bastard that she had always known him to be. He was going to try everything that he could to get out of paying alimony. She knew it for what it was, sheer spiteful jealousy, and she was disgusted by it. She went over to the drinks cabinet and fixed herself a brandy and Coke. She mused for a while, promising herself to call her solicitor first thing the next morning. She went into he kitchen and fixed herself a sandwich before going upstairs with her bags to unpack, completely forgetting to call Amanda.

Ricky sat at his studio. He had just finished sampling a tune when the phone rang. It was Shaniqua.

"How ya doin'?" she asked.

"Fine," responded Ricky.

"How's ya bitch?" she asked abruptly but with enough of a light heart to suggest that she didn't mean it.

Ricky's response came in mellow tones.

"You better have some respect," he said.

Shaniqua corrected herself and apologised, albeit quite sarcastically for the comment.

"We need to talk maney!" she declared.

Ricky braced himself. He didn't have plenty and even though he always did his best to make sure that he gave something to Shaniqua for Tanika, he knew that she was struggling and that at some point she would begin to pressure him for more money on a more consistent basis. He respected her right to do this and pledged himself to do what he could as this, he thought, was probably going to be the moment. Shaniqua spoke quietly.

"You know 'arve alwiz give ya the benefit of the daaht wiv dis maney bizniz, cos are know you don't earn a lot, but arm sorry, are gotta ave more maney for Tanika."

Ricky breathed heavily.

"How much more?" he queried.

"Are gotta 'ave samfink from ya on a manfflee."

"How much?" Ricky enquired again.

"Baaht £200 a manff," said Shaniqua abruptly.

Ricky spoke quickly and decidedly.

"Can't do it. I'm barely taking home £500 a month as it is! I can probably push it to £50 but that's all I can do."

"'S'not good enaff!" shot back Shaniqua, whom Ricky could sense was becoming more irate.

"Well I can't do any more than that," he said, sounding conclusive.

"Oh no mate! Are fink you can!" shot back Shaniqua.

"I'm not holding back any money from you!" he said, deducing this to be the point that Shaniqua was driving at.

"Aren't ya?" she accused. "How cam you didn't tell me that yer bitch had maney? An' har much of it are you gettin'?"

Ricky fumed. He thought for a second. Then it came to him. Shaniqua had always shown herself considerate to his poverty. Now that she had heard that his woman was rich, things had changed. He figured that there could only be one possible reason for such an abrupt change of heart.

"Why do you allow that Bones to mess your brain up?" he asked.

Shaniqua met the question with disdain.

"Arm sorry mate, are don't fink so! Are fink you're the one that's facked ap around 'ere! you can't even take care of your blasted doota!"

Ricky wanted to avoid an argument, he raised his offer.

"£75 a month."

"No good, ard get £200 easy if are went to the Charl 'Spoot Agency!"

Ricky exploded, he considered the very mention of the word unnecessary. Whenever that phrase was used it constituted a serious breakdown in communications between a man and the mother of his children. He considered it nothing but either a desperate measure or spite. He spat poison at Shaniqua.

"Tell the fuckin' CSA, I don't give a shit! I'm sure they'll be interested in knowing how much of your child support you're giving to that fuckin' crackhead boyfriend of yours! You tell him this from me, him and his big mouth friend Buzzard. If I ever catch them talkin' my business outta street. I'm fuckin' em both up!"

Ricky slammed the phone down hard and with disgust. He fumed. He just couldn't understand how and why Shaniqua was allowing Bones to pressure her so much. He had always credited her with more common sense than that, but he reasoned that she was still young and still possibly very gullible. It enraged him to know that the mother of his child was endangering herself in this way. He pledged himself to talk to Bones at his next opportunity because now the situation was getting out of hand. If he had the chance, he would also talk to Buzzard as well. He had never spoken to him. They had never exchanged a greeting and yet, this man had taken information about his private life to Bones. This was just not on. A warning, at least was in order. His anger got the better of him and as he looked up at the clock he figured that now was as good a time as any to do it. He knew exactly where they would be.

It hadn't taken Ricky long to spin his car round to the park. He was still fuming as he got out. About twenty-five black guys of all ages had just finished playing football on the park and another ten had been watching. Ingin was one of them, as was Bones and Buzzard. Tuesday night was football practice for Roots FC, the only all-black football team in the local Sunday morning league and as such they carried a lot of support. As the players all sat around changing and holding various group conversations, Ricky walked straight up to Bones who was surprised when he turned to find an irate Ricky up in his face.

"Why you gotta keep pressuring my baby mother for money?" he asked.

"What?" was the only response that Bones could muster.

"You heard!" Ricky fired.

The raising of his voice attracted a lot of attention and soon enough the two were stood centre circle as thirty plus black men had surrounded them expecting a scuffle to break out. The excitement merely served to raise Ricky's blood pressure some more as some of the guys' implored him to relax whilst others, most of whom disliked Bones, encouraged Ricky to hit him.

"Come oat a my face bwoy!" ordered Bones who was visibly shaken and evidently worried by the attention. His comment only bought Ricky closer up into his face.

"You need to cut the shit out!" he warned. "The next time I have to come and see you I ain't gonna be talkin'. I've got a kid to protect and I'll do anything to protect her from the likes of you. If I have to even do a bird for her, I'm ready to do it! You understand?"

Bones shook.

"Come oat me rassclaart face me seh!" he said with false bravado.

"Buss 'im up Ricky!" came a voice from the crowd "Crackhead Rass!"

"You got one warnin' and that's it!" concluded Ricky, pushing him slightly in the chest. The crowd heard the wind break from Bones as Ricky turned away. But he wasn't going far. He scanned the crowd to find Buzzard and when he did pushed his way towards him. Once close enough to him and without a single thought, Ricky grabbed his throat. His weight training was proving useful as Buzzard grabbed his wrist with both of his hands in an effort to wrest himself away from Ricky's grip. His efforts were fruitless. Ricky was too strong and Buzzard had been smoking too much crack and was not eating well enough to have the strength in his skinny body to break free.

"You! Who told you to carry my fuckin' business any where?" asked Ricky at the top of his voice.

"It wasn't me man! Serious!"

"Same goes for you! I don't know who the fuck you are, never spoke to you! But you got the fuckin' nerve to carry my business all over the damn place! If I have to look for you again I'll be swingin', you understand?"

"Ricky mine you strangle him!" shouted Ingin.

Ricky released Buzzard from his grip with a push that sent him sprawling at the same time. As the crowd dispersed, talking over the incident, Ingin approached Ricky and walked him back to his car.

"I think it was my big mouth, that made him know about Claire." he said.

Ricky didn't look at him as he spoke.

"Yes but it wasn't you that told Shaniqua. That blasted idiot Buzzard told Bones. That's the only explanation I have. Now she wants regular money from me. Talkin' about the CSA," explained Ricky.

"Bitch!" cursed Ingin.

"Yo, chill," said Ricky nonchalantly as he pushed the key into the door of his car. "She's still my baby mother."

"Sorry star," replied Ingin correcting himself.

Ricky lightened up.

"What you doing tomorrow night?" he asked. "I spoke to Claire earlier today. She's got something lined up for you."

Ingin beamed. "Seriously! You came through for me guy! Wicked," he said slapping Ricky hard on his shoulder.

"I'll come for you at eleven. Don't forget your Viagra! You old whore," smiled Ricky.

"How she stay? She have money?" inquired Ingin.

"If she's Claire's friend she'll have money. The rest I don't know. Guess you'll find out tomorrow."

Ricky gave Ingin a pound with his fists and was off, looking like a child, grinning from ear to ear. He would have clicked his heels like Gene Kelly in 'Singing In The Rain'. He was so happy. Ricky started thinking. He had no problem with Ingin prostituting himself like this. If fact he was pleased to help him out. Ingin's view on mixed relationships was one that he partially supported. If he could fuck his way into money, why not? It had been his choice to use his most marketable assets for sale and he was free to do what he wanted. It was just like the Hottentot Venus. As Ricky started up his engine and pressed the accelerator, he wondered if he would ever see her again.

six

Tortilla chips with salsa. Vegetable patties, baked aubergine. Basil and mozzarella rolls. Onion bhajis, a mint and Cannellini bean dip with cauliflower, carrots, cucumber, radishes and peppers. Squared Tofu pieces. Cheese and garlic pate mixed with herbs. Avocado pear slices. Almond and sesame nut roasts. Vegetable samosas, chinese leaves stuffed with mushrooms, cheese dips with various sauces and much more. Allison had put on an enormous vegetarian spread. Six women sat in her living room occupying every sofa space available. Allison, a tall muscular woman in her early forties sat at in the middle on a single sofa. She was an elegant woman, who dressed comfortably in a light green jogging suit. She was a woman who had spent a good deal of her life fighting the women's cause. As a radical in her younger days, she had pledged to beat men at their own game and had become a millionaire from the sale of her natural food, hair and beauty products. She had travelled the world many times over for her recipes and ingredients. She wore an air of experience and maturity that far surpassed any of her guests. To them she was a role model, someone to whom they al looked up. Someone to emulate and admire. She was a moral conscience for all of them, the sort of woman they all felt, deep down, that they should be themselves. But they couldn't because, in most cases, their men ruled their lives.

Claire and Emma sat together eagerly tucking into the large spread that rested on a large oak coffee table in the centre of the room. Katrina was American. The wife of a football agent, she was by far the chattiest. Then there was Stella, a young looking forty-five year old who bred horses with her husband. Finally there was Gina, an attractive mixed-race thirty-five year old who worked in television. Claire was particularly interested in hearing what she had to say, but was often irritated as she didn't talk much. The do was into its second hour. As the women munched away and the wine flowed, the conversation passed from the latest movies, to French men, from beautiful countries that they had visited to Italian men, from good works of art and inevitably onto black men. They were all aware of Claire's relationship and unlike most other topics of conversation, they trod carefully through this one.

"Oh I find them most strange," said Katrina in her heavy southern American accent. "I mean, are we really to believe that all they do is walk around, wearing Tommy Hilfiger, smoking weed and doing drive-by shootings? I find that hard to believe, but the Ebony magazine image - you know, with the short curly perm, a neatly shaven moustache and an Armani suit - is just as hard to get to grips with."

"But aren't black men in the states, so much more successful than black men over here?" queried Stella.

"Oh come on darling," shot back Katrina with gusto. "Take a greyhound bus across California, through Compton to Hollywood and you tell me. Black people live in pockets of abject poverty. We have the most atrocious welfare system. The Ebony jet man image is really not all that it's cracked up to be. Sure, there are opportunities in America, but you wonder, sometimes, if these guys are really up to it y'know?"

"Up to what?" queried Claire with an almost challenging tone.

"Work, darling!" fired back Katrina. "Oh come on," she punched her fist through the air from her hips. "Get up and go! Make money! They seem to spend half their lives crying racism and how American society is so bad. I mean, the Million-Man March! What was that all about you know? Just some more boo-hoo if you ask me. Don't you get that over here?"

"I suppose we do, to some degree," said Allison.

Stella sank a glass of wine.

"Oh come on, darling, we get it all the time!" she fired. "If it's not police harassment it's not enough black role models on television, or some racial attack. I mean for Christ's sake. Katty's right, why don't they get off their arses and do something for themselves instead of complaining all the time?"

"Well what about racism?" interjected Allison, chomping on a cheese dip that she had just twirled in avocado cream sauce. "Isn't that a reality for many of them?"

"OK, yeah," jumped in Katrina. "OK, we had this Rodney King thing, OK? But hell, they got their own back with O.J. I mean half of that jury was black and I know for damn sure that if it was a black woman O.J. would be on death row right now!"

"But isn't it indicative of racism that when they cry racism, we simply try to reverse the idea as a means of letting ourselves off the hook?" challenged Allison, who was by far the calmest of those that were speaking.

"Hey come on. We live in a democracy. People have choice. If you're gonna spend your life accusing people of discrimination, hell those people are gonna hit back!" spouted Katrina.

"So your saying that they oughtn't to complain?" challenged Allison. "I mean, would you be saying that about the women's movement?"

"Darling, the women's movement died years ago," replied Katrina, waving the issue away.

"But black issues are still on the agenda, doesn't that tell you something?" jumped In Claire.

"Now you're biased," said Katrina with a smile.

All the women but Gina laughed

Katrina sipped Dom Perignon then looked at Claire waving her fingers at her.

"So spill the beans," she said. "What's he like, this black guy of yours? I think you're terribly courageous darling. I bet it was one in the eye for that rat bastard husband of yours."

Allison sat up in her seat to hear what Claire had to say. She too was eager to hear about Ricky.

"He's nice," began Claire. "He's a real gentleman. He's very conscientious. He cares a lot."

"My God! A prince!" said Stella, shunting herself back in mock amazement.

"Not quite, he's human," shot back Claire with a smile. "He's very intelligent. He gives me a complete head fuck. He really fucks my brain."

"Sorry darling?" Broke in Katrina confused.

"He stimulates my brain," said Claire, correcting herself. "We can talk for hours, I love to hear him speak."

"Even when he's extolling the virtues of the once mighty African race?" asked Stella once again with slight mockery in her voice.

"He really doesn't go there very often, but when he does. I like to hear it," replied Claire calmly.

"Don't you get all this crazy angst from all these crazy black women?" inquired Katrina excitedly. "Present company excepted of course," she said, turning to Gina who merely looked at her and smiled.

"You're stealing our men from us you naughty white women!" said Stella, acting the wounded black woman with a mock smile.

Claire ignored her even though she was becoming irritating.

"I've not met many, though I understand I won't be receiving any Christmas presents from his daughter's mother," said Claire.

"He's got children then?" asked Gina.

"One," said Claire.

"Humph!" said Gina under her breath to no one in particular.

Allison eyed her intently. She had been quiet for most of the evening. She was wondering when Gina was going to say something and when she did, she worried that it might not be very respectful of her present company.

"So," said Stella rubbing her hands.

"Oh my God, she's going to ask the question!" shouted Katrina laughing.

"Is it true?" asked Stella.

"Is what true?" asked Claire smiling.

"You know! What they say?"

"What they say about what?"

"You know! These black men and their lunch boxes!"

"Oh, has he got a big dick?" shouted Claire to the amusement of everyone but Gina. "I'm sorry to disappoint you," she continued.

Emma dropped her head in disappointment, then raised it quickly before anyone could notice.

"I honestly don't think so. I think that's a myth," she said.

"Oh," said Stella, the disappointment clear in her voice.

"But they have stamina," said Claire. Emma turned to her quickly and smiled. Claire was unashamed. "They just go on and on and on," she said, eyes closed, shaking her head emphatically. "I've had more orgasms in the month or so that we've been together than I had in all the years that I was married to Paul."

"Really?" asked Emma, eyes aglow.

Claire nodded at her reassuringly.

"Wonderful!" said Emma.

"Way to go!" said Katrina.

"Wow!" said Stella.

Gina looked to the ground and said nothing.

"But honestly," said Claire in a more serious tone. "I think I love him."

Allison's eyes were aglow. Happiness reigned over her caring face.

"'sabit soon," said Katrina.

"Not for me," replied Claire. "It's a feeling I've never known. It must be. The man does so much for me."

"He'll let you down!" broke in Gina with alarming venom. So much so that all the women were shocked by her intervention.

"Sorry?" asked Claire nervously.

"He'll let you down. Mark my words!" was Gina's embittered response. "They're all the same! Just like my father! I've never known that bastard and I never want to!"

The women were stunned into silence, not so much with the abruptness of Gina's interruption but the venom with which she spoke.

"He'll do the same to you," she continued. "Fuck you, take your money, your devotion, your love, then spit you out the minute he's had enough of you!"

"You sound very bitter," said Emma, doing her best to keep her composure.

"Bitter isn't the word," replied Gina. "I had to grow up watching my mother suffer. She tried to find him, tried to contact him, more for my sake than anything. When she did catch up with him, well, he convinced her into having one night of passion with him again then pissed off. I hate the bastard."

"But surely they're not all the same. I've known some white men that have done the same," argued Emma.

"Really?" asked Gina sarcastically. "Have you really? The difference is that with white men, it's not in their blood. These black guys seem to just want to fling it around everywhere. Haven't you noticed the numbers of black single parents around? And what's worse, there are a growing number of white single parents nowadays too. All pushing their little buggies with their little half-caste babies in them. It makes me sick! This generation of black men is at it just like my father's generation. It's in the blood. They have no concept of love, dedication, commitment, no concept of family! They think and act with their dicks. It's the fucking animal in them."

Even Katrina was surprised by the sourness of Gina's argument.

"You're half black," she said. "How does that make you feel?"

"I'm not black, I'm white," said Gina. "Being half–caste means I have to make a choice about my identity and I'm sorry, but I could never choose to be black."

"But you've got black blood in you," insisted Katrina, ramming the point home.

"I'm ashamed of it. Claire, I don't begrudge you for seeing this guy. It's your choice. You do what you want to do. But he'll leave you miserable, dishevelled, with no self-confidence and lost. He'll make you love him, give all of your devotion to him and sap every last bit of your energy. Then he'll leave you alone, and even when you beg him back through tears and total devastation he'll be cold. He won't hear you. He'll be off to find some other stooge's life to mess up. You take it from me. They're no good," said Gina with gusto.

All were silent again, allowing Gina's venom to sink in. Claire looked at the floor and had a hard, embarrassed look written all over her face. Emma put an arm around her shoulder and shook it gently. Allison sat stony-faced staring at Gina. Her blood boiled. She had expected something like this from her. Gina was a spoiler. She had known her for a long time and had realised that she was a woman with built up frustrations. She was often moody and acted like a spoilt child. She wondered what the point of her outburst was. Missing out on a father for so much of her life had affected her. On top of this she had to deal with the obvious difficulties of belonging to and coming from two cultures. She respected this, but her behaviour was sometimes nauseating and unnecessary. She could have spoken with a bit more respect and understanding for the circumstances, but she had ruthlessly ripped Claire's world asunder and had done so without any remorse or compassion. Allison wasn't going to allow her to get away with it. She broke the silence with a soft voice.

"Well," she began. "I suppose, with this topic at least, yours is supposed to be the most discerning view. Being half black …" she rubbed that part in "… should make you an expert on the matter and we poor, pitiful, blind white people should respect your view. But I suspect that your picture is clouded. There is simply good and bad in all of us. Your father wasn't a good man. It doesn't mean the same of everyone of his ilk …"

"Yes, but …" broke in Gina.

"Shut up I'm talking!" shouted Allison with so much fire that Gina dropped her head and instantly remained quiet. "You're entitled to your views nonetheless," she continued. "But I think it was completely irresponsible and so totally, typically selfish of you to express them in the way that you did with the company that you are in. Your heart and your mother's have been broken, that's your tough shit. You deal with it. And dealing with it does not mean causing someone else who's in a similar position so much anguish. You've sat here for two hours and said virtually nothing. Your whole vibe feels like something from the depths of hell. Lighten up and let it go or else you'll never be welcome in my house. Do you hear me?"

Gina remained quiet.

"I asked you a question," said Allison calmly.

"Yes, yes I do," replied Gina in a quiet tone, her face bowed to the ground.

Allison had a fiersome reputation, not only for speaking her mind, but also for putting people in their place when she felt that they were out of order. The silence that hit the room suggested that this was one such moment. Allison had been responsible for the atmosphere and she knew that she had to take responsibility for lightening the air. She did so with impeccable cleverness. She reached over to a small cabinet just by the sofa she was sitting on and pulled a small leather bag from the drawer and tossed it over to Gina.

"Here," she said light-heartedly. "I know you like Givenchy. I picked this up in Italy for you."

Gina opened the bag and pulled out a small bottle of perfume. She could hardly speak. Allison dipped into the drawer again, pulled out two small boxes and tossed them to Katrina and Stella. They opened them with ravenous impatience to reveal, for Katrina, gold earrings ("From India," said Allison) and for Stella a sparkling string of pearls ("From the Seychelles," said Allison).

Once more she dipped into the drawer. She could see the excitement on both Claire and Emma's faces. She didn't disappoint them. Emma opened her present cautiously. She gently pulled aside the small amount of wrapping paper. She sat, wide eyed and mouth agape at the beautiful gold necklace that shone in her hands. She, just like the others, was speechless.

"From Paris," said Allison with a smile. She looked at Claire who had not yet opened her present.

"Go on girl, don't keep us in suspense!" ordered Katrina who was just as keen as everyone else to see what Allison had bought her. Claire pulled apart the wrapping paper to behold a small box, which she opened slowly. Inside it lay a gold chain with a small gold grafted map of Jamaica on the end. On the other side were the letters C and R engraved. Claire lifted it up and turned to Allison.

"Thank you," she said with a graceful smile. "It's wonderful."

"I'm glad you like it. I asked the guy to make it especially for you, there's only one of those in the world and even though there are many mixed relationships darling, that's how you must consider yours," Allison replied.

A tear fell from Claire's eye. Gina reached across and put her hand on her shoulder, gently pulling her head to her shoulder. Stroking the hair gently back from her forehead she spoke softly.

"I'm so sorry darling, I don't know what came over me. I really didn't mean to hurt you. Forgive me. I really do wish you the best." Emma stretched out a hand and rubbed Claire's arm with compassion. Katrina poured out another glass of wine, lifted her glass and raised a toast to Allison.

seven

Claire drove quickly along the motorway. It had been a long night. Emma, her passenger was tired. She was too. But they would not sleep yet for a good while.

"So, it's settled. You're staying by me tonight then?" asked Claire.

"Oh I don't know, I haven't …"

"Oh stop being so negative. Wear my clothes. God, I've got enough!" said Claire boisterously.

Emma held both of her breasts in her hands and sized them up.

"I don't think I've quite got the boobs for your clothes dear," she said.

Claire slapped her gently on her shoulder with the back of her hand.

"The baggy look is in darling," she said. "Where have you been for the last two years?"

Emma got serious again.

"Oh I don't know what Peter will say. He might think …"

"You're out doing what he's doing? It would bloody well serve him right wouldn't it?"

"Oh I don't know."

Claire tired of Emma's procrastination.

"Ring him. Get out your mobile phone. Call him. Go on," she said

Emma reached into her handbag and pulled out a Nokia 8810.

"OK, one can but try," she said worriedly.

She pressed the digits and put the phone to her ear and spoke when she heard Peter's voice. She was nervous and spoke timidly.

"Erm darling, do you mind if I, erm s-stay with …"

Claire, disgusted by her tone, grabbed the phone from her and put it to her own ear. She spoke brazenly.

"She's staying over with me tonight. That OK?" she said. "Tough shit if it isn't darling."

She passed the phone back to Emma.

"It's fine," she said.

Emma listened for a while then spoke into the phone.

"Yes darling, I'll be back by midday. Yes darling, your shirts will be ironed. Yes darling ... no darling ... of course darling."

Emma sent her eyes to the heavens and shook her head in disgust as she drove. Emma closed the conversation with her husband and put the phone back in her handbag. There was silence for the rest of the journey.

Once inside Claire's house Emma relaxed on the settee. She wondered what she was doing at Claire's at half past midnight. The thought faded from her mind as Claire brought in a drink for her. She sipped the scotch slowly. It hadn't been chased. Claire flicked the television on and leaned back in the settee, glanced at her watch and said nothing. Emma wanted to speak, but found Claire immediately wrapped up in the Jerry Springer show so she said nothing and sat confused.

Before long there was a knock at the door. Claire rushed to answer it leaving Emma even more bewildered. Who could be calling her at this late hour? She settled herself at the thought that it was probably Ricky and immediately became excited at the thought of meeting him for the first time, even if it was at one o'clock in the morning. As the door opened she fell back in the settee, her eyes agape, her nervousness displayed for all to see. Ricky walked in first. He smiled at her and gave a hearty;

"Hi."

To which she gave a nervous "Yes."

Ingin followed. His eyes were alight with enthusiasm. Upon noticing the cute, timed little thing now cowering in the corner of Claire's settee he beamed.

"Evening," he said in a pathetically official voice that made him sound like a policeman.

Emma said nothing. She couldn't. The shock of the moment sent her into a flurry that made her drown her scotch in one go.

She placed the empty glass on the coffee table and swallowed her last mouthful with a loud gulp and not so much as a single cough. Claire stood in the centre of the room.

"Emma, meet Ricky and Ingin. Ricky's my lover, as you know, and Ingin is ... well, as you can see, a six-foot Rasta with dreadlocks down to his arse and a dick as big as ..."

She held her forefingers out, studied them and moved them slightly further apart.

"That," she concluded. "Well so I'm told."

Emma sussed the game and tossed Claire a worried look.

"You heard right," said Ingin, still beaming.

"Oh," said Emma with a stifled giggle, brushing her hair from her forehead.

"So you're Emma?" asked Ingin in his ridiculous voice.

"I think that's what Claire called me," she responded.

"Hmm," said Ingin.

"Hmm," said Emma coyly, studying her feet.

The air went quiet. The atmosphere became heavy. No one knew what to say.

"Spose you're going to fuck me then?" said Emma in a courageously nonchalant manner.

Ingin didn't know what to say.

"If you want," he finally managed in a boyish tone.

"Fancy me then do you?" asked Emma, trying to get something going.

"Well...er...yeah!" came the reply.

"Good, 'spose that helps," she replied nervously. She stood up. Took a deep breath and held an outstretched hand to Ingin. "C'mon then," she said. "Let's go upstairs."

Ingin took her hand. He was usually an upfront sort of chap, but the complete look of bewilderment on his face spoke volumes. He tossed a worried look at Ricky who just looked away. Claire jumped in to separate them.

"Emma let's have a word first," she said, leading her to the kitchen. Once inside she placed her hands on Emma's arms. "Are you sure you want to do this?" she asked. "I guess he is a bit intimidating."

Emma said nothing, folded her arms and sighed. She thought

for a while. Claire controlled her anticipation saying nothing, allowing her friend all the space and time that she needed.

"It's not that I'm worried about," said Emma eventually, "Fantasies are no longer fantasies when they appear before you. What worries me is why I wanted it in the first place."

"Darling there's nothing wrong with ..." interjected Claire.

"Who's talking about right or wrong?" Emma interrupted her. "I could easily justify doing this. What I'm more concerned about is the good and the bad of it. I'm a married woman, I took a vow to be faithful to my husband."

"Even if he's not faithful to you?" asked Claire.

"Is that even an issue? Should I consider it an issue? What? Do I fight fire with fire? Even if I remain unconcerned about my husbands morality, shouldn't I still be concerned about my own?"

Claire spoke softly.

"Of course you should darling. But I wonder if your morality should be based on the words of ancient vows that when they were conceived assumed Puritanism for all those that took them. That assumed a woman's place was, well, forgive me, but just where you are. Those rites belong to a society that would have stoned or burned you at the stake for even thinking about doing what I know you're about to do. Emma," she continued. "I love you, you're like a sister to me. Remember the words that you spoke to me after Colin and Rosy's dinner party. You gave me strength, you encouraged me even further to a place where I have found even more freedom than I have ever known. I want to do the same for you. I arranged this for the simple reason that your husband is probably, even right now, doing the same thing to you. It's not revenge that I want for you, it's not your morality that I want to change. Darling I want you to be free. I want you to share the most valuable possession that we as poor pitiful intellectually and mentally restrained so-and-so's could have. Liberation."

Emma looked at her, leaned forward and kissed Claire on her cheek.

"Thank you," she said softly. She moved towards the door. "Excuse me," she said, "but there's a deliciously sexy young man out there that I have to liberate. From his pants!"

"Hold on a minute," said Claire. "Take these," she said,

handing her a packet of condoms that she had quickly pulled from one of the kitchen drawers. "I don't think that I can trust that young man to wear one of these."

Emma refused to take them.

"I bought some," she said with a devilish smile before she bounced confidently back into the living room. She smiled at Ricky as if to say goodnight and without a word took Ingin by the hand and led him out of the door and upstairs. Claire entered the room rubbing her hands together and looking tense. Ricky rose from his seat and held her.

"What you worried about?" he asked gently.

She looked up at him and sighed.

"He'd better be good," she said.

Shaniqua straightened both her legs. Bones was out of breath. He lay on top of her panting for dear life. It had taken longer for them to get their clothes off than it had taken their intercourse to last. Shaniqua omitted a gust of abhorrence at another one of Bones's sad bedroom performances and rolled her eyes to the ceiling. Bones rolled over, stretched over to the small table that was situated next to the bed, pulled out a cigarette, put it to his mouth and lit it. Shaniqua waved the smoke away from her face in disgust.

"You know are don't like that stuff in mar bedroom," she said wearily.

Bones ignored her, took another toke and blew the smoke to the ceiling.

"Tork t'me bleeding sewff," she sighed. She looked at him, wondering how to raise the next subject. She knew it would upset him, but she went for it anyway. "Are don't feel too good abaaht Ricky," she said tensely.

Bones eased out of his Karma and threw her a look out of the corner of his eyes.

"Wha' ya chat bout?" he asked, slightly more aggressively than his high would have suggested.

Shaniqua felt trouble in the air. But she spoke bravely.

"'Snot raaht, he ain't got no maney."

"Him rich man, wha ya chat boat?" replied Bones in no mood

to hear her grievance. "De white ting a feed 'im wid carn. As so dem stay."

Shaniqua tried a different tact.

"Did he hit ya then?" she asked with cunning. She wanted to upset him.

Bones chupsed his teeth to signify his response.

"Shoulda' beat the livin' shit outta ya," Shaniqua muttered under her breath whilst turning in distaste. A bad move. She felt the back of Bones's hand across the side of her head.

"What the fack dya do that for?" she bellowed, turning to him.

Bones raised a finger to the sky.

"Don' fuck wid me y'hear!" he warned.

"Fack off!" Shaniqua fired back.

She hardly had time to bury her head back into the pillow when the burn from Bones's cigarette inflamed her arm. She jumped out of the bed, hardly able to believe that he had stubbed his cigarette out on her naked flesh.

"You're fackin' mad!" she screamed, holding and studying her arm at the same time.

Bones jumped out of the bed and dived towards her, grabbing her instantly by the throat.

"Gyal you gwine know boat fuckin' mad!" he bellowed with fire in his eyes. "Mek sure dat bwoy gi' you de money seen!"

Shaniqua tried to wrest herself from his grip but no good, he held her too firmly. Her quick temper got the better of her and in a desperate attempt to break free, she slapped him. Her third wrong move. Bones released her, landing a quick right hook into the corner of her mouth.

"A fuck you a look fi fuck wid me?" he bellowed. "Come den no?"

He thumped her again, finding a fluid slugging motion as he engulfed her with more punches. Shaniqua dropped her head and vainly waved her arms to arrest his blows. But Bones was too slick. He landed a right into her stomach that caused her to double up. Bones pulled her hair and threw her across the room. She fell and once on the floor struggled to get her naked body up, but Bones put a stop to that by dropping his foot on her head. She let out a scream. The door flew open. Tanika had heard the thuds and frightened by them had come running to her mother. She couldn't believe her eyes. Bones ignored her and landed a fist in Shaniqua'a face.

"It's OK darlin' go back to bed!" she screamed desperately.

Tanika broke.

"Mummy!" she shouted before bursting into tears.

Shaniqua was torn, she didn't know whether to fight back or run to comfort her daughter. She was unable to do either as Bones dropped his foot on her again and again brutally stamping on her head. Shaniqua screamed. Tanika screamed louder and began to jump up and down shaking her wrists up and down in sheer terror and panic.

"Mummy!" she shouted again.

Bones tired of her noise and sent a slap across her face that felled her.

"No! God no!" Shaniqua screamed.

Bones turned his attentions back to her but Shaniqua, fired by her compassion for her daughter who was by now hysterical, fought back valiantly. As Bones stood over her, waving her arm, she was able to grab his exposed testicles. She squeezed them tightly. Bones let out a shriek of pain before hurling a series of insults at her. In the split second's respite, Shaniqua ran to her daughter, scooped her off the ground and was out of the door with Bones in hot pursuit. Shaniqua nearly fell as she ran down the stairs but held her footing skilfully. Not so Bones, who slipped and had to hold onto the banister. Another valuable respite. She made it into the living room just in time to lock the door before Bones could reach it. He thought about trying to kick it in but he realised that he was barefooted so he pushed his shoulder against it.

"Open de fuckin' door bitch! A gwine kill you tonight!" he shouted.

Shaniqua screamed through tears.

"You fackin' barstud, you're gonna fackin' pay for this! Get aaht! Get fackin' aahhta mar haass. Are got a phone in 'ear! Are'll ring the fackin' police!"

The pushing stopped.

"Bitch!" shouted Bones.

Shaniqua dropped her tone, though her tears were no less subtle.

"Just get aaht, please leave me alone."

Bones pushed the door one more time. Then there was quiet. Through Tanika's confused sobbing she could hear Bones climbing the stairs. She sat against the door, her naked body shivering. She held tightly onto Tanika both to comfort her and give herself warmth. Her breathing was heavy, nervous and unsteady. She heard the thuds of furniture being turned over in her room. She knew that what money and jewellery she had up there would be his. It mattered little. He could take what he wanted so long as he left. Soon enough Bones's footsteps were heard coming down the stairs. He said nothing. His exit was announced by the vicious slam of the front door. Shaniqua breathed a sigh of relief. She held her daughter tighter as she sat with her on the floor, her back against the cold door. She pressed Tanika's head into her shoulder, looked up to the ceiling and cried.

Ricky and Claire were outside the bedroom. Eagerly they listened. This was becoming a habit. Claire felt slightly guilty, but Ricky's eagerness to hear Emma and Ingin in action helped to convince her that perhaps listening to people having sex was fun. Plus he had wagered that Ingin would give a repeat performance and he wanted to claim his victory. Claire had warned him that Emma would be no pushover, but he reasoned that the scrawny little thing would be no match for the hulk that Ingin was. He listened eagerly. A wry smile that had been etched on his face had become concern. By now he had expected to hear Emma wallowing in sexual powerlessness, but something was wrong. He couldn't hear much. Claire was concerned too. She twirled her necklace as her eyebrows turned inwards and her face became contorted in abject confusion. She looked up at Ricky and mimed.

"I can't hear anything."

Ricky shrugged a shoulder both in agreement and also to wonder what was going on. It soon became clear. Ingin's groans though faint began to slowly become audible. Then came Emma's slurping.

"Blow job," whispered Claire, allowing her thumb to meet

with its nearest finger in a circle with the other three stuck in the air. "She's good at that!"

Ricky pressed his ear closer to the door. Ingin's groans of pleasure were becoming louder. He was confused. He'd not imagined Ingin in this sort of mood before. He had assumed that he was always in control. Emma's slurping became louder and more frantic as did Ingin's moaning. Ricky shook his head, nonplussed. Ingin was letting him down. He was surprised by a loud bellow that came from his friend.

"Oh shit! That's good, deep though, take it deep," he said in sensual tones.

Claire covered her mouth so as to make her impending laughter inaudible. She concentrated harder. Emma was doing her proud. The noise from the bedroom began to rise. Emma's slurping becoming louder and the bed began to squeak. Emma was using its spring to get a more feral suck. Ingin was in raptures, no longer able to control his ecstasy. He shook his head in disbelief. He was being laid big time and he could do nothing about it. Then the slurping stopped. The two listened intently. Emma had stopped her blowjob and had climbed on top of Ingin seizing his erection and placing it inside of her. Ingin died of bliss. His moan seemed to last for an age. Then the bed started again, this time much more violently than before. Emma was riding him like she was in a rodeo, and Ingin was helpless.

The impact of her wild fucking left him in a state of powerlessness. He could only hold on as she tortured him with wild abandon. He screamed time and time again as the combined noises of the bed-head banging against the wall and the screeching of the springs reached a furious crescendo. Emma was sweating, as was he, but she was tireless as time and again her violent thrusts sent him again and again into rapture.

"That's my girl!" whispered Claire with uncontrolled excitement. Ricky was still shaking his head in disbelief. The climax wasn't long in coming. Ingin surrendered to his passion and with a lasting cry of "Ooh shit!" it ended. But not for Emma. She had come three times and was still going strong, but once Ingin lost his erection she finally succumbed. Ingin was desperate to get her off him, almost begging her to stop. When she did stop he lay there numb. Ricky and Claire, sensing the end, made their exits quickly and quietly back to the living room, both still hardly able to believe what had just transpired.

Claire and Ricky were sitting in the living room making light conversation when both Ingin and Emma re-appeared after about fifteen minutes. The tiredness on his face was clearly visible and he didn't try to hide it. He sat next to Ricky on the sofa and placed his head in his hands.

"Drink darling?" asked Emma briskly. She still had plenty of life in her.

"Sure," sighed Ingin. "Gimme an orange juice if you've got one," he said wearily. "Stick it in a pint glass, with plenty of ice."

Emma disappeared quickly into the kitchen. Claire followed.

"Well?" she asked once assured that they were alone and out of earshot.

Emma pulled a jug of orange juice from the fridge. "Well what?" she asked.

"You know!" suggested Claire.

"You were listening weren't you?" replied Emma, pulling a pint glass from the top cupboard. Claire was hesitant.

"W…well I heard some noise," she said tentatively.

Emma pulled the ice from the freezer and liberated a few pieces from the tray.

"It was good," she said insouciantly. She touched Claire's shoulder. "My, he's big!" she said casting a smile at her friend. Claire smiled too.

Emma placed the ice in the glass and poured juice over it.

"I feel so bad," she said in a worried sort of tone. Claire became worried too.

"Really?" she asked with some concern.

"Yes," said Emma sadly. She made her way to the door with Ingin's drink then turned. "I didn't lick his balls," she said with honest regret. "Just couldn't get over the size of that cock!" she mused to herself.

Claire laughed and watched her friend exit the kitchen and place the drink gently in Ingin's hands. He sank the drink without a pause, then turned to Ricky who spoke up immediately.

"We need to be off. Busy day tomorrow for both of us."

Claire hugged him

"Really darling?" she asked with regret. "I was hoping that we could do some mating of our own tonight," she whispered tenderly.

"Sorry babes. Too much to do tomorrow," replied Ricky

Emma gave Ingin a slight hug.

"Take care darling," the women said in tandem.

"I'll probably be in touch," said Emma to Ingin, who hardly seemed concerned.

Claire kissed Ricky on the cheek and ushered them to the door. "Thanks a mill. I owe you one," she whispered to her lover.

"I'll be back to collect!" he warned jokingly.

The women waved and stood in the doorway as the guys drove off. Ricky turned to Ingin as he manoeuvred his XR2 down the long driveway. He looked very out of it. Ricky asked him if he was all right. He seemed too stunned to reply and almost surprised Ricky when he managed to muster a small "Hmm, think so."

The air went quiet again. Ricky knew what the silence meant. He knew that Ingin wasn't always playing Mr Macho. There were times when even he had to take a stop and assess himself. Ricky was pleased that whenever Ingin faced such a moment, he would act accordingly and as expected. This was one of those moments for sure. Ingin's ego had taken a battering. There was no bragging, no bravado, and no excessive testosterone, macho-laden braggadocio that issued unyieldingly from the passenger seat this night. No, there was simply silence. Ingin had closed his eyes and was contemplating life, the world and the bullshit therein and he had started with himself. Ricky knew that this wasn't the sign of a massive realignment in Ingin's chauvinist perspective on life. It simply meant that at least for the next few days, he would shut the hell up about his sexual prowess.

The simple truth lay in the realisation that Ingin had been mastered in the bedroom. He had been devastated by the ravenous desire of a woman who had simply taken what she wanted. She had laid him to waste at the doorstep to Valhalla and he could do nothing about it. He had been dominated, controlled, had the shit fucked out of him and whilst it felt good at the time, it felt like shit now. What compounded his growing misery was the fact that it had been done by a beautiful but nonetheless puny framed little white woman whom on any other occasion he would have sexed into total oblivion. Emma had set about him like a hungry panther, fed herself and in the process had clipped his narcissistic wings. Ricky realised all of this and was amused by it. He jabbed the clutch with his foot and adjusted the gears as he viewed the empty road ahead of him. He smiled and switched on the music. 'Notorious B.I.G's, Life After Death' subtly emerged from the speakers. Ricky bobbed his head, took a last look at Ingin, who was still meditating, and settled himself for the long drive ahead of him.

Emma sat in silence. So did Claire. They hardly knew what to say to each other. Eventually Emma lowered her head. Claire eyed her as it began to shake. Emma blew out a squall of breath whilst at the same time raising her head to send her hair back over her head. She looked at Claire, chewing on her bottom lip. She dropped her head again and spoke.

"I'd honestly thought we'd seen the back of this," she said softly.

"The back of what dear?" asked Claire, pretending that she didn't know what Emma was alluding to.

Emma's hand moved right to left from the wrist.

"This … this bloody promiscuous sexual activity, you know, the orgies the parties and … everything."

Claire mused for a second then spoke.

"Did I do wrong, in setting this up?" she asked with concern.

"No," replied Emma. "You've acted like a true friend. That stuff you spoke about earlier, about liberation. God. Now I feel so free. I feel so free, I'm frightened. It just feels so wrong."

The last word was said through tears as Emma dropped her head onto an open hand and sobbed. "God I enjoyed it so much," she continued through sniffles. "I felt so liberated. I took 15 years of marital frustration out on that man and now I just feel empty."

Claire looked at her half puzzled, but wanting to console her anyway. She could not understand why Emma had lapsed into apology once again. At least, she didn't want to understand it. It was a place that she had left a long time ago and had so desperately wanted her closest friend to join her. But she sighed, concluding that perhaps it was not to be.

"Shall I take you home?" she asked softly.

Emma, her face awash with tears, could only nod.

The drive to back Emma's seemed to take forever. It happened in silence. Claire tried to embolden her by playing Sheryl Crow and Hole tapes. No good. When they were about a mile away from her house, Emma pulled down the passenger side mirror, applied make up and brushed her hair. The action aroused Claire's disgust but she hid behind silence and focused on the road ahead of her. Once at Emma's gate, Claire pulled up. Emma touched her hand and issued a comforting smile.

"Thank you," she said quietly

Emma left the car and walked briskly to her front door. Claire watched to make sure that she got in safely.

"Enjoy, your life darling," she said. "That's all I ask." Then she drove off.

Emma entered the house cautiously, not wanting to wake Peter. She dropped her handbag at the foot of the stairs and kicked off her shoes. She walked slowly and steadily up the stairs passing the bathroom, which was to be her next stop, before slowly opening her bedroom door. She was surprised to notice that the light was on, perhaps Peter was still awake. She pushed the door too then stood in absolute horror at the sight that beheld her. There was Peter standing naked, attired only in a ten gallon hat and cowboy boots. On the ground, in front of him kneeled another naked body, a female body attired in nothing but a gun holster that barely sat around her waist. Even from the back Emma recognised her immediately. The Blonde bimbo, big jugs, not an ounce of grey matter in sight thing was skilfully working away at his dick. Peter was in ecstasy, but not too far good to be blown away by the sight of his furious wife standing at the door directly in front of him. He grabbed the woman's head. She had been so involved in her blow-job that she didn't even hear the door open. Peter pushed her away.

"Emma! It's not what you think! I can explain this," he said desperately.

The blonde turned round and dropped her head in her hands.

"Oh shit!" she said in her strong Texan accent, before running to her clothes on the other side of the room. "I knew this was a bad idea!" she cursed as she grappled amongst her clothes for her panties. Peter shook. He farted with nerves, then instinctively covered his erection with both hands. He was speechless. Another gut reaction moved him towards his wife. Emma raised an open hand to encourage him no further. He stopped. Emma was calm. The air became thick with silence. Emma raised a cheeky smile.

"Thank you," she said placidly.

Peter was now both stunned and confused. He held his arms wide in bewilderment.

"W…What d..do you mean?" he asked nervously.

Emma looked at him for a final second, then in an instant pulled the wedding ring off her finger and threw it at him. It landed straight in his eye. Peter screamed with pain and dropped his head into his hands.

"Thank you!" she shouted. She slammed the door too, leaving Peter alone with his mistress. She entered the spare bedroom and locked herself in. Once behind the door she leaned against it. She looked up to the ceiling, half in disbelief and half with a sharp sense of pain tinged with a hint of satisfaction. She felt tears emerging, but she battled them back. She would not allow herself to cry. The light faded as she closed her eyes. Her breathing became heavy as she fought to keep the oncoming emotional rush at bay. The clatter of Peter and his mistress and her loudly voiced frustrations faded into the distance as they scurried down the stairs and left the building.

Emma allowed the ensuing silence to sink in. She allowed her breathing to stem from within her stomach. It was more comforting and bought an immediate calm to her stricken soul. She meditated, allowing the warm feeling from below her diaphram to engulf her whole being. Her mind's eye beheld a light. An orange hue that slowly became an azure blue immersed her. Emma smiled to herself a smile that grew and eventually seemed to cover her whole face. As she wallowed in the ecstasy that her comforting spirit had laid upon her, she envisioned the days ahead. She could no longer hold back the tears, but they were tears of joy as she welcomed her liberation.

"Thank you Claire," she whispered. "Thank you so much."

eight

Claire poured hot coffee. She was shattered. Allison's dinner party, the ensuing events with Emma and Ingin and the drive back to Emma's place had taken its toll. It was now two o'clock in the afternoon and she had just woken up. She thought about making breakfast but she waved the notion away, settling for a cigarette to accompany her caffeine and promising to lunch at Pedro's, her favorite local restaurant. She had barely taken a sip of the coffee and two puffs of her cigarette when the phone rang. She wanted meditation time and didn't particularly want to answer it but she forced herself. Her wearied greeting was met with silence. She repeated her hello and a timid voice spoke back. It was Amanda.

"So the dead arise?" she opened sarcastically.

Claire scratched her head.

"Oh Amanda…I'm so sorry, I've been so busy. I completely forgot to call you back."

"No problem. 'Spect you've had that Jamaican serving your pussy on a nightly basis. Guess it doesn't leave you much time to do much else." Amanda said as if to negate her apology.

Claire mustered a fatigued laugh.

"It's not like that really…"

"Well it bloody well should be!" exploded Amanda.

Claire was stunned into silence by the outburst. Steadily the sound of crying and sniffling emerged from the other end of the telephone.

"Amanda are you alright?" asked Claire with more than a hint of concern.

"No," managed Amanda through the tears.

There was silence again but for the sniffles.

"Talk to me," encouraged Claire sensitively.

"I can't. Not on the telephone."

"Look, I was thinking of going to Pedro's…"

"Sure."

"I'll meet you there in an hour."

"Make it 45 minutes," requested Amanda with urgency.

"No problem," responded Claire.

Amanda dropped the telephone. Claire became worried. Amanda was a good friend. She girded her loins and prepared to do some serious listening, reminding herself of Amanda's fragility.

Claire made it to in Pedro's in forty minutes. Amanda was waiting for her. It was a warm day and she had chosen to sit outside. Her hair was covered with a wrap and she wore dark glasses and was puffing heavily on a cigarette. Claire noticed that she was shaking, although it wasn't cold, and could tell that she was obviously stressed. She took a seat opposite her estranged friend after greeting her with a kiss on the cheek. Amanda took her hand and said nothing. She took another puff on her cigarette as the waiter bought them menus.

"What are you having?" she asked in a businesslike manner.

"Continental," replied Claire sheepishly.

Amanda exhaled the last of her cigarette then began to dig into her handbag. Claire watched intently, noting the eagerness with which she searched. Eventually she pulled out a small plastic bottle which Claire noticed immediately were prescription tablets. Anxiously Amanda twisted the cap, dropped a pill into her hand and shoved it into her mouth drowning it with the now cold cup of coffee that she had earlier been sipping.

"What are those?" inquired Claire with concern.

Amanda allowed a short silence to pass then spoke.

"Just a little ray of sunshine dear," she said nonchalantly. "Nothing to worry about."

Claire wasn't having it.

"Amanda darling," she pursued sensitively. "What's wrong?"

Amanda dropped her head; she was about to speak but was interrupted by the waiter who took their orders. Once he disappeared Claire pushed again.

"What are those pills?" she asked gently.

Again Amanda let silence pass between them. Claire pressed her again. Amanda spoke eventually but with a hint of aggression.

"Prozac," she said, not looking at her friend.

Claire sat back in her chair.

"Prozac?" she asked, hardly able to believe it.

Amanda shook her head from side to side.

"Parrot, parrot," she said in dull fashion.

Claire ignored the protest.

"You're on Prozac?" she asked. "Why?"

Amanda looked at her with puzzlement.

"It's a cure for depression dear. Well, supposed to be," she replied sarcastically.

"OK, so you're depressed. Please, let's dispense with the games. Talk to me. What's the problem?" Claire was now becoming slightly infuriated with Amanda's attitude. She took a deep breath and reminded herself that the lonely woman in front of her needed help. She didn't want to mess up and reasoned that if her GP had prescribed Prozac for her, she was already some way down the line. Or maybe not. They seemed to prescribe Prozac for anything nowadays, she remembered reading in a magazine. She hoped that that was the case when she spoke quietly.

"Darling please, I'm here for you. What is it? What's wrong?"

Amanda allowed more silence to flow. She breathed heavily, wanting to speak but was unable to find the words. She found comfort in the fact that the waiter reappeared with their food. But that didn't last long. Neither of them ate. They sat in silence waiting for the other to speak again. Claire refused to say anything, reasoning that Amanda would soon speak. She did soon enough, although not before wiping a tear from her eye.

"Well," she began. "I guess I've answered the eternal question about my fertility."

Claire feared the worst; her heart skipped a beat. The magnitude of the moment struck her instantly. She was afraid, fearing the worst. Her immediate thought being that Alan had been unfaithful and had made someone pregnant. Amanda sensed her anxiety and immediately sought to cancel that notion out.

"When God said go forth and multiply," she began with as much wit as she could muster, "He certainly wasn't talking about arithmetic was he? Forgive me for being stereotypical but I guess black guys have certainly got that message."

Claire's whole body heaved with shock. Her eyes widened, as did her mouth. Her heart ran ten to the dozen, she trembled a little then spoke.

"Ingin?" she asked with outgoing breath.

Amanda nodded slowly. Claire had no more words.

"The condom snapped. I'm pregnant," she said, shrugging her shoulders.

Claire came back to her senses and verbalised her next most immediate thought.

"Why darling, I think that's wonderful!" she exclaimed.

Amanda pushed her sunglasses back. She wiped another tear from her eye.

"Really?" she asked coldly.

"Well why not?" asked Claire, trying to lighten the atmosphere, "You've answered the one question that has made your life such a misery. Why aren't you happy?

Amanda broke down. The tears were now in full flow. She took a tissue, wiped them and blew her nose, then mustered all the strength that she could find.

"Claire I really wish I could be happy," she started. "This is all I ever wanted. First I wanted a child and then it became a desire to at least know if I could bear a child and now both questions have been answered. Yes, I should be happy and God, even with the fact that I'm pregnant for some guy that I don't know. The fact that I had a one-night stand with him doesn't even faze me. Because I know that I can have children and that bastard of a husband of mine is the barren one, I suppose I should be happy."

Claire leaned forward and took her hand.

"Then why aren't you?" she begged.

Amanda's tears were flowing unchecked. Her face screwed up as she fought to speak.

"Where does this leave me, what life do I have now? Single parent I could do, but that bastard of a husband of mine - he'll cut me off. That prenuptial I signed. It sealed my fate. I've never worked. God almighty, I wouldn't know how to. I could possibly live without the millions. But I couldn't live off social security."

"Oh it wouldn't be that bad," dismissed Claire.

"Wouldn't it?" shot back Amanda. "I have no skills, few qualifications and no work experience. I'd go from living in a mansion to a two-bedroomed council house. Darling, you know me. The Mercedes, Harrods, credit cards. Those aren't things that I appreciate. Those are things that I take for granted. I simply couldn't live without the money. On top of that … forgive me, but the child would be, well…"

"Black," concluded Claire in a disgusted tone that Amanda hurried to dispel.

"Oh no I don't mean…"

"What do you mean?" challenged Claire who was becoming agitated.

"It's just … the stigma of it … I just couldn't deal with it," Amanda replied in defeated fashion.

Silence filled the air once again. Amanda looked away as empty lamentation washed over her face. Claire fought back frustration of her own. She too was empty. She closed her eyes almost in prayer as she struggled to find the words. Eventually they came as she was reminded by the lesson that she had given to Emma. She leaned forward, again, this time taking both Amanda's hands in hers. She spoke solemnly.

"Would that you had been pregnant by Alan," she started. "But I suppose sometimes in this life we just have to be careful of the things that we wish for. But darling, when we do receive the things that we wish for, it sometimes comes with a challenge. The challenge that faced me when I met Ricky was whether or not I should take my freedom. It was something that for a long time I had been searching for. Even though I decided to divorce Paul, the challenge of seeing a black man signalled the breaking of my chains. For someone in my position it takes a lot to see a black man. It's not just the fact that I'm rich, I sometimes only wish that that were it. No, it's the fact that I'm white. There are still too many areas of society that won't accept it, and for me to give society two fingers means that I have to be free. You've been in chains for so long darling. This is your wake up call. Your liberation is just around the corner. I think you should grasp it without fear or worry for the future. Because you will find the strength to cope and you must trust yourself that you will. It's a wonderful opportunity for you to address all those issues that have beset you. It's a chance to find yourself and straighten out that troubled heart of yours. I'll be with you darling. You know I'll be there."

Amanda looked at her blankly and pulled her hands away. She looked away sternly.

"I've considered all that," she said. "It's no good. I have nothing in me that will see me through this. Nothing. Trust me Claire. Over this past week, I've soul searched like a bitch on heat. I found fuck all. Not even a hint of inner strength, pride, moral fibre, none of those rich stand-up qualities that make you so special. No. Not me. I asked my heart to tell me who I was and what I was all about and all I saw was a credit card, a bottle of booze and a big fat dick. I asked my soul to show me happiness and bring some light in my life and all I saw was an empty darkness. I desperately searched my emotions for some form of joy, some form of happiness and all I found was sorrow and gloom. I am in the depths of hell. The one thing that I thought would bring me happiness has bought me nothing but torture."

She dropped her head, inhaled then spoke again.

"That's why I've chosen to abort."

Claire's heart jumped. For the second time that morning she was in shock.

"You're just in depression," she hurried.

"I have an appointment next week," Amanda concluded in belligerent fashion. "I wanted a baby more than anything in my life!" she squealed as a flurry of emotion broke her again.

Claire rose from her seat and stood over her. A weeping Amanda dropped her head against her friend's stomach, soiling her blouse with her tears. Passers-by wondered at the sight of a woman holding another woman as they both cried openly. The waiter appeared to remove their empty plates but was stunned not only to find them full but also to have wandered in on such a delicate moment. He didn't know what to do. He gathered their plates and touched Claire's hand.

"No bill," he whispered. "No bill."

Shaniqua sat in contemplation. She had just put Tanika to bed after spending an evening together that she had purposely devoted to her. Her daughter had obviously been affected by the events with Bones. She had had difficulty sleeping that night and in the morning had waded through her breakfast nervously and sheepishly. Shaniqua had quickly noticed the adverse effects on her and had sought to destroy them immediately. She had taken her shopping that day buying, amongst many other gifts, no less that four cuddly toys for her, which she had situated around the head of her bed. She had thought it might be a slightly extreme reaction, but what the hell? Tanika needed comforting and she would do whatever she could, however excessive, to make her feel sheltered and relaxed again. She would keep an eye on her over the next few days before deciding whether she needed to get professional or medical advice regarding her daughters welfare.

Shaniqua was confused. She sat in cold, silent desolation. She pondered the events that led to the bust up of her relationship. Her mood was tranquil. She had bravely worked through the sorrow and the hurt. Now it was a time for reflection. She was essentially a gentle woman that, hard as they were to find, enjoyed the finer things in life. Her outlook surrounding her existence was simple. Life was hard, every day - especially for a black woman. It was a struggle. It was a struggle that she met head on. Raising a child, keeping a house and putting food on the table were, for her, obvious and essential goals. She did it all without complaint, even though she knew that she deserved better.

Love was another essential quality. A quality that she knew she had in abundance. She wondered why she had fallen for a low-life like Bones. She found no answers. But that was not the issue. Hadn't she tried with him? Didn't she give him all that she had to give? Honesty, devotion, caring, food, sex, in fact anything that he desired? She had even lied for him, such was her dedication. Even though she knew that it was wrong. She had tried. She had asked little in return. Not even a compatible level of devotion from him. She had simply asked that he appreciated her efforts.

Shaniqua was easily pleased. She wanted nothing material from her men. She considered Bones lucky in that respect. Not that he had anything to give. But she knew that. She just needed him to think about her every now and then. Show some appreciation by not just taking, not just draining her energy and her emotional resources, but just sparing a small portion of his own for her. This was all that she asked of any man, regardless of his lifestyle, regardless of his outlook on life.

Life, she believed was for sharing. With friends, you shared the joys, the highs and lows of life and with your lover, the intimacy and depth of those life experiences. Life wasn't about being alone, it was about giving, about sharing, and in that respect black men were selfish. She wasn't even going to consider what white men or indeed what any other races of men were like. For her, they were nonsensical issues. She was black and could only share her life with a black man. But the truth was that they had failed her every time. They were selfish, wanting their cake and eat it. Her hard-earned efforts at making a relationship work had been shoved right back in her face and it had happened on too many occasions. This tired scenario was now not just part of her own experience, but the experience of many of her friends and many other people that she either knew or knew of. Why? She knew not. The prospect of considering it filled her with dread, as there were so many ideas, concepts and perspectives to consider.

She knew one thing though. The standpoints between black men and black women were different. In fact they were so different as to be literally poles apart. Black women want commitment, black men don't. Or at least few do. Those that do, for her were so few, that it would be easier to win the lottery than to win the love of one of them. In London at least, it was a ratio of seven to one in favour of black women. Where the hell was she going to find a decent man with those odds?

Ricky was honest, she thought, but he was a no-go area. For many reasons, she needed to put him behind her, or so she thought. Anyway she considered him no more. With a heave of her chest, she pondered the future. Where would she go from here? She was hardly able to begin musing on this subject when the doorbell rang. She jumped out of her thoughts and into the hallway. As she put her hand on the lock, she paused. Caution took hold, prompting her to find out who it was before she opened the door.

She hadn't been expecting anyone and impromptu visits came from only one person. She felt slightly afraid but reasoned that she had enough time to find a weapon if she needed one.

"Who is it?" she asked heedfully.

"Me," came the reply.

Her reaction was instantaneous. The door flung open. She had forgotten herself. Ricky caught the excitement on her face and noticed Shaniqua re-adjust her mindset. She became modest and heedful of the evident bruises on her face that Ricky noticed instantly.

"Come in," she said in a dead tone.

Ricky was slightly confused albeit happy to be in the house. He hadn't expected that reaction, even though Shaniqua concealed it very well. He hadn't expected to be invited in. He hadn't expected the warm welcoming feeling that he and been greeted with and even though Shaniqua had changed, it was still there. He hadn't expected to see Shaniqua covered in bruises either, it worried him, but he relaxed, promising himself to get to it. Ricky stood in the living room, waiting for his invitation to sit down. It came in typical Shaniqua fashion. She sat down first, folded her arms and crossed her legs. She gave him a moment then spoke.

"Gonna stand dere all nart?" she asked.

Ricky feigned coyness and took a seat opposite her. She stared at him, shifting backwards and forwards the leg that crossed over her left knee.

"This is a surprise," she said slightly aggressively. "Whatcha want?"

Ricky thought for a second, his demureness now honest.

"It's about the money…"

Shaniqua put up her hand to stop him.

"Forget it. Are fink it was PMT. Had me seeing notes. Don't warry abaaht it."

Ricky was surprised with the ease with which she dismissed the issue. But he persevered.

"Well I was going to say, I might be able to make eighty pounds…"

Shaniqua was now angry.

"'S'what I always used to 'ate abaaht you, you neva eva

listened to anyfink I 'ad to say. For de larst taarm OK? Kip you maney. Are don't wannit are don't need it. Sorry to 'ave bovvered ya."

Ricky was quiet, she knew him too well so she pre-empted his next strike.

"Don't take it personal. Are don't mean to bruise that male, arm the provider, are'll do ve best for mah doota' ego of yours. Don't fink are don't appreciate it neeva. Arve just changed me mind OK?"

Ricky dropped his head in his hands. He appreciated that she appreciated the gesture. But it wasn't enough.

"What makes you women think you can just..." he asked, evidently about to raise an issue. But Shaniqua was quick to rebuke. She knew what he was about to come with and she didn't need it. Not right now. She sprang to her feet, stuck out her right leg, rested her fisted hands on her hips and let rip.

"Don't even bovva to go vere all raaht? I do wot are do, because I can. As a hard workin', long saffrin', extremely patient, dedicated and caring black woman are can do anyfink are want! And you Mr arm all dat, loadsa flippin' testosterone, God's gift Mr Black man can't do naffink abaaht it! Are'll make decision then change mah mind because are can! Are'll give you grief one minute, then rub your back with all mah femnin charms an' sensitivity the next, because are can! If you was anybody, you wouldn't question mah decisions, you wouldn't allow them to confuse you or worry you! You would just allow me to be who are am. A simple, honest, dedicated human being who maaht just 'ave her moments of stress an' confusion! Who maaht just go off the rails every narr and den, but who for damn sure knows her own mind an' is sensible enough to recede on decision she makes that she ain't 'appy wiv! You get me? I can do whatever the fuck are want, plain an' simply because are can. Now you just fackin' well learn to deal wiv it! Bladdy Nora! You men alwiz got to be in charge!"

Ricky was slightly embarrassed by the ferocity of her castigation. His response was flippant.

"Sure Miss independent," he muttered quietly. But Shaniqua was in regal mood.

"Don't you fackin' well patronise me you pig! Yes are am independent! Why is dat such a problem? You and your kind 'ave made me this way! What a fackin' cheek! Then you 'ave the gall to object abaaht it. Arm not one o' these wimin who finks she don't need no man! But are certainly don't need your fackin' bullshit eeva! Naah, if you ain't got naffink sensible to took abaaht, Bladdy well go home or samink, but for Christ's sake don't let me really start t' kick off in 'ere!"

With that Shaniqua was out of the room and into the kitchen. Ricky heard running water then the electric kettle click on. He thought for a while, then approached her in the kitchen. He figured that Shaniqua's outburst and her bruises might be related. He would investigate. Once into the kitchen, he looked at Shaniqua. She was a proud figure, leaning against the oven, arms folded, staring out of the window.

"Cappa tea?" she asked without looking at him.

"How'd you get your bruises?" he asked, blatantly ignoring her offer.

Shaniqua thought for a second. Ricky thought he heard her say

"Fack it," under her breath.

"'Ad an argument wiv Bones," she said calmly.

Ricky said nothing. Shaniqua pre-empted him again.

"'An are don't want nan o' this. 'He put his hands on mah baby movva' crap neeva. Forget it. Are can fight me own battles OK?"

Ricky was surprised by the honesty of Shaniqua's response. He had half expected her to lie and to try and cover the matter up, especially knowing what his reaction would be. But he couldn't help verbalising his disgust.

"What made you take up with that stupid crackhead anyway?" he asked, trying to remain calm.

"'Arve bin wondrin' that meself OK? You just forget it. You don't own me; you don't belong to me. 'Snot your problem." Replied Shaniqua conclusively. "You havin' this tea?"

Before Ricky could answer, his thoughts were interrupted by the high pitched greeting that came from his daughter. Garbed In her little nightdress, she beamed as she ran towards him.

Shaniqua flinched as fear gripped her whole body.

"Come on darlin' back to bed," she said nervously and with desperation moving towards Tanika. But Ricky reached her first and picked her up. Tanika hugged him, he embraced his child with passion. Then studied her face, for he had noticed a bruise across her left cheek. He noticed it for what it was and immediately his blood began to boil. Shaniqua noticed his expression change and yet again, pre-empted him. This time with trepidation, her voice was a hopeless plea.

"Ricky, no," she begged.

Too late. Ricky put Tanika on the floor and stroked her hair.

"Go back to bed darling, Daddy will come and see you soon," with a gentle kiss and another hug he ushered her off. Tanika ran off waving as she reached the bottom of the stairs, glistening with happiness at the mere sight of her father. Ricky said no more but headed for the front door. Shaniqua chased him.

"Ricky, please don't…"

No good. In a split second he was out of the door. It slammed hard in her face. She thought to follow him, but gave up, realising the futility of her efforts. She rested her back against the door, looked to the ceiling and closed her eyes, not wanting to even contemplate the horror that what was to come.

Ricky pulled his little XR2 over to the nearest phone box. Once in, he called Ingin.

"Mission," he said without greeting his friend once he picked up the receiver.

"Who?" replied Ingin.

"Bones."

"Covering up?"

"No I want him to know who beat the shit out of him."

"Loading up?"

"Baseball bat, hammer, whatever the fuck."

"It's that bad?"

"He put his hand on my pickney guy!"

Ingin went quiet for a second then spoke.

"Come and get me," he said with fierce resignation.

nine

Bones's self-contained bedsit was a mess. A squalid little dwelling that in truth was once the attic to a large terraced house that the owner had converted into separate domiciles. There were four in all. The tenants that occupied the first three rooms each situated on a different floor were all out. It was a Friday night and there was a lot of raving and drinking to be done in Peckham. Bones and Buzzard were broke, having spent their last pennies on crack. They had invited a couple of local female bass-heads round and were about to get high in anticipation of their coming.

They both sat in silence, staring blankly at the TV. Jerry Springer was interviewing yet another jilted lover and was just about to expose the fact she too had been unfaithful - with a two-foot lesbian. Buzzard found it amusing and raised a deep chuckle. He thought he had heard a bang or a crash that seemed to come from downstairs and turned to Bones in an effort to solicit some kind of reaction but it was not forthcoming. The air went quiet again. Bones rubbed his crotch. His mind had wandered onto the women that were supposed to be coming round. He wondered if they would. He contented himself with the thought that they would, then commenced to fantasise about what he was going to do to them. That's where the crotch came in. He could hide his frustration no longer.

"Where dem rassclaart gyal deh?" he asked, eyes fixed on the TV.

"Relax, dem a come man," insisted Buzzard. He was enjoying the fact that the midget lesbian had just introduced her lover, a giant of a woman who really wasn't a woman, but, she insisted, a hermaphrodite. Bones focused harder on the show, wondering what the hell the world had come to. It was his last peaceful thought.

In an instant, there was an almighty crash that signalled Ricky and Ingin's violent entrance. Both men were startled, Bones so much so that he fell of the chair as he spun round in shock to see just what had taken the door of its hinges. Bones, too, was shaken. He shot up to a kneeling position on the bed that he had been lying on, breaking wind at the same time as the avenging figure of Ricky flew at him. With baseball bat in full swing, Ricky, his face a picture of extreme ferocity, expertly and whilst still in motion adjusted his frame to send a sweet knock of the bat across the side of Bones's head. It threw him across he bed. The crunch of the wood against his face was painfully audible, as was his scream. His mouth turned red as blood gushed from it. Bones had neither the strength nor the inclination to spit out his teeth. Once dislodged they merely fell out of an open mouth that struggled for breath amid the terrible realisation of what was happening. The blanket on his bed was reddened also with the gush of blood that emerged from his mouth. He just fell over, resting his head onto it. Buzzard fared no better. His desperate attempt to meet the onslaught of Ingin's terrifying warrior-like appearance was futile. Ingin waved a baseball bat in his direction and caught him squarely with a bang to the face that immediately split his bottom lip.

As Buzzard reeled, he felt the mighty retribution of Ingin's bat across his back, the notification of his pain a disgusting and pitiful yelp. Bones sought to raise himself up. Ricky, with amazing self-control, allowed him to crawl to his knees before sending another whack across this face with his bat. Bones fell again, this time against the wall, before flopping back onto the bed. Ingin discarded his bat to deal with Buzzard once again. As he lay face down trying to rise up, Ingin's boot stamped his head repeatedly back into the ground, before landing more kicks into his stomach. Buzzard was quickly finished, as was Bones. Ricky couldn't resist giving him another taste of his bat and did so with ardour, sending his victim helplessly into unconsciousness.

Ricky stood over him heaving. Ingin was cool, his breathing quiet. He looked at Ricky then headed for the door. For the last time Ricky surveyed the carnage of Bones' little room. One carcass lay in quiet repose awkwardly across the bed in a pool of blood.

The other, twisted and quiet, was lying in extreme pain on the floor. Ricky followed Ingin out of the room down the stairs and through the main door that was hanging off its hinges and into his XR2. Throughout the ordeal, both men had said nothing.

Tina and Cherry were two small and very wry white girls. Tina was about five foot six and was once a bombshell. During her working life she enjoyed eating out, saunas and going to the Gym. One evening she went to a party, smoked a little dope and got hooked. She hung with black men because she figured that that was where all the drug action was. She wouldn't go out with a black guy unless he was doing drugs, partying and living the fast life. Now she was unemployed and had two mixed race kids, one for Bones, who spent most of their time with her mother. The drugs had made her thin and unhealthy. She smoked forty a day and even though she was only twenty-three years old, she didn't give a shit about her future. Life was about sex, drugs and black men and she was pursuing it to her ruin.

Cherry was of the same ilk. She used to be a dancer, attempting to hit the big time backing some famous singer, but it never worked out that way. She only ever got to show her talent at clubs. One night she caught the eye of an East End gangster. He showed her the ropes. She enjoyed a few good years as a mobsters moll, knew the entire goings on of the underworld before being turned out of his life when she was no longer of use. Just like her friend, she turned to black men in order to maintain even a slice of the "good life" and just like her friend had two mixed race kids that spent their time either in foster care or with her parents. They had both dressed up to the nines this night, in short skirts and black tights. They wore sports jackets, Tina's a white Adidas and Cherry's an un-ironed and quite dirty Blue Umbro. They approached the front door of the house and looked at each other in both shock and trepidation as they beheld the state it was in.

"What the fack 'appened 'ere then?" asked Cherry of her equally bemused friend.

"Fack knows," came the reply. "Fink we oota go ap?"

Cherry breathed heavily, anticipation for the night's possibilities getting the better of her.

"Probly naffin'," she said as she continued cautiously into the house.

The women climbed the stairs and both breathed a sigh of worry as they beheld the state of the door that led to Bones's room.

"Fack it!" said Tina in a resigned whisper.

"Fink your right," whispered her friend. "Les get aaht ov' it."

The two ladies quietly turned round and tiptoed back down the stairs. Once out of sight or earshot of Bone's room they sprinted for dear life out of the house and into the street.

16th April 1998
Our ref.   DPADD021.1.kk   your ref.

Dear Mr Hinds

RE: Divorce proceedings Mrs C. Flower and Mr P Flower

I write with great concern at recent developments concerning the above. My client, Mr P Flower, has instructed me to write to you to re-appraise the situation. You may, under the circumstances, find these matters rather unusual, but as ever I act in the best interests of my client.

In short, my client is disturbed by your client's recent behaviour. It has led him to question her mental health. Whilst he does not fear that there is any great cause for alarm at this stage, he believes that as a result of her recent actions, it does beg questions as to her intentions with the divorce settlement.

I'm sure you accept that five million pounds is a substantial sum as a divorce settlement. There may still be questions as to her legal right to claim this money. It is, after all, based on providing her future security once the marriage is annulled. This is of course on the proviso that the sum is spent with due regard to the prescribed restrictions placed by my client.

With these matters at the foremost of his mind my client now requests that your client considers one of two options.

(1).   Abandon her claim for divorce. Or
(2).   Accept that he will oppose her claim for financial remuneration. This would mean her repaying all monies already given to her or spent on her behalf.

I mentioned that these matters are quite unprecedented, but my client feels that your client's behaviour merits such an extreme response. Rest assured, he will do all in his power to ensure that both his rights and his interests are protected.

I look forward to receiving a response at your earliest convenience.

Yours sincerely

D. Noble
Partner

Claire fumed as she read the letter. It had arrived by first post that morning and she had scanned it whilst wading through a pot of natural yoghurt, the final part of a continental-style breakfast. She had wondered, when Paul had mentioned his misgivings about her relationship with Ricky, at what he had meant. It was now clear, in plain black and white, for her to see. An accompanying letter from her solicitor had arrived with it. It was short and to the point. It's words echoed more than a slight hint of concern on Hinds's part.

"I attach a letter, which arrived on my desk today," it read, "I think we should arrange to meet."

From Hinds' perspective it was an easy shot to call. Weekes and Noble were the best. Paul Flower was a very rich and powerful man. There was little more that needed to be said. Claire was not so easily frightened. She knew her husband for what he was. A very self-serving and lecherous man who would stop at nothing to get his own way. The sentiments that his solicitor had portrayed on his behalf were just so much gloss over a very rotten core. Paul had been infuriated by her relationship with a black man. These weren't just about the very normal issues of control and manipulation, no; this was something deeper and far more putrid. She considered the matter further and perhaps with a hint of confusion. For her to place her husband in the category of racist was difficult to do. He had always managed to maintain a particularly objective view about the plight of black people on the very few occasions that they discussed had such matters. He never seemed to have a problem employing black people, even though they were a small employment statistic in his large enterprise and he certainly had never shied away from admiring a black woman - that at least was for sure.

She was able to conclude after a moment's consideration that this was about something else. Ricky was a torment to Paul, but she could not put a finger on why he was such a thorn in his side. Her anger however was no less restrained. Claire was a woman of many moods. Some events angered her but not enough to solicit a reaction. Other events would not upset, but would solicit a reaction from her, some slightly calmer than others. But this occasion was the worst of both cases that Paul, in the latter stages of their marriage, dreaded. Had he been with her now, he would have been able to predict her very next move. Once she laid the question of Paul's motivation to rest for the while, she made that move without hesitation. Her first phone call went to Hinds. He was available and spoke to her quietly and with concern.

"I just read your letter," she began. "What do you think?"

"I think he's fallen off his trolley actually," replied her solicitor. "What did you do to upset him?"

"Got a boyfriend," replied Claire, emphasising her puzzlement.

"So he's jealous?"

"Maybe. But my boyfriend's black."

"So he's not only jealous, he's offended?"

"It seems so."

Hinds allowed a thoughtful moment to pass between them as he withdrew into contemplation, then spoke with an investigative tone.

"This boyfriend of yours, what's he like?" he asked.

"Well he's not the way that Paul is inferring, that's for sure."

"Decent chap? Good moral character…?"

"And then some."

"Good. We may just have to prove it. If Paul is serious about all of this then we're going to have an almighty scrap on our hands. In truth I don't think any court in the land will believe his arguments, however…"

"Go on."

"Your husband has got money. Need I say more?"

"Yes Malcolm I'm afraid you do."

"Look, you can buy a decision with the best lawyers, if you have the money. I wouldn't be too complacent about this. Paul will be seeking to prove that you intend to blow the settlement on this boyfriend of yours. I've seen it before. If he has to play the race card he will. He'll drag your boyfriend's character through the mud and yours too. Every wrong thing that you or he ever did can be dragged up and made to look much worse than it was. He will have to make a pretty damned strong case against you, because that settlement is your legal right. However… well. I think Paul is clutching at straws. In my opinion he may only have grounds to contest the settlement if you had not made a significant contribution to the relationship. Let's just not be complacent shall we."

"Where do we go from here then?"

"I assume you don't intend to comply with his requests?"

"Malcolm, please."

"Just checking. I'll draft a response, then we'll meet."

Claire closed the conversation then immediately called Paul's office. She had lulled her mood for the chat with Hinds and now that she had become even more enlightened, her rage was now further inflamed.

"Paul Flower please," she said to the receptionist that picked up the phone.

"I'm sorry, he's in a meeting," came a robotically sweet but patronising voice, "Can I give him a message or get him to call you back?"

"You can bloody well tell him that it's his wife and I want to speak to him now!" exploded Claire in raw mood.

"Er … I'm sorry Mrs Flower, he er … left instructions that he was not to be interrupted."

"It'll mean his life if he doesn't speak to me. Yours too, you little hussy, if you don't get him on the end of this phone right - and I do mean right - this minute!"

The receptionist swallowed noisily, the gulp of which could be heard even over the phone. Claire seethed as the phone went dead for a few seconds. Pretty soon she was talking to Paul.

"You complete and utter bastard!" she greeted him.

"You got the letter then?" asked Paul quietly and without concern.

"You are a sick man you know that? How could you?"

"How could you? I can take the separation darling…"

"Don't call me darling!"

"I can take the separation. But I can't take you philandering with that black boy with my money! I can't allow that."

"Oh come on Paul. We both know that it has nothing to do with him or my relationship with him. Why don't you come clean? Tell me what it is?"

Paul went quiet. He hadn't expected Claire to be so keen and so astute. He certainly hadn't expected her ire to subside so quickly. He expected a challenge, but not one that was born of so much wisdom. When he did speak, he did so with more than a hint of hesitancy and nervousness.

"I...I don't know what you're talking about."

"Don't you? I think otherwise. You have some serious internal shit to resolve, you know that?"

"Do I now?"

"Yes you bloody well do! And I suggest you deal with it. You are a grown man of some fifty odd years. Please. It's time you stopped sulking."

"Is that so?"

"Yes it is. Deal with your issues. God forbid that we could even ever be friends after all this. But hey, Let's at least try and find those still waters eh? Let's at least try and have some peace about our lives. "

Paul went quiet again. Claire said nothing. The quiet frighteningly emphasised a chilling expectancy down the phone from both sides. It frightened Paul and he quickly sought to leave its presence.

"I have to go, I'm in a meeting..." he said.

"You can't run from this," warned Claire. "You can try to punish me as much as you like. But those ghosts are going to keep haunting you."

"My dear beloved ex-wife. Spare me the lecture. You have a week to respond to my letter," closed Paul, who had clearly decided to ignore the conscience in him that Claire had so masterfully awakened. She knew him too well. He was shocked by her astuteness. He had resolved to fight it and at least for now, he would do the best he could. But deep down Claire's words had rung bells within him. His greatest fears were about to be realised and at such a difficult stage in his life, he wondered silently at the wisdom of challenging them.

Claire replaced the receiver gently. She walked over to the drinks cabinet and poured herself rum. She held the glass firmly in her hands as she walked over to her balcony to survey the emerging morning. She took a sip. Her heart sank. She had loved

Paul once. He had been the world to her. She remembered their wedding and in a split second relived the blessedness and sheer exultation of the moment. The joining in love of two hearts, two spirits that really believed that they were meant for one another. She wondered at what point it was that he had lost his innocence, and at what point she had lost her love for him. She concluded that those moments had been corresponding.

She took another sip as she eyed two young lovers ramble below her balcony in sweet delight at the apparent joy of love between them. Paul had that once. But he had sought to deny it. Like so many other men, he had sought to dispute the validity of his heart. He had become cold and very callous over the years. But she knew that the innocent, charitable, universal child that lies within us all was now tugging at Paul's heart. It would not die; it now simply wanted to live again. It simply wanted to breathe again. She knew, as she took another sip, that he would seek to stifle it. But at his peril. She breathed a sigh, perhaps in hope more than anything else before returning to her breakfast.

Ricky was depressed. He was a peace-loving guy. He never considered himself to be a violent person, even though whenever push came to shove, he could and would show his mettle. But it hurt him every time he had to resort to violence. Once, he had beaten up someone that had insulted Shaniqua. His conscience could not let him rest and even though he had defended his then-girlfriend's honour, he still went back to the guy and apologised to him. He abhorred violence, but he did what he had to do. He felt no pride or glee at what he had done to Bones, but it had become a matter of honour. Where he came from, this was how these matters were settled. It wasn't lawful, but it wasn't criminal. It was about something that society could never understand.

When he thought about how much Tanika meant to him, he knew there would be no apologies this time. It didn't stop his heart from grieving and as he lay on his bed, staring blankly at the ceiling, he was sorrowful. Shaniqua crossed his mind a couple of times too. He couldn't help but admire her for the way she had worked through all that she had suffered over the past few years. He couldn't help acknowledging that he had had some part to play in her suffering. But she was a tough and feisty girl... he corrected himself: woman. He didn't mind admitting to himself that he missed having her around. Her savvy, streetwise, attitude-laden exterior was a part that she played well. It helped her through her tumultuous life, but he felt a great deal of caring from her and somehow, just like all those years ago when they first met, his feelings for her were beginning to register again.

This brought his thoughts to Claire. He hadn't seen her for a while. They had spoken a couple of times over the telephone, but hadn't gone too deep or for too long into conversation. He searched his feelings. He liked her a lot. He loved being around her. He loved her style, her strength of character, and in fact her whole aura awoke something positive within him. But there was something missing. There was something that Shaniqua had that Claire didn't, but he couldn't quite put his finger on it, even though it was glaringly obvious. He had been seeing her for a couple of months now and was quite pleased that despite that, his identity was still intact and that, in fact, so was hers. He tried to picture himself in five years time and kissed his teeth loudly and gave up, when he didn't see her there with him.

He moved to his music system and switched it on. His latest tune needed lyrics laying down so once he pulled out the words to 'Deliverance' and after setting his DAT machine to record, he ran the heavy roots dub beat, that he had recently put together and begun his poetry.

"Men and people couldn't teach me what I know,
Life is about searching for the glow
In your heart that spells freedom and liberation
The breaking of mental chains and spiritual emancipation.
I didn't feel like a slave, till I grew up
And the picture of a peaceful world blew up
And began to see the reality,
Of the morality
Of a world that seems senseless, empty and proud
Got to try and be different from the crowd
No chains around my hands and feet
But I ain't free and see no liberty

Cos what we see with our eyes
Is merely lies
And what we see with our hearts is where it starts.
Can't stress about what another may think
Maybe that's why they drink
Maybe that's why they smoke
Maybe that's why they inject
Maybe that's why they sniff
You tell me your view, as if that's they way it is.
Whilst your heart doesn't know how to live.
Breeding fear and trembling seems to be your mission
Your goal pursued without intermission.

Give me deliverance from this nonsense
Give me deliverance from this shame
Take me away from the confusion
Where still rivers align to nature's fusion

My heart taught me to listen
To the quiet voice of coalition
It's not about right or wrong, that's simply to do with perspectives
It's about good or bad and what your heart and mind gives
To the world and to your fellow strugglers
Too many brothers and sisters is simply smugglers
Stealing the energy of my soul
Making my downfall their goal
But you're a timorous demon,
Spreading illegal semen
You're a lost spirit
Who just couldn't kick it,
With the beautiful ones, the angelic ones
The one's who want to give; the one's who want to live.
Maybe that's why you hate
Maybe that's why you slate
Maybe that's why you love money
Maybe that's why you're untidy
Your mind gave up
And your heart said fuck it

The world would be a better place
If you kicked the bucket
But while your histrionics
Creates more manics
I live, I give

Give me deliverance from this nonsense
Give me deliverance from this shame
Take me away from the confusion......"

The phone rang. Ricky turned the music down and answered it. It was Shaniqua.

"You fackin' barstud!" she screamed down the phone. Ricky was astonished. He tried vainly to get an explanation from her but Shaniqua was mad as hell and having none of it.

"Who the fack d'you fink you are!" she howled. "Who the fack tode you that you can run my flippin' life!"

"Shaniqua," Ricky said finally and as calmly as possible. "What the hell are you on about?"

"Bones! 'Arm tookin' abaaht fackin' Bones!"

"What about him?"

"Look don't play de fackin' arse wiv me! Did are tell you are wanted him in fackin' casualty? Did are tell you are wanted him facked to shit!? Did I?"

"I didn't do it for you."

"That's mah fackin' problem! What 'appened between me an' him was none of your fackin' business! You're not my fackin' bravva!"

"No, you're the mother of my kid and he hit my kid."

"Isn't that just your fackin' problem though? You never gave me any credit for being a woman that could stand up on her own two feet. Soot aaht fings f'meself. Never gave me any fackin' fought when it came to decidin' what was de best fing for me. Always up in your own flippin' self! Like you have t' be de fackin' man!"

Ricky was bewildered. He rued Shaniqua's view of his actions. He tried sarcasm as a means of justifying himself.

"So you still love him?"

"Don't took so fackin' stupid, is naffin' to do wiv him, you barstud! Is abaaht me! When you gonna fackin' understand? Thas why are tode you t'piss off in the first place! Arm mah own independent woman, are can soot aaht me own problems! What the fack makes you fink you're mah fackin benefacta? Why you fink you gotta soot aaht mah problems?"

"Shaniqua look…"

"No you look! Step aaht ov mah laarff OK? Are don't want naffink t'do wiv ya! Fack right off!"

"What about Tanika?"

"Are'll be facked if you ever see her again! Step off!"

Shaniqua replaced the receiver viciously. The continuous dialling tone echoed eerily sending a shiver across Ricky's perplexed mind. Without thinking, he dialled her number. Shaniqua was quick to answer. She didn't even give him time to speak.

"Are mean it. Don't fackin' call here, don't ring, don't fackin' write! Are want you aaht ov mah life for good! And are mean it!"

The phone slammed down again. Ricky dropped his head and allowed the confused high that Shaniqua had put him on to settle. It quickly became a daze. His heart pounded and he shook. He rose from his chair and paced around the room stopping at the mirror that occupied the far wall. He walked over to it. Ricky surveyed himself for a second before sending his fist right into it, cracking it to pieces. He then sat down on the edge of his bed. Dropped his head into his hands and allowed his mind to go blank as even the darkness began to spin.

ten

Amanda left the Harley Street clinic in a daze. She had a shoulder bag and a suitcase, but didn't need them. The abortion had taken place over an hour ago and whilst there were no complications, she signed herself out of the surgery and bundled herself into a waiting cab. She had disobeyed the clinic's instructions and had gone alone, convincing them on her arrival that her boyfriend was waiting outside and would continue to do so throughout the ordeal. She had secretly called a cab to meet her halfway down the street and she was now out of breath after the brisk walk with the bags to meet it.

Claire had offered to accompany her to the clinic but she had declined the offer, not even contacting her as to the date of the operation. She had convinced herself that Claire really didn't care about her plight and that in fact, if anyone else knew about it, they wouldn't care either. She felt alone. A massive bout of depression had set in and she was feeling desperately sorry for herself. But this was no whine, no sulk, and no childish chip on her shoulder. She grieved. She grieved at the fact that she had destroyed the one thing that she had, for the greater part of her life, sought. She had cried throughout the operation at the thought of what she was doing. She grieved at the fact that her marriage was all but destroyed and that throughout married life, the bringing of a child into their lives ought to have been, next to the marriage ceremony itself, their proudest moment. She was no less than a million miles away from experiencing that joy. She grieved for her life, trying to figure out how she had ever gotten into the situation that she was now in. She wanted to start over again and tried to methodically undo all the aspects of her life that had gone wrong. But there were too many and now she felt so tired. As the taxi driver took her bags and stuck them in the boot she climbed in and slumped back on the hard leather seats, angling her head to look out of the window.

"Where to luv?" asked the driver once settled into his cockpit.

"Knightsbridge," she replied with an exhausted tone. "I'll direct you."

"Goin' away then?" asked the driver, ready to make conversation.

Amanda said nothing. The driver was undeterred. He was a talkative sort of chap and liked to give his passengers the benefit of his opinions. He was exactly what Amanda had feared. A London cabby! 'Please not now', she begged almost in prayer. A prayer that wasn't answered. He was soon out of the stalls.

"Y' maart as well be away!" he began. "Are mean, oo wants to stay 'eya? This cantry's in the dog aahse darlin' are tell ya. Rule Britannia? Rule mah toilet! Ah mean what we camin' to eh? Bring back Mrs Fatcha thas wah are say! Look. You got ya loony lefties disguised as serious politicians. New layba? Don't make me larff! Are mean, what 'ave they dan since they been in powa then? Naff all! Trains are late; unemployment's got no steadier, the Germans 'ave boot our motor industry and her majesty's filth are at an ool tarm low in morale. Are mean what 'ave we got to look foowud too but anarchy? Are mean yuv got ya Mooslim fraternity, basically gettin' everfink they want, houses, mosques, plannin' permission, 'cos if ya don't let em ave it they'll cry racialism. Your flippin' Africans are ool turnin' ap 'ere on student visa's wivaaht a single fought of goin' back 'ome arfta cos their cantry's are ravaged and war torn. An' yer blacks? Well bladdy Nora! They're all yardies 'int they? Shoot ya soon as look at ya. Are tell yoo wot. Is their kids leadin' our kids on the wrong parff are tell ya! Wiv ool this rap jangle banny business. Snoop Doggy Dogg singin' abaaht committing' ool soots of crarms. Are mean how do they let that stuff in the recood shops thas what are wanna know? Can't they see is affectin' the minds of the kids? Avin' said that, you wouldn't wanna 'ave kids in this day and age would ya? Are mean not wiv the fret of nuclear war loomin' everytime Saddam decides he needs a bit o maney. Not wiv the leader of the free woowd gettin' his kicks in the oval office of a mornin'. Are mean bleedin' ell, suppose in the height of extreme sexual passion, he gets his leg over and knocks the wrong batton. You gotta fink abaaht these fings though int ya though? Are mean cam on. Clinton's a flippin' sex maniac and Yeltsin's a drunk, what 'ope ave we got eh? Nah, not a good tarm to raise kids at all. Are mean unemployment, violence, street crime an' then in ovver parts o' the woowd nah, famine, starvation, war, what 'ave the kids got to live for eh? You got any kids then luv?"

Amanda remained in silent disbelief.

"Don't 'spose you 'ave," he continued regardless. "'Scuse me, but you don't seem the soowt. Too busy spendin' ool that filfy looka seems lark."

Amanda just wanted to tell him to shut up, but she had neither the energy nor the nerve.

"Arve' got two little uns, lave em 'tbits. Andrea and Carleene. Four and seven," continued the cab driver. "D'you know, there is naffink, are mean naffink betta, than camin' 'ome arfta a hide days work…"

"Left here," mentioned Amanda in a vain hope that the necessary interruption would throw him off his intended line of discussion. No such luck.

"Camin' 'ome arfta work…" he continued "…and havin' them two beautiful little fings ran t'meet you at the door. They grab y'legs and squeeze the daylights aaht of 'em. Little smiles on their faces, screamin' Mummy, Mummy, Daddy's home. It's luvly."

A tear rolled down Amanda's cheek, unnoticed by her driver who was too busy watching the traffic. Amanda's heart changed. Another tear fell from her eyes, but she wanted him to continue.

"Andrea, that's the baby one, ahh mah God she's so clever. Y'know we … me and the missus lark, we put a little maney t'gevva and bort a computa. 'Sgood t'ave one around the aahse y'know. And are tell ya, she watched me for ten minutes on that fing and before long she was working that mouse lark she'd taken a training course. They learn so quickly these kids. We was ap in the loft the ovva day and she's pulled aaht these little baby boots. Bought back a lot ov memories are tell ya. Her first pair ov boots. 'Daddy', she says, 'look my boots, my boots', lavly. Lav her to bits are do. Mah littoo darlin'. Arve put maney away f'them goowls, determined that they'll 'ave a decent future. I'd die for 'em. Which way luv?"

The driver looked in his rear-view. He had been talking, but had almost forgotten that he had a passenger. He looked at Amanda properly for the first time. He noticed a pretty but tired face that was twisted in pain. She was bathed in tears. Tears that she hadn't even bothered to wipe away as she had dropped the side of her head against the window and was blankly watching the passing traffic out of the corner of her eyes.

"You all raaht lav?" the driver asked with concern.

Amanda continued to stare out of the window.

"Take the next left second right and third left, pull up in the middle of the street, I'll be fine," she responded.

The driver said no more until he had reached Amanda's destination.

"Fourteen-fifty then," he said cautiously as he pulled up.

Amanda got out of the cab. She stood in desolation with her arms folded and legs crossed, shivering slightly in the breeze. She paid him with a twenty-pound note and took the bags from him without looking him in the face, unconcerned that he had begun to search his pockets for change.

"Thank you," she said, before stumbling off down the quiet street.

Once inside the house, Amanda dumped her bags at the door. She entered her living room, heading straight for the drinks cabinet. She poured a vodka and downed it in one go. She then stood motionless and held the glass firmly between her two hands. She broke down. Her chest quivered for a second before a stream of tears leapt from her eyes. She didn't hold back this time. She bawled quietly at first, transfixed staring at the floor. In an unconscious effort to compose herself, she squeezed harder at the glass. It shattered, cutting her hands and causing blood to pour from them. She didn't feel it though she dropped the glass pieces instantly, before composing herself slightly and entering the kitchen. She ran the tap over her bloodied hands, picturing a child in her mind's eye as she did. She broke down again. She turned off the tap and staggered out of the room, her hands still bleeding.

Once back into the living room, she threw herself into the settee and allowed herself to drift on an ocean of dejection, picturing, what would have been her child and repeating over and over.

"I'm sorry darling, I'm so sorry."

Ricky and Claire sat together watching the television aimlessly. There was nothing on. Ricky had called her in a somewhat depressed state. She had echoed his emotion and soon they were together at her house. The atmosphere was slightly thick. It had been so long since they had actually shared the same space that they hardly knew how to deal with each other.

Claire was slightly nervous and this was only made worse by Ricky's complete silence. He stared at the television vacantly. He was watching the programme but it was clear to Claire that he just wasn't with it. He seemed to be in a world of his own. Her occasional snippets of conversation were returned with grunts or short acknowledgements that turned to silence when she realised that he just wasn't listening. Claire began to become edgy and slightly irate. She wanted communion with him. It was particularly necessary, as she had a slight feeling that their relationship was somehow on its way to nowhere. Ricky was too distant. The manner in which he had spoken his very few words to her that evening reflected coldness and a separateness that she had not known before. She knew that he was troubled, but she was not happy at the way that he simply kept his feelings to himself and did not want to share them with her. She felt locked out. She nudged him.

"You OK?" she asked sensitively.

"Sure," he replied in disinterested fashion.

"So why the hell won't you talk to me?" she challenged gently.

Ricky turned to her, pretending confusion with a plastic smile.

"Sorry?" he asked.

"Talk, gab, rabbit? You know? To me?"

Ricky laboured another smile and turned his head back to the TV He didn't need her sarcasm, not now.

"Guess I don't feel like talking much." He said hoping to see the issue off.

"Well I do," persisted Claire. "I'd like to talk to you, I mean God knows when we'll get another chance."

Ricky detected more than hint of sarcasm in that statement. It also sounded like a complaint. He stifled his immediate ire accepting that he was going to have to engage in some kind of talk or end up in an argument.

"So what do you want to talk about?" he replied nonchalantly.

Claire thought for a second. She was being challenged.

"Us," she said nervously.

"What about us?" replied Ricky, not taking his eyes off the television.

"Well we haven't managed to spend an awful lot of time together over the last month. I was wondering, you know, if there was some kind of problem?"

"No…No problem at all."

"I don't know, it seems to me that there is."

"What brings you to that conclusion?"

Claire dug around for an answer. She really didn't have much of a clue as to the reasons why. She was relying on intuition but just couldn't word her emotions. But she tried anyway.

"Well," she began, almost stumbling over her words. "We haven't spoken on the telephone an awful lot. Maybe I live too far away for you to come round more often. We hardly ever go out together…I don't know, we're just not functioning as a real couple would." She released a breath of mollified air; she had done quite well under the circumstances.

Ricky fumbled around for a response. This really wasn't an issue that he wanted to entertain right now. It was all too much hard work. He certainly didn't want to release his true feelings, even if he did know what they were. But he tried not to offend her.

"Well I guess I've been busy, you know?" he mustered.

"Too busy to even make a phone call?" Claire challenged.

"Guess so," Ricky replied with an insouciant shrug of his shoulder.

Claire began to become incensed, but she tempered it.

"You're patronising me Ricky. Please, you know me better

than that. Give me some respect here," she said gently, but with enough force to inform Ricky that she was not playing.

"Look." said Ricky. "You're creating a problem where there isn't one. I've been busy. Had a lot on my mind and not having any money doesn't help."

"And you'd sooner just deal with all that on your own?"

"Well who else is going to help me?"

"Now you're insulting me."

"Claire look. I don't want this OK?"

"What are you hiding?"

"Please."

"What are you hiding?"

"I'm hiding nothing."

"No I think you're hiding something," Clare persisted.

"What am I hiding?"

"I think you're hiding the fact that you're afraid of this relationship."

"Really?"

"Really."

"Go on."

"Well I think money is a problem. You've made it quite clear to me that you don't want my money, you don't want me to help you with your financial difficulties. Now that's a trait that I admire in you. But when it prevents you from not having … I don't know … enough petrol in your car to come and visit me, then I think you're just using it as an excuse."

"Excuse me," Ricky retaliated. "But how many times have you been to Peckham?"

"As many times as you've invited me."

Ricky resumed his silence.

"I know that you have to work, I know that you have your daughter and I know that you have your music. I know you're a busy guy but there's nothing wrong with a call every now and then, just to let me know that…"

Claire stopped short, not wanting to presume anything. Ricky jumped on the issue quickly.

"You doubt me," he challenged.

Claire remained quiet.

"Yes, I think I do," she said finally, with guilt in her voice.

"Yes, I doubt that you love me."

"Why do you doubt me?" asked Ricky, seemingly with the upper hand.

"My colour," she confessed. "I think you have a problem with it."

"And how long have you thought this?"

"I suspected it the very day we met and all you've managed to do is confirm my fears."

"How so?"

"Come on Ricky, let's stop playing games."

"No, how so?"

"Because we're having a relationship that doesn't exist. Because you don't contact me and because we spend no time together. Because you avoid being with me."

"Boy, you sure are paranoid," shot Ricky with sarcasm.

"Really..? I wish I were. Search yourself. Picture us on the High Street somewhere, walking, talking and holding hands. I don't know, along Peckham High Road, or in Brixton, Notting Hill anywhere where there are black people. They're looking at us wondering, what the hell is going on? Another mixed relationship. How do you feel? Suppose I bought you a sports car and happily took my place in the passenger seat whilst you drove. We stop at traffic lights and a car full of young black women pulls up. Don't you just feel like the sell out? Picture this one. We turn up at the Black Comedy Jam and the comedian makes a joke about white people, the crowd's in stitches, how do you feel? Or maybe this one: we're at a night club, reggae music is the order of the day, loads of brothers with sisters, dancing and winding up themselves, you know in that sexy rhythmic way that you do? I'm the only white person in the place. I can't dance to save my life, but I try because I like reggae music. I look so stupid. But worst of all I'm with you. I mean isn't that just your worst nightmare? How about this one…"

"OK you've made your point," said Ricky, waving her to silence.

Claire waited for Ricky to speak. He couldn't. He quietly fumed almost hating Claire for her aptitude and the clarity of her imagination. She was glad he couldn't speak, for she had something else to say.

"Darling," she said, taking his hand. "These are things we can work through. I have my hang ups about these things too, but I'm prepared to face them. The question is really … do you want to?"

Ricky looked at her with longing. He heaved a sigh and shook his head slowly. Claire leaned over and kissed him. Then said no more.

Eventually, Ricky's mindset had adjusted enough for him to engage in normal conversation.

"How's Amanda?" he asked.

"Pregnant, depressed, on Prozac," replied Claire.

"Pregnant? So she finally made it?"

"She answered her eternal dispute."

"That's nice."

"She doesn't want to keep it."

"Why?"

"It's not for Alan."

"Oh shit. So she finally got caught?"

"Guess so."

"So who's it for?"

Claire said nothing. She made her expression ironic and turned her head so that Ricky could see. It took a second to click.

"No," he said, half in shock.

Claire merely nodded her head.

"Fuck," was the only thought Ricky could assemble.

"You can't tell him," Claire pleaded.

Ricky could say nothing. He thought about the issue. In a way both of their prayers had been answered. Ingin was to have a child by a rich woman. Amanda was to have a child. But it just wasn't going to work. Claire became worried by his silence.

"Ricky, you can't tell him," she repeated. He looked at her with melancholy.

"I know," he admitted reluctantly.

Claire allowed the issue to fade from their thoughts, then sought to lighten matters.

"How is the degenerate anyway?" she asked in pleasantly upbeat tone.

"He's good," replied Ricky. "He helped me beat the crap out of a basshead the other day."

Claire shot up.

"What?" she asked in disbelief.

"The guy put his hand on my daughter," explained Ricky, "I wasn't going to let him get away with that."

"Are you alright?"

"I'm fine."

"Did you beat him up badly? Suppose he calls the police?"

"Apparently he did, I heard that he went to the police station but they immediately arrested him."

"What for?"

"Possession of a class A drug. The fool forgot to take the shit out of his pocket. Then they called him up on one of their computers and found a string of untried offences as long as his arm. He's awaiting trial now."

"They completely ignored his complaint?"

"The police haven't knocked my door, at least not yet."

Claire hugged him.

"Let's hope they don't," she said softly.

"How's Emma?" asked Ricky.

Claire's face brightened up.

"Oh, she's filing for divorce."

Ricky looked worried.

"Don't worry," said Claire comfortingly. "He didn't find out about that night. No. In fact it was the same night, that she went home and found her husband with another woman. Quite a little irony," she concluded smiling. "How's Tanika?" She asked.

"She's OK," replied Ricky.

"And her mother?" asked Claire. The question seemed to register concern with both of them. Claire sat up to study his reactions and measure his response. She was good at reading body language and for some reason she felt that she ought to read his. She noted that he began nervously.

"She's OK," he said with outgoing breath.

"Just OK?" she pushed.

Ricky was in no mood to undergo the third degree he knew was going to arrive if he didn't continue to discuss Shaniqua so he continued.

"The last time I spoke to her, she threw a wobbly. Told me

that I was never going to see Tanika again. Going on about her independence."

Claire shot up in total surprise.

"What?" she exclaimed. "Is she nuts? Why?"

"Because I beat up her boyfriend."

Claire was quick. She looked at him accusingly.

"The crack-head," she deduced.

Ricky dropped his head.

"Yes," he admitted. " He heard about us, tried to screw Shaniqua for money. She must have refused. He knocked seven shits out of her and hit Tanika in the process."

Claire became saddened. Her aura dropped as she sent her eyes to the floor.

"Why has us being together affected virtually everyone we know so negatively?" she wondered aloud. "Paul's just the same, he's been acting like just a complete arsehole lately."

"Really?" asked Ricky, inviting her to continue. Claire registered his concern but did not want to allow the conversation to leave Shaniqua so she switched the subject back quickly.

"What's wrong with her?" she asked. "Doesn't she realise that you absolutely love Tan..."

Claire stopped in mid sentence. Ricky hardly noticed. He wasn't used to people speaking then just suddenly stopping so he didn't pay the matter the notoriety that he should have. Hence his surprise when he eventually turned to Claire and discovered a tear was falling down her face.

"What's wrong?" he asked in surprise.

Claire allowed a second's tranquillity to pass then spoke.

"Have you been spending much time with her, since I saw you last?" she asked accusingly.

"No," stated Ricky categorically.

"She still loves you," she proclaimed through a sniffle.

Ricky, though he tried, was unable to hide his elation at the revelation. Claire spotted it.

"And I think you still love her," she added.

"Don't be silly," pleaded Ricky. "She's the mother of my child and that's it." Curiosity got the better of him. "So why do you think that?" he asked.

More tears flowed from Claire's eyes though she admirably kept her emotions in check.

"She argues independence as a reason for holding back probably the one person in the whole world that means anything to you. Psychology is a funny thing. Especially where we women are concerned," she wiped a tear away.

"Go on," implored Ricky.

"Well, sometimes, and often as a last resort, we tend to invert what we really mean. You know. Say one thing and mean the other. She probably does want her independence but not from you. She is simply holding your daughter as a hostage. You defending your daughter's honour probably didn't help much. She wanted you to protect hers. It would have shown her that you still cared for her. Shaniqua is a sensible woman, from what you tell me of her. She knows better than to endanger Tanika's welfare by withholding her from you. It's just a gambit. She'll hold out for as long as she can, hoping to get the reaction from you that she needs." Claire wiped further tears and reached for a tissue to blow her nose. "Well," she said calmly. "I knew I'd have competition but not from her."

"I don't think that's the case…"

Claire moved closer to him and placed her palm on the side of his face.

"We'll see darling. We'll see."

"Well what makes you think I still want her?" he asked. "Cos I don't."

" I guess I've known it for a long time but I've just tried to ignore it. Remember that night in Reading? Shaniqua makes your eyes shine and your face light up. You enjoy even the very thought of her. But she makes you cry too. That's love."

Ricky shook his head. He was about to speak when the phone rang.

"Just ignore it," he pleaded.

Claire did as he requested. But the phone rang too loudly and for too long for Ricky to speak and for Claire to hear him over it. So he gave up and signalled her to answer it. She moved across the room and put the receiver to her ear. She had no time to even greet the caller for the shock of the terrified shrieking voice on the other end of the phone. Ricky noticed Claire's face adjust with horror as the voice on the other end spoke hysterically through a rush of tears.

"It's Emma! Claire come quickly! It's Amanda. She's dead!"

eleven

Amanda's home was a hive of activity. Ricky and Claire pulled up sharply after the hour or so's drive to her dwelling. The yard was littered with police vehicles, both marked and unmarked. They were checked at the gate by a uniformed officer who eyed Ricky intently, abruptly ordering them to turn round. Claire was already a picture of distress. She was in no mood to be messed about and insisted on being allowed to go in. The officer refused and she jumped out of the car and went completely berserk, knocking the cap off his head in her frenzy. Another, evidently more senior officer approached them and carefully listened to her pleas, but it was only the emergence of Emma and Allison, and confirmation from them that she and Ricky were friends of the deceased that made him realise her purpose before allowing them to stay.

Emma threw her arms around Claire. It was evident that she had been crying as her face and eyes were a mass of red. Her hair was tousled and she was unsteady. Allison looked no better. Strong woman that she was, it was obvious that this was all a little too much for her.

"It's terrible," whimpered Emma. "We came to visit her, saw the Mercedes so we knew that she was in. But she wouldn't answer the door. So we went round the back to see what the problem was and…" Emma broke down again but persevered through the bolt of emotion that had hit her. "There she was, lying on the floor."

Claire emitted an "Oh God," before breaking down again and embracing Emma a second time. Ricky stood motionless. The pain in his face was manifested for all to see. Allison approached him.

"You're Ricky then," she said calmly.

"Yeah. You're..?"

"Allison." She held out her hand to shake his. Ricky took it. "Sorry we had to meet like this. I've heard a lot about you," she said.

Claire released Emma from her embrace.

"I want to see her," she said bodly.

"I'll go with you," said Allison

Ricky stepped forward also. Emma stayed behind. She had seen enough and was simply too distressed to see any more. Another uniformed officer checked them at the door.

"It's OK," said Allison. "They're with us."

Once inside they walked into the living room. It was sparse. A female police officer was there with the coroner's assistant. Amanda's body was covered. Claire faltered again, but mustered enough strength to approach her. The WPC stopped her.

"Are you sure you want to?" she asked.

"Yes," replied Claire.

The officer knelt down beside the body and once Claire was ready, drew the blanket back. Amanda's body was twisted, her eyes still open and her face, though ashen white, looked peaceful. Ricky took a step forward and craned his neck to see her. This was only the second time that he had been in her company. The fact registered. He looked away with sorrow.

"What happened?" asked Claire of the officer.

"It's not a suspicious death. It looks like suicide," she replied. She didn't need to go into any more detail than that. She wasn't allowed to and she didn't want to.

"She left a note," mentioned Allison.

"Can I see it?" asked Claire of the officer.

"Sure," she said, picking out a piece of paper enclosed in a plastic evidence bag.

Claire read the note then broke another time.

"Oh my God," she cried with pained torture. "Oh no."

Ricky moved forward and held her just as her feet gave away. He hugged her. She fought for consciousness, the rush of her tears not allowing her to faint. Whilst holding her Ricky took the note from her and scanned it.

"FORGIVE ME MY FRIENDS," it read. "YOU KNOW I ALWAYS WANTED TO HAVE A CHILD. IT WAS MY ALL-CONSUMING PASSION. TO BE WITH HER NOW IS MY ONLY

DESIRE. IT MATTERS NOT WHETHER IT BE IN THIS WORLD OR THE NEXT. I LOVE YOU ALL. REMEMBER ME. GOODBYE."

Ricky handed the note back to the coroner's assistant without looking at her. He hung his head and shook it, desperately trying to hold his emotions under control. Claire's tears had soiled his shoulder. But he held her ever more closely as her crying became a wail of uncontrolled passion.

Ricky lay in silence on his bed. With hands placed behind the back of his head, he stared blankly at the ceiling. He was torn asunder and could only allow blank meditation to run through his brain. Life had suddenly become a nightmare. He sought to relate the unfortunate recent events in his life back to that night at Crinkles when he met Claire. Ricky concluded that before that night, life hadn't been so bad. He had heard many people, whether in real life or on the television, talk about the many problems that being in a mixed relationship could cause and some of them were real horror studies. He considered his own plight to be bad enough. Sure, racist thugs had not put a petrol bomb through his letter-box or sent shit through it. He had not received any 'hate mail' and no one had sought to burn down his little flat. But he might have been able to bear that more than what he was having to go through right now.

His beloved daughter had been lost to him. When he pictured her smiling face looking up at him after not having seen him for days, or when he heard her chuckles as she chased a bouncy ball around the house, he was shattered. His gut wrenched. He could not imagine how Shaniqua could ever be so heartless, knowing that Tanika meant the absolute world to him. At times he thought of going round to her house and beating the shit out of her. But he didn't want to really do that. It wasn't his style and even if it was, the very picture of the lovely Shaniqua grimacing from a hefty left hook from him only caused him greater pain. Still, he knew now why some men were prepared to go to such lengths.

He had heard stories like this before, but never paid them any mind as he never ever, for the life of him, imagined that he too could end up in such a pitiful situation. A situation where vindictive and selfish baby mothers kept their ex-boyfriends from seeing their children. Who could not for the life of them see the sense in even allowing the man to see his child for even a small period of time maybe at weekends. There was never any justification for that sort of behaviour. Nothing short of child molestation or child abuse from the father justified the withholding of contact.

Nothing like that had occurred between Ricky and Shaniqua, he would never harm her. He could never harm her. Keeping Tanika away from him was a completely selfish act. There was his sweet innocent daughter, being punished for no fault of her own, but rather being held hostage by her mother in a bid to secure his compliance. He considered doing what so many men, so many black men have done in the past and just forgetting about them - blocking them completely out of his life. He had poured scorn on the way that many guys, even some that he knew, were prepared to go down that route. But he had a little more sympathy for them now. In many of those cases he reasoned that the majority of them were brave men. Men who, even though they loved their children, even though their children had meant the world to them, were prepared to sacrifice their relationship simply to get away from the obnoxious behavior that the mothers of their children displayed. The way they used children to secure a man's love or conversely to punish him was simply objectionable.

According to Claire's assessment of the situation, the former was Shaniqua's reason for witholding contact. Whilst the thought brought a modicum of a consolation to him, it was an act that he could not condone.

Ricky steadily eased himself out of his reverie by pledging himself to see a family solicitor in the morning. This was a fight that he was not going to give up on so easily. It might cost him a packet, but he would try and secure legal aid if it were possible. Even if he couldn't, he reasoned that if he was prepared to die for his daughter, he could easily go broke for her. The phone rang. He shifted over to it, praying that it would be Shaniqua, but it was not. The deep voice of an obviously excited middle-aged white man appeared on the other end of the line.

"Is that Ricky Jackson?" he asked.

"Who's this?" Ricky asked cautiously.

"Mike Stone, I own Rugratz Recording Studio." He said.

"So?" Ricky replied hardly caring.

"I heard your music."

"And?"

"I think it's cool."

"And?"

"I've got a contract with a major label."

"So?"

"I passed your tape on to them."

"So?"

Mike Stone was becoming pissed off with Ricky's petulance.

"Look," he said, his patience now gone. "I know loads of people that would jump at the opportunity. You hardly seem to give a shit so guess what? Just forget I rang OK?"

He was about to put the phone down when Ricky snapped out of his doldrums, fully realising what was going on and changed his tone.

"No wait," he said. "I'm sorry, I've been going through a difficult time. Didn't mean to take it out on you."

Stone was forgiving. He brightened up immediately bringing the excitement back into his voice.

"So this recording studio have been looking for someone to remix a couple of their numbers. Right now they're working with some big stars. I let them hear your tape, because I tell you what, it knocked the shit out of me. Great stuff! Matey boy at Arista was just as excited about your music. He asked me to speak to you. They want to give you a deal."

"Really?" asked Ricky, bemused.

"No shit. They want to meet you."

"When?"

"Soon as possible."

"Well I've got a few things on right now. I've just lost a friend. So I guess I won't be in the right frame of mind. Can they hold on a couple of weeks?"

"Sure, no worries. But they're keen to get you started. A couple of weeks will be fine, but I think you'll be in the studio straight away. I'll tell them to prepare a contract in the meantime. Five hundred pounds is their usual pay-out on a remix. But don't worry. You'll get plenty of work.

"Cool."

"So look, bell me here at the studio in a couple of weeks yeah? I'm in the book."

"Sure."

Ricky caught the man again just before he signed off.

"Tell me something?" he asked. "How'd you get my tape?"

"A woman called Amanda," he replied. "I don't know her very well. I guess you could say … well, I met her one night at a club."

Ricky's heart skipped a beat.

"Sure," he said in disbelief.

"Nice woman she was," continued Stone. "But she was married to a fuckin' mobster. Still I was surprised that she kept my number. She called me and sent the tape over. Told me to listen to it. Reckoned you had potential."

Ricky replaced the receiver. He was floored. Now it was on. He just could not believe what the woman had done. In taking her own life, she had probably saved his. There were no more words to describe how he felt. He lay down again, wondering at how strange and how unfathomable human nature was.

Harry Blanchett was a small round man. He looked a lot older than he actually was. For a man of twenty-five years you could easily have mistaken him for fifty. His brown hair was receding and he wore round glasses. At five foot seven he had a round face and a double chin. He was tubby, but not overly. He was your average nerd, fidgety and accident prone, but for all that there was no mistaking the fact that he was a brilliant architect. He stood nervously at the door of Paul Flower's office, adjusting his tie and straightening both his tweed jacket and black slacks. He even rubbed his shoes against his calf in an attempt to make them shinier than they were already which was an impossible feat, for, as frumpy and unfashionable as he was, he was a meticulously tidy dresser. When he was completely satisfied with himself he knocked the door and waited.

He had no idea as to why he had been summoned to the boss's office. He figured that he might be in trouble. He had just finished a project for a large company and though he hadn't gotten wind of any problems, he shuddered at the thought that someone may have complained about him and that now Mr Paul Flower of Flower Architectural Enterprises was now going to fire him.

He jumped at the sound of the strong voice that issued from behind the door instructing him to enter, which he did instantly. He had never seen the inside of Frankenstein's office, as Flower was known to most of his staff. He surreptitiously took a second to survey the absolutely stunning design of it. It was a large room. Before him lay a host of leather settees and a drinks cabinet to his left. Chinese, African and Middle Eastern ornaments adorned it and they sat elegantly in the subtle light that shone onto them from inside the cabinet. At the far end of the room sat Flower in a leather rotating chair that moved when he moved. He looked like a mighty being behind the thick semi-circular mahogany desk, placed in front of a set of very large windows that overlooked the elegant city of London behind him. Flower used an envelope opener to empty the stale tobacco from his pipe into a marble ashtray on his desk. He beckoned Blanchett to sit down which he did quickly and without hesitation. As he talked, Flower stuck new tobacco into the pipe.

"Harry, how are you?" he asked.

"I'm fine," Blanchett replied, nervously running his finger between his neck and the collar of his shirt, which all of a sudden had begun to feel too tight.

"How do you like your work?" Flower began, lighting his pipe and strolling up and down in front of him. Blanchett feared the worst.

"It's a great profession." He quickly became lost for words. His mind hanging on a tender thread that he was about to slip from. But he composed himself quickly and found more words, feebly sycophantic though they were. "It's the best job I've ever had and this has got to be the best firm I've ever worked for."

Flower smiled.

"Good. Good. I'm glad to hear that," he replied, moving over to the side window. "Because I want to promote you."

Blanchett flinched with shock. He shot to his feet, forgetting himself.

"Mr. Flower..?" he began.

"Don't get up," ordered Flower gently.

Blanchett sat back into the chair with decidedly more haste than he had done the first time. He pushed the rim of his spectacles back into his face and sat tensely, eagerly awaiting Flower's next words.

"I received a call yesterday from Lord Judd. They were terribly impressed down there at Radio-Link with the way you handled the design for their new headquarters in Hertfordshire. They'll be throwing their next four contracts my way," he said with a smile.

Blanchett forgot himself again and shot to his feet.

"Oh sir, I'm so pleased ... " he began.

Flower approached him with an outstretched hand, which he shook tentatively.

"Not as pleased as I was when I got that call," explained Flower. "Lord Judd's a very powerful man. He adds a degree of political clout to this operation. The future's bright," he said with a cunning smile. "Congratulations. You're now Head of Overseas Development."

Blanchett shook slightly. Flower noticed a degree of misgiving in him, which he decided not to address instantly.

"Sit down," Flower ordered in a gentle whisper.

Blanchett complied. Flower walked over to the drinks cabinet.

"Drink?" he asked, leaning aside to reveal the impressive array of beverages. "Take your pick," he concluded.

Blanchett scanned the bottles.

"I'll have a Cockspur," he said feverishly, holding his thumb and forefinger aloft but slightly apart. "Just a small one."

"Aah," said Flower with a smile. "Barbados's finest! Got this in '93. Beautiful little island. Obviously a drink that you would recognise. Isn't your wife from Barbados?"

"My girlfriend."

"Of course, your girlfriend. You haven't known her for very long have you?"

"Three months."

"It's obviously going well. You're obviously in love. Heard she's quite a stunner." Flower held out open palms, which he moved up and down around his chest area. "Big."

Blanchett resented the implication. Although a frail sort of man, he wasn't one to have people take the piss, regardless of who they were. He bit back.

"Yes. I met her in a night club," he said, in a tone less timid and more conversational. "I remember your wife was there that night, talking to some black chap. Seemed to be having a good time."

Flower passed him his drink and stared menacingly into his eyes. Blanchett looked away, his trepidation gone.

"I sense your reluctance to take the position," Flower suggested, waving the possible ill feeling away.

"It's a position I'd love to have Mr Flower, but I feel it will keep me away from…" Blanchett hesitated, but admonished himself for doing so, before finding the word. "…Sharon. I mean, I suspect the job would take me abroad quite a lot."

"Well, take her with you. I'll pay her expenses."

"That's very kind of you…"

"You're the man I want for this position Harry."

"I'm very flattered."

"Look, discuss it with her. Come back to me in a couple of days."

"Yes. I will. Thank you."

Blanchett rose to his feet again, sank his Cockspur and headed for the door. Flower broke the icy silence.

"Tell me something Harry," he mused.

Blanchett turned from the door that he was just about to open.

"Yes Mr. Flower?"

"If I may be so bold. What is it you see in a black woman?"

Of all that was said in the time that they had been together, this was by far the most staggering thing that Flower had come out with. It pierced him. Rumours had been rife, right throughout the corporation, that Flower was having a terrible time dealing with the fact his soon to be ex-wife was seeing a black man. He looked deep into his eyes and saw his pain instantly. That question had come from the heart. He adjusted his mindset and resumed his place in the chair to address Flower who was perched against his desk, tightly hugging his glass of whisky.

"That's an odd question," he began thoughtfully. "The same thing I see in any woman really." Blanchett pushed his spectacles to his face again. Whenever he did that it was either a sign of his nervousness or his desire to concentrate. The latter was very much the case now. "Women are women," he continued. "And I believe that men are made for women. So, when you meet a woman of colour that attracts you, if you're … I guess liberated enough, I mean mentally, to ignore what people may think … well, that's as natural an act as if she were your own colour."

Flower rose to the debate, his concern quite evident.

"What about the differences? I'm sure you'll admit there are differences?" he queried.

"Of course there are, but those differences are superficial, cosmetic. People may see them as obstacles but they're not really. It's all about respect. Now surely, you shouldn't have to work hard to respect someone that you already admire? Sharon's differences bring a newness about my life and in some ways I guess mine do hers."

"What about your identity?"

"My identity is revealed to me in a different light. My knowledge of myself is merely expanded."

"But you have to change. You have to adapt."

"Who says I do? I have to be myself. I may have to rediscover myself in order to fully appreciate her. She will have the same battles, but you just have to want to. Look. I'm not going to stop listening to R.E.M, U2 or the Smashing Pumpkins…"

"Who?"

"The Smashing Pumpkins, they're a band."

"Oh."

"I'm not going to stop listening to the Smashing Pumpkins and start listening to The Mighty Sparrow, just because I'm seeing a black woman. I'll appreciate The Mighty Sparrow and she'll appreciate R.E.M. But the truth is that we'll have a very varied record collection. Relationships are about accepting your partner for who they are. Why should the rules change just because you have someone from a different culture?"

"Suppose you fail to respect one another's differences?"

"Then we fail."

"You know Blanchett, there's something inside of me, forgive me, that just argues that it's not right."

"Forgive me, but that's your ignorance. But why listen to the voice of right or wrong? Right or wrong is a misconception because they're based on perspectives. You can justify any action as being right or wrong. But I tend to see good and bad as a better denominator. Mr Flower, I strongly believe that the measure of our worth is based on how we human beings treat one another. Therefore it makes perfect sense for us to define our actions, not in terms of what's right or wrong, but what's good or bad. If you bring happiness, joy and pleasure to another human being you've done some good. If you bring offence, hurt and pain to another, if it's not for their own good, then you've done bad.

We must also deal with the voice of reason. Why should we ever be concerned about the way people choose to live their lives, when it is simply not our place to judge? But to wish our fellows every happiness and lend support when making decisions that they feel are the best ... for them? Let adults be responsible for their children, but let us all be responsible for the decisions that we make in the way that we choose to live our lives. I have an inner voice that tells me, I have a right to do as I please. I have an inner voice that tells me not to bring hurt to another human being and I have an inner voice that tells me that no-one has a right to condemn me when I do good. Now, the role of these voices may seem subjective because they keep me in check, but collectively, those voices are my freedom. On that basis Mr Flower, I simply cannot hear the people that tell me that dating a woman of a different culture is a bad thing."

"But it's about culture."

"Culture, history, heritage and everything is important. But it's more important to acknowledge the context into which these issues are best placed. Culture helps you to understand who you are, but I'm afraid the argument doesn't rest there. The solutions are found in the areas I've tried to outline to you. Freedom of thought, freedom of expression and freedom of choice."

The frumpy little nerdy looking man had totally bewitched the high-powered multi-millionaire. He spoke like a wise old sage. Flower was humbled, he wanted more. He took a seat next to Blanchett and spoke quietly.

"You've heard about my wife...?" he asked, not needing to explain further.

"Yes Mr. Flower, I've heard stories. If you don't mind my saying so. I think that your wife spent a lot of time in your marriage feeling somewhat subjugated. I suspect that she probably used a lot of that time constructively in terms of getting herself together. I don't believe that she has chosen a black man because he is good in bed, or because she wants to somehow feel trendy and with it. I don't believe she's dating him to somehow get back at you or for any other false and selfish motive. I believe it is indicative of a state of mind that is free enough to no longer give a damn about what anybody thinks. She simply likes him. Unlike in the days of your marriage. I believe she is truly free."

Blanchett rose to his feet as he noticed Flower slightly drift to contemplate on his words.

"Life's a funny thing," he said in conclusion. "I guess we can't always believe what society has taught us over the years. It's too dangerous and threatens the cohesiveness of our existence. The truth is inside all of us: we just have to hear it. Give your ex-wife wife the respect she deserves. She's been through a lot."

Flower raised his head and forced a smile. He thought for a second. Then heaved slightly. Conscious that Blanchett was only inches away and could see a distinct change in his persona, he quickly sought to regain his authority. He stuck out a hand and shook Blanchett's.

"Thank you Blanchett. Give your madam my regards," he said.

"The position..?" queried Blanchett not needing to say anything else.

"It's there if you want it. If not, I'm sure we can squeeze you in somewhere else."

"Thank you Mr. Flower."

Blanchett threw him a childish smile as he left the room. Flower smiled back, raising his glass to him in the process. He took a sip of his whisky before losing himself in contemplation.

twelve

Claire was alone. She was agonising over the coroner's report into Amanda's death which, two days following her suicide, was still not forthcoming. She was having a terrible time of it. Ricky had been calling her consistently to offer her comfort, though he couldn't always be with her. She had also received numerous phone calls from friends either offering their condolences or wanting to discuss the matter in some detail. None of it made her feel any better about the situation.

Claire felt as though she had let Amanda down at a crucial period in her life when she needed her companionship and friendship perhaps more than ever. She hadn't been there for her and it was cutting her to the bone. Every so often she would break down and cry. It was difficult not to. Amanda was the only thing that entered her head, the only person that she could think about. Time had stood still; life had become nothing but a fleeting shadow. Amanda's death had numbed her and dealing with it was not easy. She considered the issues once again as she had done a million times. Amanda's failing marriage, her perceived inability to have children, her alcoholism, that night with Ingin, her subsequent pregnancy and obvious loneliness. Amanda's cry for help that she had ignored, as she had done a million times before. She could go on no more.

She broke down again and allowed the tears to flow. She was interrupted by a knock at the door. She grabbed a tissue, quickly dried her eyes as best she could and went to answer it. It was Alan. She could have accommodated bad feelings towards him, as the common perception in their circles was that he had been responsible for the conditions that gave rise to Amanda's despondency. But she had little time for that. As he walked in, she immediately put her own grief to one side and hugged him.

Alan took it, running his hand down her back as he did. Claire didn't notice the slight lack of emotional content in the hug. She thought he cared.

"I'm so sorry Alan," she said as she embraced him.

He said nothing.

"It's a nightmare," she continued. "An absolute nightmare."

"I was passing really," he said finally as he released her. "Just wanted to see you. Find out how you're coping."

"I'm fine. It's such a terrible situation. But, I guess death is just as much a part of life as life is itself. I'll be OK. Have you heard from the Coroner's office?"

"Not yet. But I guess it'll be soon."

"How are you getting on with the funeral arrangements?"

Alan looked worried.

"You know I've not even started to think about that, I've been so busy…"

"Do you want me to take over for you?" Claire asked.

Alan eyed her darkly.

"I could do with some help," he said. "As you know, Amanda was an only child. Her sole remaining immediate relative is her mother. Well…"

"Of course she's too old," pre-empted Claire.

"And bound to the resting home that she's in," he said placing his hands in his pockets. "How's your divorce going?"

Claire stopped, surprised by the question. Why Alan had even raised that issue amazed her. He had never openly showed much interest in her life and she felt it rather strange that he was doing so now. Nevertheless, she paid the question enough respect to stumble out an answer.

"Paul's being awkward, but I guess that's probably run-of-the-mill stuff. It'll happen."

Paul moved towards her holding her by each elbow.

"That's good," he said. "Situations like that can be difficult."

Claire sensed that he was pretending to be concerned. She began to become worried, releasing herself from his touch.

"The funeral arrangements…" she pressed once again.

"Y-yes, yes of course," replied Alan, remembering the notion. "Maybe we can work on it together. Perhaps we can go by the undertaker's tomorrow."

Claire's concern grew. Alan was not showing the level of concern over his wife's death that she felt he ought to have.

"W-well I can take care of it."

Alan was insistent.

"I have to fly out again on Thursday, so I've only got a couple of days. I could use your help. There's lots of running around to do."

That was the final straw. Alan could not even think to cancel his work appointments. She would have forgiven him, if she even thought for an instant that he needed to work so as not to confront the reality of his wife's death. The indications were, however, that he had done so already and by now, was well over it. Alan revealed his hand by his next move. He placed one hand on her elbow this time. Stared at her intensely, first studying her face, then eyeing her bosom and back to her face. Claire flinched, sensing that she wasn't going to like what was to come. She didn't.

"I've always admired you Claire," he said touchingly, moving closer to her. "Amanda spent a lot of time just eating my money. She wasn't a good wife. She never cared about what I wanted. Life to her was about using me. She was a selfish woman. Not like you Claire, you were always so much more attractive than that bitch."

Claire recoiled in horror. If she had reacted like a horrified, but helpless woman, perhaps pushing him away, or pleading with him not to proceed, Alan would have welcomed that. It would have at least given him something to work on. But Claire was not that kind of woman. The horror subsided in an instant. The vexation that replaced it sent an impulse that resulted in a fierce slap around the side of his face.

"You bastard!" she roared.

Alan's astonishment was evident. Claire gave him no room to breathe.

"You never cared about that woman. You absolute bastard!"

"Claire I…" Alan began whilst rubbing the side of his face. The ferocity of the slap made it tingle.

Claire was tingling too. With anger.

"Don't you even try! Get out of my house. Out!"

"Claire please…"

She dived at him, throwing uncontrolled punches in his direction. Tears began to fall as her fury reached a crescendo of noise and violence.

"Get out!" she screamed. "Get out!"

Alan could do no more than comply. He straightened his clothing and nervously edged himself towards the door. Claire had caught him a beauty of an uppercut across his jaw and he was rubbing it gently.

"Don't do anything for Amanda. I'll take care of it all! You bastard! You don't even have to be there!" she bawled.

Alan sought to capture some kind of dignity.

"Sort it out then. You bitch. If it was left up to me…"

Claire stared at him, tears soaking her face. But she was ready for his verbal onslaught. It didn't arrive. Alan thought about his next statement.

"Never mind," he said in a slightly softer voice than he had previously spoken in. He thought for a second as he placed his hand on the door handle. He turned to Claire. "Just tell me one thing," he asked. "The suicide note…"

Claire's response was instant.

"Yes. Yes she had a lover!" she proclaimed proudly. "…And he did something for her that you could never do! He gave her a child."

Alan's face took on a callous look. He waved a finger in the air.

"I thought so," he said calmly. "Because the last time I fucked her … well let's just say, it wasn't in a place where babies come from."

His statement initiated a second instantaneous reaction. It didn't seem possible that her anger could rise. But it did. She picked up a Buddha, one of her prized ornaments, and slung it at him with an alarmed cry of "You fucking heartless bastard."

Alan ducked just in time, as the solid bronze implement hit the door, denting it instantly. Alan arose with dignity.

"Look," he said nonchalantly." I've got an idea. Why don't you invite him to the funeral? I'd love to meet him. I'd love to meet the great stud this great stallion that relieved me of my life's biggest handicap. I'd like to shake his hand. At least before I knock his block off for putting his genitalia where it didn't belong."

Claire found calm too.

"I'll do my best to make sure that you do meet him."

Alan nodded his head and smiled.

"Good," he said, buttoning his jacket before leaving the house. He pulled the door to gently. Claire dropped her head. She now knew all of Amanda's worries. Claire felt Amanda's plight. Where Amanda had been was a place that she had escaped from. It bought little comfort to her already grieving soul.

"Dexter! Ricky! Come eat!" Ingin's mother was in buoyant mood. It was Sunday afternoon and she had just cooked. Ingin lived alone but his mother had saved a spare room for him at the family home figuring that he was probably the sort of son who would, at some point in is life, need to return home. Ingin appreciated the gesture because it meant that he had another place to rest and could easily access his mother's delicious cooking, especially on a Sunday. Ricky had passed by and had just finished explaining Amanda's death. He had originally planned not to speak to him about it, but Ingin was his best friend and besides he deserved to know. Ingin was devastated. Hard man though he was, he had feelings. His eyes had watered as Ricky recounted the sad tale. He had enjoyed his brief encounter with Amanda and had made light of the fact that the condom had burst when he made love to her. But this nightmarish outcome was too much even for him to bear. He lifted up his eyes to Ricky after wiping away an emerging tear.

"So why she have to kill the yout?" he asked desperately.

"The shit got too much for her. If the husband found out it would have been all over for her."

"Specially when he find out is a half-caste pickney," said Ingin.

"That too," echoed Ricky.

"S'all some fuckin' bullshit," murmured Ingin.

A momentary silence got the better of them, then Ingin spoke with fervour.

"You goin' to the funeral?"

"Yeah. Claire's making the arrangements, she'll want me to be there. But hell. Feel like I should go, you know how I mean?"

"Well I'm up in that shit too then," Ingin replied sternly.

"Dunno if that's a good idea," said Ricky cautiously. "Claire tells me the husband's gunning for you."

Ingin raised a difficult smile.

"Well he gone finally get to meet me then innit? If he wanna fuck wid me... well," Ingin said with a slight shrug of his shoulders. "Only one ting dat bodder me doh."

"What's that."

"These fuckin' white people and their funerals though. Five six people at most. When we black people have fi we ting, the whole community turnin' out."

"So what you sayin'?" explored Ricky.

Ingin dropped his head.

"Nuttun I 'spose. I just feel like the girl deserves more than that you know what I mean? And the yout."

"Ain't a lot we can do about it though."

"I dunno, you know."

Ricky threw a glance at Ingin. He had known his friend for a long time and was well aware of his ability to make an unreasonable situation reasonable and an impossible situation possible purely because he felt passionate enough about it. He had an idea of what Ingin was thinking and was about to air his feelings when Ingin's mother cut the atmosphere again.

"Dexter! I'm telling you for the last time! De dinna ready!"

"Come let's eat 'fore she blow a gasket."

"Ingin look..." said Ricky trying to deal with the previous issue.

Ingin paced towards the door, not looking at him.

"Ricky man look. It was my yout too."

Ricky decided not to touch on the subject again. At least not for now. His mind turned to another issue that he had wanted to raise with Ingin. He trod carefully.

"You know what happened to me the other night?" he began.

"What?" asked Ingin, rising to go and eat.

"Some guy from a recording studio told me that he heard one of my tapes and passed it on to some guy from Arista records and now they want to sign me up to do some remixes," he said, sounding curious and puzzled at the same time.

Ingin was unsuspecting.

"That's good. I told you you're music was happenin'. You been sending your tapes all 'bout then?"

"That's just the thing. I haven't been. This music production thing I only do it for a hobby. Damn. The only person that has been pushing me to try and do it full time … is you."

Ingin staggered inwardly. Ricky went for the kill.

"The guy got the tape from Amanda," he said, allowing the drama of the revelation to do its job.

Ingin looked hesitant initially then smiled softly. Ricky began to feel warm inside. He waited, saying nothing, for Ingin to confess - which he did without hesitation.

"The tape in your car, that night when we met Claire and Amanda for the first time," he said.

"You took it," said Ricky.

Ingin became loud and even slightly aggressive.

"C'mon Ricky man, you know me," he pleaded. "I wasn't going to let a chance like that slip. That night at 'Crinkles was a lucky night. We met two millionaires. You think I was going to leave there with just a soil in my pants? I figured the woman was only up for a one-night stand anyway. She was just fulfilling a fantasy. Fuck it. She was going to do more for us than that if I could've helped it! Yes I took the damn tape and I told her, just before we got down. Pass it on! She was rich, she had to be connected!"

Ricky became grim.

"She did pass it on. Hooked me up big time," he said.

"That's why we need to make sure she gets a good send off. She was a good woman," said Ingin with feeling. "A good woman."

Mrs Stewart had outdone herself. As Ricky and Ingin took seats at the table they both eyed the spread with relish. Jerk chicken, rice and peas, roast potatoes, vegetables, coleslaw, potato salad, curried mutton, roti's and a pineapple punch drink had their mouths watering. Ingin's father, an old greying man with a hardened face, sat at the head of the table. A dish of ground food that included boiled dumplings, yams, sweet potatoes and a large cho-cho had been prepared for him specially. Ingin's young sister, Tanya, a sixteen-year-old, and his brother, eighteen-year-old Nathaniel, were there too. Mrs Stewart had invited one of her church sisters, a plump woman who went by the name of Sister Sterling. It was she that blessed the table. Once the formalities were out of the way, they all tucked in.

"A lovely service dis marnin' Sister Sterling," opened Ingin's mother.

"Bway Pastor Brown really have the anointing you know Sister Stewart."

"Me know man."

"When the Holy Ghost start to move, Sister Stewart."

"Yes man."

"I really feel de spirit of de Lard this mornin'"

"Yes man."

"Sister Mac really feel the spirit too man."

"Me know man."

"Pass the coleslaw please," interrupted Nathaniel of their guest.

"Wait. You don't see Sister Sterling talkin'?" said his mother.

"When you gwine tek dem nasty sitten offa you 'ead bwoy?" asked Mr Stewart of Ingin.

"When I good an' ready," replied Ingin, tucking into a piece of chicken.

"Sister Mac, she really lego de tongues this mornin'"

"Yes man."

"Go out last night Ricky?" asked Tanya

"Why you askin' big man question, like you an' he is size?" interrupted Ingin.

"If I did have a scissors I woulda chap dem arf right no," said Mr Stewart.

"Coleslaw," begged Nathaniel.

"I'm only askin' the man a question."

"Nah, I stayed in."

"But why you have to wear dem nasty sitten pan you head bwoy?"

"Goin' out tonight?"

"Dad you've been asking me that for nearly, what? Seventeen years now."

"Can I just get some flippin' coleslaw?"

"De choir really get whe this marnin' too."

"Yes man."

"Unnu dutty Rasta. Back home we used to run unnu down."

"I'm going to Ezekiel's next week."

"No you're not."

"…And when de spirit drop Sister Stewart. What a ting!"

"Seventeen years you have dem blasted supum inna yuh 'ead?"

"Why not? Kirsty Simpson goes every week."

"Cynthia, yuh have any scissors boat de place?"

"Coleslaw now!"

"Kirsty Simpson's not sixteen."

"Sister Beecham doh!"

"Oh yes man!"

"Ain't you women got no brothers in the church?"

"Shut up bwoy! 'Fore me go look a scissors!"

"Chuh, I'm just going reach for the coleslaw me'self then."

"Coming with me Ricky?"

"Nah, I don't think so."

"You ain't goin' to no Ezekiels."

"When she put arr mout cross dat song."

"Yes man."

"Den tell me supum. You no trip over dem supum when you a walk?"

"No. But I keep shutting them in car doors."

"Right that's it. I'm reaching for it."

"You can come with me Ricky. You an' Shaniqua's been mash up now for the longest time."

"Don't even go there Tanya."

"See one a dem a fall out deh! Warn me pull it out?"

"…And when Brother Lynch start to pray!"

"At last a brother!"

"Never liked her anyway."

"Shaniqua's big woman to you. You ain't got to like her!"

"Brother Lynch preaching at the funeral next week. You know."

Ingin pricked up his ears. He looked at Ricky who had

already clocked his thoughts. He wanted to convince Ingin out of what he knew he was planning, but too late.

"Will your church take on a funeral?" he asked his mother.

The talking stopped, everyone attracted to Ingin's topic of conversation.

"Who's dead?" asked Tanya.

"None of your damn business!" snapped Ingin. "Mum?"

"I shouldn't see why not. Eeh Sister Sterling?" she replied.

"Well das what the church deh deh fa?" she said.

"Ricky what you saying?" asked Ingin turning to his friend. "Talk to Claire no?"

"I can talk to her, I don't know if she…"

"Tell her it's for me man," interrupted Ingin.

"So who dead?" asked Mr Stewart.

"Just an' old school friend."

"Who fa pickney?" he pushed.

"You wouldn't know her. She's white," said Ingin as he tucked into another piece of chicken.

"Why don't they go to the flippin' Methodist then?" asked Tanya somewhat perturbed.

"Why you got to worry about that? You de Pastor now?"

"Why white people always got to be into everything black? Crikey, they're even taking over the churches now!"

"Tanya, de Lard don't know colour you know," intervened Sister Sterling gently.

"I don't care!" snapped Tanya.

"White people funeral?" asked Ingin's mother.

"Yes," replied Ingin defiantly. "So what's the problem?"

"Nutting," she said calmly. "What you tink Sister Sterling?"

"We nuh have no time fi prejudice inna de church sah," she replied in commanding tones.

Ingin's mother looked at him intently. She turned the issue over in her mind as she did so. Her conclusion, at least to Ingin, would be predictable. He knew his mother well. She wasn't perfect by any stretch of the imagination. She was often brash and unreasonable, chatty and into people's business. But she approached her faith with enough conviction to keep her along the right path. He knew that Sister Sterling's words would register with her. So when she finally said.

"I will have a word wid Pastor Brown fi you."

"One prablem doh," said Sterling, reminded of something. Ingin looked up at her, worried by her tone. "White people funeral different from ours y'know?"

"How so?" asked Mrs Stewart.

"Dem no view body y'know?" she warned. "Cyaskit close mah-sa."

"For real?" asked Ingin.

"Hmm, an' at the burial? Nobaddy nah pick up no shovel," she claimed. "Dem juss' put the sitten in de groun' and garn a dem yard. A doh even feel she dem do food arfta needa."

Ingin was worried, fearing that these revelations might mean that the idea was a no-go.

"Well we wudda juss' affi show dem how prapa funeral kip," said Mrs Stewart, undeterred. "Dexter, you juss gimme de numba fi de person who a organise it. You see? Me will tark to dem."

Ingin's soul rested. Nathaniel stood up and reached for the coleslaw. His mother slapped his hand.

"Have manners bway!" she said. "Never stretch you han' across de table."

Tamika, Chantelle and T had joined Shaniqua in her garden. It was a pleasant day and as usual the children were at the end of the garden pulling one another to bits.

"So what's the dealio wiv your old man?" asked Tamika of Shaniqua.

"Bones is aaht of it man," replied Shaniqua, hardly interested.

"I heard Ricky and Ingin give that boy some licks," jumped in T.

"Facked him raaht ap," said Shaniqua studying her nails.

"Arm sorry goo, but are don't know what you was doin' wiv 'im anyways," came Chantelle.

Shaniqua considered her response carefully.

"Too many goos fallin' in lav wiv de Jamaican accent insteada de man, are guess are was one of dem,"

"Not every Jamaican's fool lark 'im doh!" shot T.

"'Course not," Shaniqua defended her statement. "Arm jus sayin' if ar've learnt anyfink, is to check how de person is raava dan de way dey present themselves to ya."

Chantelle leant forward and touched Shaniqua's knee reassuringly.

"At least you tried lav. Too mach o' dese bladdy black men don't know what dey've got till dey lose it," she suggested.

"But what we suppose t'do doh?" entered T. "When our men keep letting us down like that doh?"

"Keep on dreaming lav," said Chantelle. "Dat knight in shining arma will turn ap one day. We gotta juss keep on believin' and keep on carryin' on."

"But is he ganna be a black man doh?" queried T. "Naff o'de black sisters just seem t'be sellin' aaht nah doh. Can't faarnd a decent black man, buff! Dem Garn go look a whitey."

"'Cos dey treat you betta doh innit?" suggested Tamika. "White man'll die for a piece o' black skirt. Once deyve got one, man dere showrin' you wiv tings. Are know a black goo at college, got herself a white man an' she don't want for naffink."

"Yes bat is she 'appy doh?" asked Shaniqua.

"She seems t'be," replied Tamika.

"All dey do is eat aaht you pussy an' spen' maney on ya doh. Arve 'eard white man lav eatin' pussy," came in T.

The comment bought laughs and a high five between T and Chantelle.

"Breakfass tarm in de moonin'!" they said in tandem obviously sharing a private joke.

"Well is all dat sam women want innit?" T concluded.

"Yes bat are don't fink dem wimin can be 'appy doh," observed Shaniqua. "Are don't know how dey can be 'appy. Are could nevva imagine layin' down wiv a white man," she waved her shoulders in disgust. "Can't imagine it. It just feels narsty."

"Nah. Is bein' able to accept de fact that dere different innit? Adjust lark," came in Tamika.

"No way. Are ain't adjustin' naffink," said Chantelle. "I'm black, mah man's gotta be black. Are don't care. Are still 'old aaht some 'ope for my people dem. Know what are mean? Are mean look. If every black sista took a white man... are mean cam on. We'd be extinct innit? Pure half-caste pickney rannin' baaht de place. Don't know where dey belong. Litoo green eyed monsters thas wha' are cool 'em!"

"Das juss cruel arm sorry," said T

"Narr it ain't!" defended Chantelle.

"Narr das wicked man, you ain't gotta cool 'em dat!" said Shaniqua with more authority than T.

"Oolraaht," said Chantelle with one hand in the air. "Took abaaht bladdy politicoo correctness. Bladdy Nora!"

"Betcha din fink you would ever be under the 'ammer did you?" asked Shaniqua.

Chantelle threw her a look that probably signalled the end of their friendship

"She's raaht doh! We gotta preserve de black race, can't just sell aaht lark dat," said T.

"Sounds a bit prejudice doh," considered Shaniqua. "Are mean, the KKK and the BNP took lark dat all the tarm, preservin' de race an' that."

"Yeah so? Naffink wrong wiv dat. Are mean are ain't preachin' 'atrid, even doh are can't stand white people. Bat they've got a point, arm sorry. Black people over here and white people over dere innit? What we mixin' for?" said Chantelle.

"Yeah even the black Muslims say dat an' ool," justified Tamika.

"But is just colour that separates us doh innit? Are mean arfta ool we're ool 'uman innit doh?" challenged Shaniqua.

"Are fink dere de devil 'imself if you arx me," said Chantelle fervently. "An' dere narsty an' ool."

"'Are fink white people are wicked. Are fink Chantelle's raaht are fink dey do cam from de devil. Just look at the way they facked ap de planet. Are mean the way they got so mach power in de first place. Look at the American Indians, look at the aborigines. Look at black people, slavery an' ool dat. Wicked people man. When you fink of ool de fings dey did to as? Are mean, dey used to cut the baby aaht of pregnant slaves 'cos dey didn't want the race to continue. Fling slaves overboard, middoo passage to lighten ap de loads on de slave ships, cat black men's dicks off 'cos dey didn't want dem t'breed." Tamika was in full swing. "They used to bury slaves in sand up to their necks and kick dere 'eads off lark footbools. Naff tings dey did to us man! Den dey took control of Africa innit? Ool de land, ool de gold, that's how Europe got so rich and Africa got so poor. When you fink of ool dem fings, how can you lay down wiv a white person an' keep your conscience clear? Are don't know."

"Yes but shouldn't we learn to forgive?" asked Shaniqua.

"Forgive wha? Goo you mad?" asked Chantelle.

"No! Are tell you what," jumped in T with gusto. "Are could forgive dem raaht, but de problem is dey keep doin' de same fing. If dey could make us slaves again dey would. Look at ool de racism. Look at de way dey still treat us. 'An dere still creamin' it aaht of Africa, tookin' baaht international debt an' ool dat! Are watch mah Chanoo Four news you know! Borrow dese fird world cantry's maney den charge loads of interest to keep dem poor. That's what they do."

"But de racism doh, police brutality, discrimination the lot," came in Chantelle. "Nah man. How you suppose to go an' wrap ap wiv one dem, knowin' das how dey stay?"

"But not ool of dem are lark dat doh?" queried Shaniqua.

"D'ere ool racist if you arx me!" exploded Chantelle. "Dere the flippin' enemy mate."

"Are don't know," said Shaniqua thoughtfully. "The enemy can't be someone dat loves you doh surely?" she inquired.

There was quiet. The question made everyone think. Chantelle spoke up first, but with less gusto that she had been speaking up till this point.

"Thas if dey really lav you," she said.

"If they do, then I suppose it's alraaht den?" pushed Shaniqua.

Again the women fell silent. T found a response first.

"'Spose you're free to see who you want innit? It's a free world," she said. "Not our place to judge."

"So why are we judging?" Shaniqua asked.

Again the silence fell. Chantelle found her voice first this time.

"Are don't care, are ain't datin' no white man an' thas it," she said.

Tamika studied Shaniqua carefully. She was pained, she could see. She reasoned that her pondering had come from somewhere. It was an issue that was troubling her. It could have only have come from one place.

"How's Ricky?" she asked gently of her.

Shaniqua looked up at her, then looked away saying nothing. Tamika was quick of the mark. She knew what was going on there. Shaniqua had been trying to get into Ricky's head. Since he had started dating the white woman Shaniqua had not been the same. She had mentioned on a few occasions that she felt that Ricky had probably lost his mind. She had not realised the extent to which Ricky's relationship had affected Shaniqua, but it was becoming quite clear now. Maybe the events with Bones had bought it home to her, but to Tamika it was evident that she was missing him. She tried to comfort her whilst at the same time check for a reaction to confirm her suspicions.

"I'd really like to see you and Ricky get back together," she said softly.

Again Shaniqua looked away. But it was the longing in her eyes that confirmed it all for Tamika. Shaniqua excused herself for the toilet. She went upstairs but walked past the loo into her bedroom. She knelt at her bed and pulled a metal box from under it. Once uncovered it revealed a collection of photographs, letters and odd bits of memorabilia such as cinema tickets, Valentine's cards and so on. Relics of her past relationship with Ricky. She dug deep and pulled out a small Polaroid picture. It was of herself, Ricky and Tanika when she was a year old. She stayed their on her knees studying the photograph, before staining it with a tear that had surfaced and run down her cheek before lodging itself there. More tears followed as she reminisced about her life with Ricky. Tears that she did not even bother to wipe away.

thirteen

Ingin, Four Star and Mattik were playing dominoes at the King Centre. It was evening. They had stumbled into the Youth Club hours, but the urge for a game of dominoes and the need to be out of their respective abodes had defeated them. There were games of table tennis and pool going on at the same time. The twenty or so young teenagers were somewhat surprised at their presence, but they didn't give a damn. The youth worker had hinted politely that they weren't wanted, but after Mattik had convinced her that attendance was very low and that their presence would be appreciated, she gave in.

Hip Hop music jumped out of the speakers that were situated in the corners of the room. Four Star disliked it, complaining that it was upsetting his game. But in reality, this wasn't about a game of dominoes, it was about Ingin wanting some company. He needed an opportunity to take his mind off of the Amanda situation, which had affected him deeply. Ingin was a rogue. There was no denying that. But essentially he was a man with a heart. He was an emotional guy and could easily make an open display of his feelings when deeply impressed by a situation.

Children were no joke to him. He cared about every one of his children, albeit by several different women. He was a man without qualifications and though highly skilled in a number of trades, his one regret in life was that he couldn't make enough money to take care of his young ones the way he wanted to. But he did try. He enjoyed good relationships with the seven mothers of his children and despite his initial anxiety about possibly making Amanda pregnant he looked forward to enjoying the same kind of relationship with her. The fact that she was a white woman was of little consequence to him. In fact, he welcomed the idea.

The fact that she had money made him exited and he would have exploited that fact. This was not the centre of his grief. He grieved because he had lost a child. Two women had lost his children by way of miscarriage in his younger years. Those were difficult enough situations for him to deal with. But the burden that rested on him amid the nightmarish scenario that had unfolded was too much to bear alone. He hadn't been comfortable being alone since he had heard the news.

He had been gripped by a bout of depression, the likes of which he had never known. Amanda's was a sad tale and would have taken it to heart even if he hadn't played a role in it. But he had. He considered and asked God if this were a judgement. He had begun to know the meaning of pain. He reasoned that eternal punishment certainly didn't have to be in any way akin to a physical anguish. No. It was more than likely an emotional one. He wondered if he was somehow being rewarded for the many years of playing the field and causing so much distress to so many women. He believed that life was a circle. That what went around came around. He was humbled by the experience, convinced that this was his time. He shoved his dominoes onto the table in indolent fashion not saying an awful lot. The others players noticed that this evening he was somewhat distant and it was upsetting the vibe. Four Star sought to address it.

"How you gettin' on wid de rich ting man?" he asked in his heavy Bajan accent.

"You got me mix up," replied Ingin quietly without looking at him." You mus' be on about Ricky."

Four Star wasn't buying it.

"Nah man! Whe' you talkin' boat?" he said excitedly. "Oi hear you manage t'groin one a deh ole arse!"

Ingin said nothing.

"You sly likkle rasshole," said Four Star with a cheeky look on his face and turning to Mattik. "He en't warr seh nutting, but oi bet he kill the li'l bitch with fuck!"

Ingin shook his head in disgust at the coincidence of the statement.

"You rasshole," continued Four Star. "You tink oi don't know you?"

"Man I've stopped messing about. Ain't right," said Ingin with resignation after just making up his mind.

Again Four Star wasn't buying it.

"So what you a rasshole reform character now?" he asked, banging a domino on the table. "You need t'move you rass an' stop play de arse wid me." He turned to Mattik. "You believe dis guy here doh? He run arung, groin out half de tung, den he retoire an' tell people it ain't roight. Man come outta here wid you rasshole non sense!"

Mattik was in a more philosophical mood.

"So you got a white ting now Ingin? Me, I fuck the white women dem, but boy don't ask me to make my bed wid one a dem," he wondered.

"Boy all Pussy red y'know! Dey only for groinin'" stated Four Star in agreement.

"White woman love a fuck man! Specially from black man." Continued Mattik. "Deh fuck anywhere, any rahtid time."

"Love give blow job too," suggested Four Star.

It was soon clear that both Four Star and Mattik were talking to themselves. Ingin could hardly hear them. He had switched off.

"Black woman give blowjob too."

"Some."

"The liberated ones."

"Oi give you a rasshole joke roight. Oi fuck a l'il whoite ting de odda noight roight. Bitch tell me she 'en go gimme no blowjob roight. Oi have to arx she if she tink she is any rasshole black woman. She 'en gi no rasshole blow job."

"What she say?"

"Man she have to suck de boy! Wha' wrong wid you?"

"Black woman suck dick but they know better than to look rasshole kiss after doh!"

"You roight."

"Want fuck when they all on their period. Ain't no rahtid black woman gonna do that!"

"Some."

"OK some do. But at least they'll wash the ting out after. White women. Give dem a hankie fi wipe de pussy dey happy."

"You roight as cant."

"White woman can't cook needa. Got to have my rahtid groun' food an' shit. I don't know any white woman can cook proper West Indian food."

"Well das anudda ting dere. Pure rasshole chips you gon' get from dem. Oi use to fuck anudda li'l white ting. One noight she invoite me rung de house seh she gon' cook f'me. Tell me she gon' cook Jerk chicken. I gone rung dere, man oi tell you, diss rasshole come in loike hot rubber. The rasshole chicken 'ent cook roight an' de Jerk, man up till no' oi dunno wha she callin' jerk, if y'arx me is pure black pepper she mix in flour. "

"Nah man, dey can't cook man. Next thing you walkin' the fuckin' dog too. Why they love dog so much man?"

"Walkin' de rasshole? Next ting you sleepin' wid it, eatin' wid it."

"Out the same spoon!"

"Man dey duzz be all kissin' rasshole! Den warn come kiss you too!"

Ingin's mobile phone rang. A table tennis ball landed on the table that they were playing on. A pretty young black girl came and collected it from Mattik who had caught it.

"Thank you," she said sweetly before going back to her game. Four Star leaned forward.

"Bigga darta dat y'know!" he said quietly.

"Man you lying. Look how she grow!" Mattik started with surprise.

"She well fuckable now man!" said Four Star, getting to the crux of his conversation. "Eff oi neva know she daddy oi be right up in dere. Expan' dat li'l pussy!"

Ingin threw him a look of disgust before answering his mobile phone. It was Ricky.

"I spoke to Claire," he said. "She sorted things out with Pastor Brown. Funeral's next Friday."

"Cool," said Ingin. "So how you doing wid de baby modda?" He asked with concern.

"Fuck all. She won't speak to me. I've written to her twice. Nothing. I think I'll have to see a solicitor, to try and get a contact order or some shit."

"That's not good. Gimme her number. Maybe I can talk some sense into her."

"Anything," said Ricky, who immediately passed on Shaniqua's number to him.

Ricky signed off and Ingin immediately dialled the number. Shaniqua was surprised to hear from him. But her tone was pleasant.

"Narss t'hear from you," she said after the 'how are you's' were out of the way.

"There's a funeral at my mum's church next Friday," said Ingin wasting no time. "I'd like you to come."

"Ricky ganna be dere?" she asked, smelling a rat.

"Yes, but Ricky's not the reason I'm asking you to come." Ingin replied.

"What is it den?" Shaniqua asked with puzzlement.

"You'll see. Just be there. For me yeah?

Shaniqua agreed then hung up. Ingin put his phone back in his pocket.

"Who dead?" asked Four Star.

Ingin looked at him blankly. Then spoke softly.

"It ain't about whose dead," he said. "It's about who's still alive."

Both Four Star and Mattik pierced him with confused scrutiny and screwed up faces.

"Wha' de arse you been smokin' boy? Sung loike you goin' loopy n'rashole," said Four Star eventually.

Ingin smiled to himself, shuffled the dominoes then shared them out.

"Pose," he ordered calmly.

The Virgin Megastore was packed. Ricky had taken some time out to hunt for a CD. He was comfort shopping and The Wu Tang Clans 'Wu Tang Forever' had done the trick. He eased his way past a host of teenagers who had just left school and were hanging about by the entrance to the store. As he approached the entrance he noticed a huge security guard that eyed him intently. The look on his face was unnerving, but it instantly turned to shock and a level of nervousness as his gaze left Ricky and moved to whatever was behind him. His eyes widened before turning away in almost embarrassment. Ricky was tempted to turn around to see what it was that had given him such a shock, but he waved the notion away and carried on towards the exit. He had made the right decision, for whomever it was, decided to make themselves known to him. Ricky felt a slight tap on his shoulder; he turned and nearly died of shock.

"Didn't you see me in the store?" asked the Hottentot Venus.

Ricky took a second to gather his thoughts and answered nervously.

"No."

"Don't know how you managed to miss me," she said with a smile. "You were virtually standing next to me. Wrapped up in your own thoughts, I guess. You do remember me don't you?"

"Yes you're the woman from the night club."

"Yes, then I saw you again in Browns."

Ricky nodded his head and smiled. He took a second to allow the surprise of the moment to pass. She held out a hand, which he took lightly.

"Sharon," she said.

"Ricky," he replied.

Ricky couldn't help looking her over. He couldn't believe that such large breasts lay on a body that was otherwise well constructed. Not overly fat or thin. But very ripe. He realised what had frightened the security guard. It was his own sexual appetite, because this was what Sharon was able to extract from any man without even having to move. She was pretty too and that just made life even more difficult. She had a cute, childish smile that was set on a face that oozed maturity. Ricky deduced that she was in her early thirties. Her friendly manner only made her more appealing. Whoever the guy was that she met at the club, was certainly one hell of a lucky fellow, he thought.

"Fancy something to eat?" she asked, her effervescent smile not receding.

"Why…sure," replied Ricky, startled at the offer.

"This way," she said, walking off. "I know a good place just around the corner. Yam Yams. Great pizzas."

Ricky followed, somewhat bemused. He had not really even

met the woman. This was the first time that they had spoken. But throughout their few casual encounters he had noticed something of a bond between them. A mutual attraction of sorts, though he had no clue as to its root. He suspected that she hadn't either, but he delighted in the fact that they were about to find out. They had reached Yam Yams within a couple of minutes, enough time for Ricky to find out that she was still with her boyfriend. He couldn't help feeling slightly disappointed.

They ordered food. She had a large pepperoni pizza and he a straight cheese and tomato. She sat opposite him. As she took off her jacket he noticed every guy in the place turn around. Most of them were with their partners, who were not amused at the attention she had derived from their men. Ricky admired the way she took it all in her stride. She didn't seek the attention and when she did get it, she handled it like a pro, by just simply ignoring it. Once settled, she rested her elbows on the table, made a bridge out of her clasped hands and rested her chin on it.

"So how's your girlfriend?" she asked with a cheeky smile.

"She's good. We're going through a difficult patch right now though," Ricky replied.

"Really?" she queried.

"Well I don't know if you remember the friend that she was with at the club? Well she died recently."

"Oh dear."

"Suicide."

"How horrible, why did she kill herself?"

"Long story."

"Your friend. What's her name?"

"Claire."

"Claire. She doesn't like me does she?"

"You noticed."

"She probably thinks I'm after you."

"She did mention it."

"She doesn't have to worry. You're a nice guy and everything but I'm happy with Harry. He happens to know her."

"She did mention something like that. But she couldn't remember where it was she knew him from."

"At the club he was doing his nut too. But by the time we

saw you guys in Brown's, he'd remembered. She's the wife of the Managing Director of the company that he works for."

"Small world. I think she'll be his ex-wife soon though."

"Yes. Harry told me about the rumours. She'll get out of that marriage a wealthy woman. You bagged yourself a right one there didn't you? A black man's dream."

"Is that so?"

"I jest."

"She calls you The Hottentot Venus."

Sharon laughed.

"Charming. She's read some black history then?" she said rather smugly. "An interesting analogy. The Hottentot Venus. A seventeenth century African woman that caused a sensation in London because of the extraordinary size of her bottom. Married into the aristocracy and ended her days as a fairground attraction in some freak show. She obviously wishes ill of me. Wrong body area though."

Sharon grabbed her huge boobs and dropped them one the table with another cheeky grin.

"I'm certainly more boob than bottom," she concluded.

Ricky couldn't help savouring the conversation. He stared nervously at them and scratched his head in a clumsy fashion.

"So how ... er ... how big are we talking here then? Like er ... D cup size?" he asked pathetically.

"Typical man. That's got to be the most asked question ever."

"Sorry I ... I'm just ..."

"... Fascinated, I know. Actually I'm a double H size."

"Is that ... like ... er, H for heavy?"

Sharon looked at him confused.

"Is that like D for dummy?" she asked.

Ricky tossed his fingers in the air and looked away to hide the volume of his ineptitude.

"J-just wondered," he said.

Silence ensued. She allowed his embarrassment to fade, giggling slightly to herself. The waitress served the food and Ricky, once over his little abashment spoke up again.

"I bet those things have given you problems in your life time," he said a great deal more seriously.

Sharon accepted the seriousness of the question as painful memories wrote albums across her face.

"Life definitely hasn't always been a barrel of fun," she began in a sombre tone. "I got raped by my father when I was thirteen. He would barge his way into the bathroom whenever I was taking a bath and just sit there shitting and staring at my chest. One evening when my mother was out I suppose his passions just got the better of him. Made me swear not to tell her."

"Did you?"

"Yes for all the good it did. She didn't believe a word of it. So he would come to me on a regular basis. Gang bangs, rapes, I've had it all. I suppose Dexter told you about school days. I left home when I was eighteen. Guys on my estate would be knocking my door at all hours of the morning. When I wouldn't answer, they'd just kick off the door. I just got to a point where I just couldn't be bothered anymore. I'd lost the appetite for sex a long time before that, so I'd just let them do what they wanted. I just made sure I protected myself. I thought about heading for Amsterdam, Germany or the States, you know, somewhere where I could make some money out of these things but I said 'Sharon, you can do better than that so don't give up and strive for what you want.' I've only ever wanted to have a normal life. You know, a house a husband, kids. But with these things, if I hadn't taken care of myself, the only thing I would have been assured of is the kids."

"So no steady boyfriends?"

"Yes loads. All black and all no good."

"So now you're anti-black?"

"No. Never. I'm black myself I could never be anti-black, but please. Why does choosing a partner have to be some great political decision? I simply need love and I need to give love. I'm a woman for Christ's sake. You men tend to forget the fact that you're only human. But with the white thing, there are so many black women in my position. What the hell are we supposed to do? Wait for hell to freeze over whilst you brothers get your act together? The truth is you've got white women on your cases now too and that shortens the chances of black women getting their fair share. There's a serious man shortage as it is, so no wonder black women get up in arms.

The sad thing is that most of you guys have no idea of how to treat a woman. Once upon a time it was just black women doing the single parent shuffle. Now, just look at how many single white women there are pushing prams around, only this time with little mixed race children in them? After all this time you guys are still thinking with your dicks, look how long we've been telling you. Now those poor besotted little white girls are learning about who it is that really rules the ghetto."

"And what he rules it with," agreed Ricky.

"For sure."

"So it's not a money thing with you and this guy?" challenged Ricky.

"All I want, all any woman wants, is stability. I'd be a silly bitch if I lived my life in such a way as to allow a man to supply that for me. On the other hand, you know you get these well-off black women that go on about how they don't need a man. Crap. They only ever get to that conclusion once they've amassed enough material possessions. They really need to address what it was they wanted a man for in the first place. You'll never find me on this 'man got to be the provider' crap. But you do want a man that has his life together, why not? I admit I used my boobs to snag a man, and he's not a pauper, but in truth that's all immaterial. You come with nothing, you leave with nothing, that's life. Harry probably thought that he could pay me to allow him to bury his head into a pair of fifty double H's every night. Fair play to him, he's a man. But he soon realised that that's not the way it'll be. So how are you getting on?"

"OK."

"You don't sound so sure."

"Well, I don't know if it's what I really want."

"What was it, jungle fever?"

"Probably."

"You shouldn't have done that to her. You're probably in her system now. It'll be difficult to get rid of her."

"What makes you so sure?"

"Either it was jungle fever on her part or she was serious. If it's serious watch out. She'll never be able to let you go. That's how sensitive white women can get with black men."

"So why is that then?"

"I think that she's the type of person that seeks truth and wants what is inherently good. You embody that for her. It's your blackness."

Ricky, though stumped, respected her philosophy and sought more.

"So what is blackness?" he asked.

"Well it's not about having big dicks, big backsides, smoking dope, listening to reggae music, being good in bed, being exotic and so on," she began. "Some white people become attracted to those stereotypes and those are the ones that lose out a lot of the time. Others are attracted to the stuff that really makes us what we are."

Ricky was in total reverence of her view. He agreed with every word, but pushed for simply wanting to hear more.

"Our in-built belief in freedom, justice, equality, truth and all that stuff," she continued. "Essentially it's our closeness to God. I guess you're closer in that respect than the people you hang around with, which I guess, is what attracted me to you. We've probably got the same colour aura. But this is what Claire sees in you also. Remember, European society was built upon two things, Paganism and Darwin's theory of evolution. Europe is the only continent in the world that doesn't wholeheartedly accept the presence of a God. That makes them a lost people. Claire's a seeker. She seeks truth and freedom and she finds that in you. I suspect that your problem is that you have too much Malcolm X in you, too much Marcus Garvey and all that Black Power stuff. Isn't it funny how the stuff that once freed us can become a chain around our necks? But the truth is that times change and we need to evolve. Malcolm X evolved to embrace white people. Hell, even God moved on. One minute it was an eye for an eye, the next minute it was turn the other cheek."

Sharon mused for a second.

"Frightening isn't it?" she wondered.

"What?" asked Ricky, confused.

"The fact that even God evolves."

"What makes a mixed relationship work?" Ricky asked not wanting her to drift from the issue at hand.

"Two things," she replied. "Either one party has to sell out or conform to whatever the dominant culture of their society is or the most dominant person within the relationship or… both parties know themselves. Harry and I are different. But despite that we learn to co-exist. We've learnt to accept that it's our spiritual conditions that are important. I think we human beings are too shallow, we never seem to ask questions about our existence, we just seem to get on with life as if it were our God-given right."

"Isn't it?"

"Not if we're not prepared to seek truth and to evolve and develop what is essentially good within us. Our goal should be the pursuit of eternal and long-lasting peace, union with nature and love towards our fellow human beings. Why the hell are we clouding the issues with race, ethnicity and all that other bullshit? Those things are just a politician's meal ticket. Somewhere along the line, we're all being fooled. Black people have had to fight for legislation to protect our rights and I accept that. But the fact that black and white people can fall in love and find common ground despite their differences has done more to get us pitiful specimens to the sort of place that we should be. Remember that's why they killed X and King: because they wanted to bring people together. The BNP, the KKK, they want separatism. They're offering a false economy. It's no good for them and it's no good for the human race."

"So are you saying it's wrong to date someone of your own race?" challenged Ricky, thoughts of Shaniqua not a million miles away.

"Hardly," she replied. "Look. Some people need to date someone of their own race. They just need to. Nothing wrong with that. But there are other people that don't have that need. That's OK too. I simply believe that we are all free to make our life choices. When it comes to your choice of partner, that choice should be made out of love not hatred."

Ricky mused for a second, allowing the notion to hit home.

"Remember," she continued. "Bob Marley was mixed race. He taught us black consciousness, but he never taught us to hate anyone. Our adversity should have developed us. Few of us have really reached where we should be. We should be greater thinkers, seasoned philosophers all of that. It's a poor show when we seek to treat white people in the same way that they have treated us - to act as if they are not here, act as if we are superior to them, act as if they're not allowed into our societies and into our lives.

Sure, we have rules, but most of them want us to teach them our ways, that's part of the reason they're attracted to us. I've heard some black people talking about only black-on-black relationships, and the only justification they can give is some feeble talk about preserving the race. That sounds too much like the KKK if you ask me. What they should be talking about is preserving the culture. But they're still off the mark because they think black-on-black relationships are the only way to do it. But let's face it. Black people won't become extinct. If slavery couldn't kill us nothing will, who said it? We don't die, we multiply. Black culture fed and still feeds the world. Hell, my people need to be a lot less insecure."

Ricky sat back in his chair and smiled. She noticed the complete look of admiration on his face.

"Thought I was all tits and arse didn't you?" she said with a huge grin. "So did Harry," she continued. "Whatever kind of person he was before he met me, he's different now. Hey I'm a bona fide black woman. I'm just doing my job here."

Silence descended. Ricky felt a wave of admiration at the revelation of this woman who was clearly made up of more than she had been given credit for. They ate up, paid for their meals and left. Outside, Sharon slung her bag over her shoulder and turned to Ricky.

"Guess I'd better be off," she said, holding his hand. "I'd leave you a number but it doesn't look as though I'm going to be around much. Harry got a promotion; It's going to take him out of the country for a couple of years. He's asked me to join him. His boss loves him to bits and he just won't tell me why. Anyway, you take care."

She kissed him on the cheek and lowered her voice to emphasise her seriousness.

"Look. Just try to be the black guy that that Claire thought you were. In fact, that goes for any woman that you end up with. Positive, good and definite in your intentions. Be that way always.

There are a lot more people depending on you than you think. Bye."

Ricky returned the kiss and let go of her hand slowly. He watched her, check the traffic before crossing the road. Before long she was gone. Disappeared into the large crowd of people that had descended upon the high street that day.

fourteen

Apartheid had descended upon the Missionary Church of Christ. It was a small Pentecostal denomination with a large congregation but only one branch. Ingin's mother had worked vigilantly to encourage members of the church to attend a funeral for someone that no one knew. She did well. Most of the congregation had turned out. They were mainly black people. Mrs Stewart had convinced them that there was going to be a lot of upper-class rich people attending and that they needed to give a good impression. They filled the left side of the church. To the right, white people, many of whom hadn't a clue as to what they were doing in a Black Pentecostal church in Peckham. So they all sat together. Tears and sniffles were audible from that side of the church. Perhaps no more so than from Emma and Claire, who sat together on the front row, next to Alan. All of Amanda's friends had turned out. Colin, Rosy, Peter, Allison, Gina - they were all there. Claire was glad to see them. She picked up a programme that Tanya Stewart had grudgingly prepared at college.

She opened it to find a full programme that she and Ingin's mother had consulted over. For more reasons than one it was going to be a long and difficult service. The atmosphere was thick as the congregation awaited the arrival of the coffin. Emma looked around the church. She noticed Ingin and Ricky standing together on the 'black side'. Ricky was doing his best to deal with the overwhelming emotion of the moment. Ingin was already crying.

She looked behind her at the 'white side' to grab a glimpse of who had arrived. It was literally everyone that she knew, including her estranged husband, who tossed her a quick glance before turning his pained face away. He hadn't bothered to bring his mistress she noticed. Not that it would have troubled her one

The Home Going Service
Of the late
AMANDA GILLIAN POULTER
17 February 1955 - 20th April 1998

Precious in the sight of the Lord is the death of his saints
Psalm 116:15
At
The Missionary Church of Christ
130-135 Jubilee St
Peckham.
On
1 May 1998 at 11.00am
Officiating Minister: Rev J.T Brown

Interment at Henley Road Cemetery.

Refreshments Afterwards
The Holiday Inn.
Gloucester Road. Peckham. London.

iota if he had. She nudged Claire when she noticed that Paul had arrived also. He looked a noble figure in black. He hadn't noticed them as he was busy assessing the situation that he had found himself in. As indeed were most of the white people. This was a new experience for the majority of them and the mixed emotions of the funeral coupled with the feeling of being in an alien environment caused much anticipation amongst them.

Emma passed her gaze around the great building. An old Methodist church that had not lost any of its historic beauty was filled to the rafters. Even the balconies were full. Amanda had many friends, but so it seemed did Ingin, Ricky and Mrs Stewart.

They had conspired to give Amanda a regal send off and the atmosphere was hot and supremely conducive for such an event. A choir sat behind the large pulpit with Pastor Brown the musicians and a collection of finely attired elders from the church. They all appeared ready for business. Shaniqua eased her way quickly into the church. An elderly gentleman moved aside for her and she squeezed herself on the back row. She looked across at the 'white side' and wondered what the hell was going on.

Within minutes the organist started playing. Pastor Brown standing at the altar indicated for the congregation to stand up by raising his hands, and as they rose the pallbearers entered the church bearing the coffin. Steadily they marched down the aisle. A slight crescendo of sniffles and sobs emerged from the 'white side'. Claire broke, Emma held her tightly with one hand whilst using the other to attend to her own tears. Alan stood stoically, with hands in pockets, showing no emotion at all. Over on the 'black side' Ingin stood in silence allowing the tears to rain down his face. Ricky held firm desperately trying to hold it in.

The pallbearers placed the coffin on a trolley at the head of the church, just below the altar, before walking steadily to the back of the church. Pastor Brown signalled for the congregation to be seated. They duly obliged. He adjusted the microphone and spoke into it. Pastor Brown had a very commanding aura that would often become more powerful when he was at his pulpit. He was a short, sturdy man of fifty-four years. Grey fluffy hair rested on top of a stern visage. A rounded, well fed man who seemed to ooze an inordinate amount of physical strength, despite his maturing years. His voice was deep and authoritative. He spoke with a heavy Caribbean accent. His tone, though very aware of the circumstances, was upbeat.

"Let me thank you all in the name of our Lord and saviour Jesus Christ for attending the home-going of Amanda Gillian Poulter," he began. "This is a difficult time for the family and friends, but we know that our dear Amanda has found rest and we must rejoice in that. Let us sing our first hymm 'The Lord's my Shepherd.'"

The congregation rose. The musicians played and the 'black side' sung. The 'white side' needn't have joined in even if they had known the tune for the black members of the congregation sang with gusto, sending a great crescendo of noise around the large church. Their rendition was rousing, adding to the thick atmosphere that had descended upon the church. They were a congregation used to this kind of situation. They were fervent worshippers and approached their praise with fervour. As the hymn drew to a close and the voices faded there were isolated shouts of "hallelujah" and "praise God." Some were feeling the spirit already. A few of the white people looked across with eyes gawping in wonderment at the behaviour of those whom had lifted their voices in praise. They wondered if they were among mad people. Others caught the bug and felt uplifted in their hearts. The home-going service of Amanda Poulter had well and truly begun.

Pastor Brown announced that next Deacon Bruce was going to say a prayer. The black people bowed their heads and closed their eyes. The white people followed suit. A tall dark-skinned black man, one of the elders stood up behind Pastor Brown, and with a mighty voice began his prayer.

"Oh dear Lord," he began. "Bless us this day as we commend to you the soul of our dearly beloved Amanda Gillian Poulter. We can only trust, dear Lord, that her heart was right with you and that you will take her dearly departed soul into your tender hands. Lord, teach us the meaning of life. Help us, oh dear Lord, to accept that we are only here for a short time and that we need to take inventory, take stock of our lives while we are here merely passing through." Cries of "Hallelujah," and "bless him Lord" emanated from certain quarters of the 'black side'. The atmosphere was thick again. Deacon Bruce found another octave and prayed with increasing passion as he delved deeper into himself for words. "Bless us this day Lord. Teach us the way. Help us in this divine moment of your truth. We are nothing without you Lord, we are putty in your hands. It is given unto us once to die. Help us Lord in your holy name. Amen." Another "Praise God' came from the congregation. It was Sister Stewart.

The congregation settled once again on Pastor Brown's instruction before he called Emma to read a scripture. Claire held her hand tightly as she rose to her feet. The congregation was still. Emma strode to the pulpit. A finger tucked into the bible at Matthew 5:3, the scripture she would read. Pastor Brown gave her a hearty smile and adjusted the microphone once again for her. Nervously and without looking at the crowd, she placed the bible onto the pulpit. She was a bag of nerves and clearly distraught. She had offered to read the scripture but at this moment she wondered what had possessed her to agree. She took a deep breath as another "Bless her Lord" came from the congregation. This emboldened her slightly and sensing no hostility, but encouragement from the 'black side', she began timidly. Her soft sensuous voice polished the thick air and as she read, she thought of Amanda.

"Blessed are the poor in spirit for theirs is the kingdom of heaven," she began softly.

"Blessed are they that mourn, for they shall be comforted. Blessed are the meek, for they shall inherit the earth. Blessed are they which do hunger and thirst after righteousness for they shall be filled." She stopped and wiped away an emerging tear. Cries of sublime encouragement issued from the congregation. Emma took a deep breath and glanced over at Claire, who, even through a sad face was able to raise a smile at her. She was encouraged once again. "Blessed are the merciful for they shall obtain mercy, " she continued. "Blessed are the pure in heart, for they shall see God. Blessed are the peacemakers for they shall be called the children of God. Blessed are they which are persecuted for righteousness' sake for theirs is the kingdom of heaven. Blessed are ye, when men revile you and persecute you and shall say all manner of evil against you falsely for my sake." Emma took the last verse slowly, dipping her head over the pulpit to view Amanda. "Rejoice and be exceedingly glad for great is your reward in heaven. So persecuted they the prophets which were before you."

At the very second that she closed the bible an enthusiastic "Praise the Lord" emanated from a good portion of the 'black side'. Emma stepped down from the altar, aided by Pastor Brown, who took her hand. She walked past the coffin, dropped her head into her hand and sat in her seat as tears flooded from her. Claire held her tightly and rocked her gently whispering "Well done."

Pastor Brown called for another hymn and in seconds the church was alive with the sound of a full congregation singing 'Guide me, O thou great Jehovah.' The atmosphere was now well and truly unified. The white people had settled, emboldened by Emma's reading. The service had stepped up a gear. All apprehensions were gone. The vibe was becoming less and less dense and more celebratory, almost enjoyable.

The choir was called up next and graced the proceedings with a zealous rendition of 'Wings of a Dove' for which at it's conclusion the 'white side' was moved to applaud. The order of service called for a series of individual tributes from Ingin, Gina and Claire. The black side was surprised when Pastor Brown introduced Dexter Stewart. He was well known as the son of one of their eldest and most respected members. A few people wondered what role he had played in the deceased woman's life, but only for a second. Boldly, he took to the puplit and once there, opened a piece of paper that he drew from his pocket. Ricky had written a poem for him to read which he had offered to do with little thought or apprehension. Alan looked up at him with one eye almost closed. He breathed nervously and scowled inside at the thought that this was probably the man that his wife had committed adultery with. He would deal with it later. Ingin opened the piece of paper took a deep breath and spoke.

"This is for Amanda. I knew her briefly."
He coughed to clear his throat.
"Shadows disappear in a haze of sublime confusions.
The light is dim now before the azure blue cloud greets you.
Restoration is complete, there is no longer need for fear.
Unsubstantial light meticulously weaves it's way through the Cimmerian.
Cold and gentle at first causing sublime stupefaction
Before it's luxurious rigour bathes you.
There is no body now, though there is life.
There is no mind but there is thought.
There is no heart now but there is feeling.
There are no eyes yet there is sight.
When rapturous emotion engulfs the essence that you are

And beautiful whispering immerses your being.
Remember me.
Remember the silent moments that made us.
Remember quiet stagnation that built us.
Remember the faultlessly enigmatic second that softened us.
And I will be with you.
The cerulean radiance has enshrouded you now.
It's cold has teetered away and its warmth has caused you delight.
There is no face but you smile.
You have no voice but you sing.
No ears but you hear the music.
No hands but there is touch.
What of this warmth that surrounds you?
What of this bliss that has snared you?
It is love.
It's bending curves encase you
Sifting eagerly throughout your being
Merging your force and making you his.
You are love.
I shall see you in the wind.
Hear you in the rain.
Touch you through the snow
And feel you through the sun.
And as you experience the desire of ages
As you wallow in the ecstasy of his universe
And the wonder of his blessing.
Remember me."

Ingin wrapped up the piece of paper and stepped down from the pulpit. There was no applause, even though the solemnity of the words had hit home. Pastor Brown stepped sedately to the pulpit.

"Thank you young man," he said. "We are blessed by your words. Now Regina Tate will sing for us."

Gina stepped courageously to the front and before the coffin. Pastor Brown handed the microphone down to her. She said nothing before she began her accapella.

Her rendition of Whitney Houston's 'I Will Always Love You' was heartwarming. Gina had a powerful voice that moved the congregation. She sang with ardour prevailing through emerging lamentation as she sang the last verse.

The whole congregation applauded her. As she passed the microphone back to Pastor Brown, she looked into the coffin. Gina took a rose from one of the wreaths that lay around it, laid it on Amanda's chest and kissed her. Hands covering her eyes to hide her weeping, she paced slowly back to her seat. Pastor Brown too was moved. His voice gave a slight tremble as he himself wiped emerging teardrops from his eyes. He composed himself and welcomed Claire to the pulpit to read the eulogy. She arose and stepped gingerly to the altar. Once at the pulpit her first look was to Ricky who gave a slight nod of his head to issue encouragement. Her voice trembled as she spoke. She did her best to control it and steady her shaking hands as she laid the piece of paper onto the pulpit. She tilted her head to meet the microphone and simply read.

"Amanda Gillian Sextsone," she began, "was born to parents Gerald and Amy on the seventeenth of February 1955. She was an effervescent child who enjoyed her schooling, leaving St Peters Collegiate with 5 O'levels. After leaving school she went on to study with hopes of making it in the world of fashion design. She never made it as her love for her then boyfriend and soon to be husband Alan Poulter took over her life and in July 1981 they were married. Amanda enjoyed married life and loved children…" Claire stopped. The congregation watched her face cringe. Her body trembled and her head dropped into her hands. She cried. The moment had defeated her.

"Oh bless her now Lord," came a cry from the 'black side'.

"Be very strong now Claire," called Allison boldly from the 'white side'.

Claire lifted her head. Pastor Brown leaned forward and handed her a tissue which she graciously took and wiped her tears.

"I'm sorry," she told the congregation.

"You go on sister!" called Sister Stewart.

Claire composed herself and spoke again, this time ignoring the written words.

"Amanda was my friend," she said in a tender voice. "I loved her. Many of her friends Emma, Allison, Gina, we all loved her. She brought a breath of fresh air to our lives in a way that really, no one else could. She always had a smile for you whenever and wherever you saw her. She lived life to the full, determined to get all that she could from it. But the one thing that she wanted most in the world was denied her. She loved children and she wanted a child of her own."

Alan grimaced. Claire was unapologetic.

"Amanda felt pain. A lot of pain. But she would never let it show. Preferring I guess to hide her distress, in many respects for fear of distressing those that were closest to her. But inside she grieved and I suppose we, her friends, never really knew how much. In her last days she was alone. We couldn't help her. True to form she chose to bear her troubles on her own. But she left us with many many happy memories." Claire inclined her head to look at Amanda in the coffin. "We'll never forget you darling." Her voice broke with sobs "I just don't know why you had to go," she closed through weeping.

Moans of compassion emanated from the congregation. Emma cried too, as did Gina and Allison who struggled to maintain herself. Ricky, seated on the front row, rose to his feet and approached the pulpit. He held out a hand to Claire who took it as he led her down. He embraced her. Shaniqua winced. She had finally identified Ricky's lover. Paul winced too for he had identified Claire's lover. Claire took her seat again and Pastor Brown called for another hymn. The assembly rose to its feet as the church resounded to the tones of 'How Great Thou Art'. When the hymn was sung and the convention resumed their seats, Pastor Brown approached the microphone. It was time for the sermon. Brown himself seemed broken. He was a seasoned professional and had officiated at many funerals. But today he was greatly humbled. This had not been the normal run of the mill occasion that he had been used to. Amanda had received an ardent send off. He knew that it was now time for him to complete the task. He prayed in his heart as he approached the microphone. He placed a bible on the pulpit. Then spoke in solemn but mighty tones.

"The lord gave me a message to give to the congregation today," he began. "It wasn't the sort of message that I might normally preach either for a regular Sunday service or, I suppose, for an occasion such as this. I asked; 'Lord, why have you given me this message to preach?' And he simply told me to trust him. As I look at our fair gathering today. I believe that my question has been answered. Let me make no apology for some of the things that I say, for they are said with love and reverence for this occasion, the passing of our dearly beloved Amanda. But I would like to begin this sermon, that I have titled 'Life is Love and Love is Life' with an admonition."

He spoke calmly and with self-assurance.

"If you believe in what they call evolution, you know this idea that the world started from some explosion and then we evolved from animals. Then let me tell you straight away you're barking right up the wrong tree and you probably won't appreciate what I have to say," he said.

A vicious "amen" emanated from the 'black side', which everyone knew was directed at the 'white side', all of whom sought desperately to ignore the challenge. A thrust of passion made Pastor Brown's voice rise as he spoke his next words in true preacher fashion.

"I want to tell you today that I didn't come from no fish! I'm not the descendant of no monkey and the world didn't just appear!" he growled. "Let me tell you this. God made the Earth! God made Man! God made everything!"

The majority of 'the black side' erupted in a triumphant chorus of 'amen's', 'hallelujahs' and 'praise the Lords'. The 'white side' was certainly moved but remained perfectly quiet. Pastor Brown was becoming even more animated. He wiped emerging sweat from his brow with a handkerchief. He banged hard on the pulpit as his voice reached another crescendo in order to overcome the wave of Pentecostal Christian passion that had filled the atmosphere, which by now had become red hot.

"I cannot begin to tell you what it feels like, to know that there is a God!" he roared. "I cannot begin to tell you of the comfort that it brings to my soul, especially in times of crisis! In times of distress and in times of trouble! We don't just believe, we feel him, we speak to him! We have communion with him and, praise the Lord, we know he lives!"

Another volume of cheering arose from the 'black side', most of whom were now ecstatic. One woman, a frail looking lady, became so overcome, she jumped to her feet and started dancing and shouting "Hallelujah!" before releasing a volume of incantations in the tongues of the Holy Spirit. Pastor Brown waited for he throng to settle and spoke resolutely but more quietly this time.

"Brothers and sisters let me tell you, I feel the spirit of God here today. Oh yes! I feel the Lord is with us to bless this occasion," he said, wiping more sweat from his brow. "You know, from time to time, as I go about my ministry, many people ask me the same question. They say, 'Pastor Brown what is the meaning of life? What is our purpose? Pastor Brown why are we here?' Indeed, the very question on our minds today and in our hearts is life and death. It is for all of us, the issue of the day. Life and death. Oh praise the Lord. We understand, from our very limited understanding that we are born from our mother's womb. We live for a short while and then we die. Life to some of us, means getting up in the morning, getting the children off to school, going to work, coming home, Coronation Street, Bingo, night club, whatever. Whatever there is to do, we do it. We come home, go to sleep and wake up the next morning and … well … the same thing. We do that for a number of years then we get old, we get sick, we die. That's it. Well my friends I'm sorry to have to inform you today. It's a bit more complicated than that."

His voice rose again. His finger pointing uncontrollably at the crowd who were hanging upon his every word. His countenance full of indignation. His voice a roar that made the room vibrate as he cared little for his closeness to the microphone.

"It's a bit more glorious than that! It's a bit more special than that!" he wailed. Hallelujah! It's a bit more enlightening than that! Praise God! When the Apostle Paul wrote to the people of Corinth on the subject of death, he said.. 'Behold I show you a mystery'..."

The 'black side of the congregation caught on and repeated the verses of 1: Corinthians 15: 51 to 55 that they knew so well.

"…We shall not all sleep, but we shall all be changed, in a moment, in the twinkling of an eye, at the last trump; for the trumpet shall sound, and the dead shall be raised incorruptible and we shall be changed. For this corruption must put on incorruption and this mortal shall put on immortality. So when this corruptible shall have put on incorruption, and this mortal shall have put on immortality then shall be bought to pass the saying that is written, death is swallowed up in victory. O death where is thy sting? O grave where is thy victory?"

"Can you see my brothers and sisters?" Pastor Brown continued. "Can you see where I'm coming from?" Though clearly audible because of the microphone his voice became a whisper. "Life has so much more value than that which we place upon it and death has less value than that which we place on it. Our African heritage has taught us that death is a time of celebration. Because we want to celebrate the fact that our departed have gone on to a better place and we black people, in the Pentecostal church have retained some of that ethic. There is sorrow in these times, but we take it for what it is, a joyous occasion, a time of celebration when we know that our loved ones, if they are right with Christ, have moved on to Glory. Praise God."

Another chorus of 'amen's' and 'hallelujahs' emerged from the 'black side'.

"But I don't want to dwell too much on the issue of death," he continued. "I want to talk about life. I began by saying that I have been asked about the meaning of life. Our purpose for living. And I myself have agonised over this issue many times. Now I have the answer. In response to the question, I have often repeated to the questioner that our purpose is to love one another. That is true." He raised a finger in the air. "But there is more," he said softly.

He moved closer to the microphone and allowed a momentary silence to sink in. His timing was perfect. He knew that the congregation was waiting on his every word. He allowed more silence to dwell, and then he spoke very softly as he wiped more sweat from his brow.

"I'm here to tell you today. That life and love are the same thing," he said. "I see that even some of my flock seem confused by what I just said," he deduced with a smile. "Hang on in there. Pray for me now and I'll reveal it to you, the same way that God revealed it to me." He then banged hard on the pulpit and bought his voice to a mighty snarl that made some people jump.

"I said life and love are the same thing!" he roared. "God gave us life! God gave us love! The meaning of life is to love one another. But that should be natural. You talk about human nature? Human nature is love. Hear me now! I said human nature is love!"

'The black side' was in raptures once again. Pastor Brown was animated. The 'white side' sat, nonplussed, but equally uplifted.

"Christ said that God is love. He wasn't talking about his personality! He wasn't talking about his manner! He wasn't talking about his attitude! No! He was talking about his very essence! The thing that makes him what he is! His make up! His very life force! We are flesh and blood! God is love! Come on now it's the truth! I told you already about that evolution stuff! Don't believe it! Don't you believe it! It's a million miles away from the truth!"

Another bellow of elation erupted from the 'black side.'

"When God made man. The bible says he breathed life into Adam. Praise God!" Pastor Brown's tone lowered. "He put his life force into Adam. You know if you take a balloon and blow air into it. That air came from within you. That's what makes the balloon expand. God breathed life into Adam. His put a little bit of himself, his breath, into Adam. That's what made him live. Love made him live. Love makes us alive. It is God that is within us and it is he that makes us live. Oh hallelujah! When mankind turned to sin, there was not one that was holy. God would have destroyed us but he sent his only begotten son that we should not perish. But have life. You know sometimes on TV, they show these horror movies, have you seen them? 'Night of the Living Dead?' 'The Evil Dead' They've even got a rock band called the 'Grateful Dead'. How sad."

The black side of the congregation erupted in a fit of laughter. Brown's timing again was perfect. He did not speak until they were done.

"You know, you see the ghouls, like in Michael Jackson

video's. Man they look sick. Man they look ill. Long yellow teeth. They're bony. White faces. No colour. Bloodless. Now I'm not talking about white people, don't take me out of context here. I'm not for a minute preaching any form of racialism. Don't take me to the Race Relations Board" he said smiling. The congregation laughed. The 'white side' breathed a sigh of relief.

"Walking around with their arms straight ahead of them," he continued. "Hell-bent on destruction. Looking to cause some kind of trouble. Whoever made those movies, wasn't too far away from the truth were they? 'Night of the Living Dead.' Let me tell you brothers and sisters, the world is full of these ghouls, these vampires. You see them everyday. You work with them,"

The 'black side' broke out into laughter again.

"Oh yes," said Brown with a smile " Yes, you do. You shop in the same stores as them. You eat in the same restaurants as them. You drive on the same roads as them. They're alive but they're dead. They walk and talk, they eat they sleep. But they're dead. Because they have no love in their hearts. They have no God. That's why the world is the way it is today."

His voice raised again as he marched brazenly around the pulpit area.

"But love makes you smile!" he howled. "Love makes you sing!"

The 'black side' once again threw itself into exhilaration as the greatest surge of spiritual energy descended upon the church.

"Love makes you happy!" he continued "Love makes you joyous! Love makes you peaceful! Love makes you want to forgive! Love makes you want to help! Love makes you considerate! Love makes you care! Come on now! Love makes you feel! Love makes you cry! It doesn't make you kill! It doesn't make you hate! It doesn't make you hurt another human being! Death makes you do that! Death makes you hate! Death makes you abhor your fellow human being! What we call death is merely the passing away of the flesh into a new dimension of existence. What death is really, is what makes our existence so difficult. It is hate. Love is life, hate is death. My brothers and sisters I say to you: you have no other purpose on this planet, but to love. Love yourselves, Love one another and love your God. I see so many white people here today and it is a joy. It is a blessing to see both races mixed together under one roof with one accord. My only regret is that it is a situation such as this that has bought us together. Let us look forward together my brothers and sisters to a brighter day when we will greet each other together in the sprit of divine love that God has placed within our hearts."

A chorus of hallelujah's rose once again from the 'black side'. Pastor Brown raised a chorus. The musicians played and 'the black side' sang. The 'white side' stood in reverence at the way in which Pastor Brown had turned the occasion of Amanda Gillian Poulter's funeral into nothing less than a celebration. They were no less overcome with emotion. Many were in tears as they held each other, savoring the vastness of moment. The 'black side' was rapturous. Many held their hands in the air as they sang and swayed as they sent the song into another emotional gear. Brown sang fervently as did the choir. Another trickle of a tear rolled down Ingin's face as he turned his head to view the outpouring of emotion and praise. He looked at Ricky who caught his glance and lifted a fist to signal their triumph. Ingin had achieved his goal this day. Amanda had been sent off to her destiny in style. It was no more or no less than he could have wished for the mother of his deceased child. Claire and Emma hugged each other tightly. They had never experienced a moment between the two of them, throughout the whole of their long friendship that was more captivating or more splendid than this. Pastor Brown viewed them, smiled and gave thanks to God knowing that of everyone in the congregation, theirs had been the greatest burden.

Gina left her seat, Allison followed her. Emma lifted her head and saw them heading her way. She released Claire from her grip slightly to allow them in and the four women hugged each other and wept for dear life. Ricky turned around to behold Shaniqua. He was surprised to see her but he raised a nervous smile in her direction. She gave him a confident one back. With a nod of her head she looked away. She would speak to him later. It was then, for the first time that day, that Ricky became overcome. He could not stop the tears that fell from his eyes. He had to look away. Shaniqua noticed his tears. It made her cry too. She wiped her tears away just before the elderly brother that she was sitting next to put his arm around her and shook her gently for encouragement. She didn't know him, but she felt his love. She rested her head in his chest to absorb the comfort that she felt from him, but she could only think of Ricky.

Pastor Brown waved his hands in the air. The musicians brought their music to an end and the singing faded out. The last cries of 'hallelujah' and 'praise God' and the last of the sniffles of crying faded to as Pastor Brown gave instructions for the viewing of the body. Alan Poulter sat in the front row with Claire and Amanda absorbing the condolences as the congregation trickled past. Poulter did his best to seem interested but he had his mind on other things. He noticed Ingin disappear around the back of the church as the congregation became smaller and smaller. When it seemed OK to do so, he stepped out of the church in the direction that Ingin had gone in the hope of catching him before he went. Claire was somewhat shocked at the way he had flown from the church, but she was unable to debate the issue for too long because in an instant her former husband was standing before her.

Perhaps in any other situation she may have been hostile towards, him but the honest look of compassion written upon his face was too much for her. Her reaction was instinctive. She had spent many happy moments with Paul in Amanda's company. Some of those moments, admittedly, she would have rather forgotten, but there was never any love lost between Paul and Amanda. Besides this, Paul had another reason to hug his soon to be ex-wife. He did so with power. She hugged him back. He wanted to console her and she was happy, on this occasion to accept it. He whispered in her ear.

"Everything's going to be alright now darling. I promise you," he said.

Another tear fell from Claire's eye. She believed him. He gave her a final glance before taking his leave.

"I won't be going to the interment," he said. "But you'll hear from me," he said with a slight smile.

In the corridor at the side of the church, Alan Poulter noticed Ingin end a conversation with Shaniqua before heading into the men's toilets. He followed him determined to seize his moment. Once inside, he noticed Ingin alone, standing before a receptacle, release his flies and commence to urinate. He feigned the same thing occupying the receptacle next to him. Ingin ignored him and concentrated on his releasing his piss. Alan took a look at Ingin's penis and cringed. He was even more agitated. Ingin could feel his malevolence. Poulter spoke in dark tones.

"Did she like it then?" he asked coldly.

Ingin looked at him with distaste. He knew who he was.

"What?" he asked aggressively.

"You're the bastard that thought he could fuck my wife aren't you? Impregnate another man's woman. Don't you people do anything else?" he asked venomously.

Ingin seethed, but he kept his exterior cool. He stepped back, his willy still in his hand and, saying nothing, sent a shower of hot urine down the back of Poulter's trousers. He was not amused.

"You fucking black bastard!" he wailed in shock at what Ingin had done. "You fucking animal!"

"If you can't even respect the sanctity of the occasion," Ingin said. "Neither will I."

With a mighty haul Ingin grabbed an aghast Poulter by his collar and dragged him violently into a cubicle, locking the door behind them. A young Christian brother came into the toilet. He stood at the receptacle and listened fearfully as screams of agonising pain emerged behind the closed door. He finished urinating quickly and ran out of the toilet, forgetting to wash his hands. Eventually Poulter and Ingin emerged from behind the doors. Alan's face was bloodied and bruised. Thick, red blood streamed from his nose. His clothes had been messed up. Ingin was barely scarred, barely ruffled. He grabbed Poulter once again and threw him against a wall. Alan was breathing heavily, shaking and nervous.

"No more, please I beg you no more," he pleaded wearily.

Ingin grabbed both his cheeks with one hand, dug his fingers into them and moved within kissing distance of his face.

"If you don't want any more, then you do one thing for me," he said through gritted teeth.

"Anything," said Poulter, a vision of fear and trembling.

"You bury your wife. You get over to that interment, you pick up a spade and you bury your wife. You dig like you never dug before. You got that?"

Poulter nodded in compliance.

"I was watching you throughout the whole of that service. I couldn't see an ounce of emotion come from you," accused Ingin. "You never cared about her in life, you don't care about her in death. Why do you think that she had to come running to the likes of me? You're the animal. You call people like me animals, wicked, savage. But the way you treat even your own wife. Amanda didn't kill that child. You did. You have a grudge against me. Boy, you can't even begin to match mine for you. You dig for dear life at that interment. You bury that woman. Or I'll bury you."

Ingin released him from his grip and approached the door. He took a last look at the pitiful sight before him.

"You just be there. Or I swear to God …" raged Ingin. But he could say no more. There was nothing else to be said. He kissed his teeth and departed.

Once alone, Poulter stood over the sink. He looked himself over in the mirror and dropped his head. He was beginning to feel more than the bruises that Ingin left over his now aching body.

fifteen

Shaniqua had made her way to the interment. It was a cold day. She didn't have to go but curiosity had gotten the better of her. The crowd, hardly as big as the congregation in the church, stood around the burial area. She eyed Ricky. He and Claire stood together. She eyed Claire too. Making no judgements, she wondered at the two of them. Were they happy? Did he love her? Did she love him? Possibly the occasion had mellowed her outlook on their relationship. Once upon a time she might have shown pure aggression, pure hostility towards her, but not now. She felt a slight hint of respect for her. She looked noble and elegant. It had nothing to do with her dress, nothing to do with her status, nothing to do with her colour. It was something that she carried from the inside. Her aura was positive. She realised this and finally admitted it to herself and she would fight the notion no longer.

As the casket was lowered into the ground, the crowd sang. Pastor Brown was in fine fettle. He had been a mountain this day and he was winning everyone's respect. Claire poured out more tears. Ricky held her tightly, whilst watching Amanda's burial with an agonisingly twisted face. Ingin stood alone, feet apart and hands fixed together just above his crotch. He stared menacingly at Poulter who had done a poor job of cleaning himself up. A couple of people had asked him about the blood on his clothes but he had simply declined to answer.

A couple of family friends picked up spades in readiness to cover the casket. Poulter took a worried look at Ingin, who eyed him with a raised eyebrow. Poulter needed no more telling. He picked up a spade, loosened his tie and his collar and began the work. He dug for his life. Eagerly he picked up piles of dirt from the mound that lay around the hole in which Amanda had been laid. He was relentless as a wave of frustrated energy surged through his body. Many of the onlookers noticed his manic digging spree conscious that it was this moment more than any other throughout the day Poulter was ruing the loss of his wife. Ingin smiled, but couldn't help feeling it for him.

A family friend approached Poulter and offered to take the spade from him sensing that he was becoming tired. Poulter refused. He caught his breath again and resumed burying his wife. His manner became more frantic as he seemed more and more to lose his coordination, sending piles of earth anywhere. He was no longer concentrating on the job at hand, but rather seemed to lose himself in the activity. He dug faster and faster spraying earth everywhere. Some of the crowd were forced to move back or dodge flying earth. He heaved and began to whine, like a dog. His facial expression now contorted. Soon it became too much, he screamed. Dropped his spade and collapsed in a frenzy of tears. He called his wife's name over and over again as he knelt over the hole in the ground. Friends came to his aid.

Claire stayed still, wrapped up in Ricky's consoling arms. She felt no pity; neither did she feel any form of hatred for him. His chickens had come home to roost as he finally yielded to the piety of the moment. Two friends helped him to his feet and carried him away from the burial scene in tears. Ingin dropped his head, desperate to keep his sorrow in check. Ingin moved to the front, picked up the spade that Poulter had dropped, and continued where he had left off. Soon the job was done. Amanda was buried. Members of the crowd laid their wreaths. Claire, Allison and Emma took time to carefully arrange them neatly around the burial area. Soon it was all over and the crowds began to disperse. Pastor Brown shook Claire's hand who in turn thanked him for a wonderful service. Emma too, shook his hand. Ricky went over to talk to Ingin. They gave each other a hug initially but could not speak before Ingin alerted Ricky's attention to Shaniqua. She had approached Claire and they were talking. Ricky flinched nervously.

"Oh shit," he said. "That's all I need."

"Don't worry," said Ingin. "I asked her to come, and I think she knows why I asked her. If I know her well enough, she'll be doing just what I expect her to be doing."

"And what's that then?" asked Ricky curiously.

"Wait for the shout," encouraged Ingin.

"You're beautiful," said Claire to Shaniqua.

"Fanks," she replied pleasantly. " Arm sorry wiv met at such a bad tarm."

"I'm just glad we met," said Claire with a tender smile. She paused, choosing her next words carefully. "He's a smashing guy. You're lucky."

Shaniqua dropped her head to the ground.

"He loves you," she said reassuringly. "Probably more than anything else in the world. He loves his daughter too. He needs you both in his life. I tried to show him another woman's love and I think, in all honesty, he tried to be real and to respect the fact that he was in a relationship, regardless of my age or my colour. He's genuine like that. But I'm afraid I'm not the one. You are. You always have been. "

"How d'you know?" asked Shaniqua.

"I saw you in the tears he cried. Whenever he withdrew himself from me spiritually, I knew he was with you. He overcame the taboo of this mixed relationship quite admirably. You saw him in the church and here. He didn't disown me when I needed him. Just like he's never done you or his daughter. I thought about using my money to hold onto him. But I knew it wouldn't work. He's not about that. The man's about love. Real love, real caring, real honesty. I think he just got a bit confused."

"Jungle fever?" asked Shaniqua.

"I hope I wasn't an experiment. He's too truthful a guy to play that sort of game. I'd like to think that I did something for him. That my colour wasn't the only attraction."

"You're a beautiful woman y'self," admitted Shaniqua.

"Thanks," said Claire humbly. "I try."

"Did you lav him?" asked Shaniqua tenderly.

"I still do," Claire replied. "I think I always will. But loving someone means that you might have to let go in order to allow them the freedom to do what their heart desires. I won't beg Ricky to stay with me. I am satisfied that I didn't lose out to my colour. I lost out to another woman." Claire took Shaniqua's hand as a tear rolled down her face. "Take him," she said. "Care for him and do right by him. He needs you. He's a seeker and he desires to know himself. He sees that in you. He couldn't see himself in a white woman, only in you, a black woman. But that's OK. That's valid too. When it's love, it's always valid."

"I don't believe it," said Ricky astonished as he beheld Shaniqua and Claire hug.

"I do," said Ingin with a smile.

They watched in awe as Shaniqua and Claire held hands. They saw them exchange a few words in parting before kissing each other on each cheek. Claire departed with Emma, Allison and Gina who were stood waiting for her. They watched Shaniqua stand alone, momentarily contemplating, before scanning the area for Ricky and approaching him once he came into view.

"I'll be by the car," said Ingin.

He strolled off, without looking back. Shaniqua stood by Ricky and folded her arms not knowing what to say. The wind blew gently tossing Shaniqua's hair slightly.

"Ready t'be a farva narr?" she asked not looking at him.

"Always have been," he said. "You know that. Do I still have to do it from a distance?"

Shaniqua turned to confront him.

"No," she said. Her expression changed, she became a picture of vexation. She stabbed a finger in his chest, her passions got the better of her. "Just as soon as y'learn t'put some value on marr existence!" she said. "Just as soon as you learn t'respect me f'what are am, wiv me moods an' me ways! Just as soon as y'learn t'accept that I am nothing…but love. What ve preacher said was true. But we women. We know dat, we feel it, we live it. Ricky, we can't do naffink else! We ain't built to do naffink else! You men can hide it wiv your macho bullshit…" she was now in tears. "Wiv your 'got to be ve provarda' shit! Waddaya see in us? Naffink but devotion, tenderness, caring, affection, humility, strenff and beauty. The very essence of nature and the very beauty of creation, God's gift to this planet, God's gift to you! An waddaya do wiv it? Treat us lark ve very shit under y'feet. We can only love and when you turn you're backs on us … it hurts. Are had t'take Tanika away to prove somefink to you. Are fink y'know now what it feels lark t'be alone, to know what it feels lark when samone you lav makes aaht that they don't care. You took me vere Ricky an' arve been vere an ooful long tarm. Fings got so bad are had t'give my love to a no good, lowlife stinkin' natta that smoked his livelihood away on crack. Thas 'ow bad it got. Fought are could change him. Look where it put me. You learn t'respect where arm camin' from. Is the highest mountain to climb and is the deepest ocean to swim in. But ool are want, ool any woman wants ... is t'see you tryin'. Can you do that? Can you try f'me Ricky? Can you?"

Ricky's eyes had swelled with tears also. He was lost for words. She threw her arms around his neck and squeezed him tightly. Ricky pulled away from her, not too much but enough to stay locked and to see her face. She saw his tears and knew his response. She kissed him. He in turn locked his lips into hers. There was no more to be said. Shaniqua pulled away from him.

"I'm not goin' t'the reception. Are tode mar mam ard be back f'Tanika about now."

"I don't feel like going either," said Ricky.

"Cool," she said wiping a the tears from her face and raising a slight smile. "'Arm cookin' Ackee and Sootfish tonight. 'spect you at araand eight," she said, letting him go.

"Don't you need a lift?" he asked.

"Pablic transpoot mate," she smiled. "Eight o'clock."

Ricky stood alone and watched her walk away. His mind was in a daze. He beheld what she called God's gift to him as she slenderly eased her body through the graveyard. In an instant she was gone. He contemplated for a second. Breathed a heavy sigh and walked to his car. He registered a feeling in his breast that he had not known for a long time. He smiled gently to himself.

Claire sat at the table as the waiters served the food. Few of the black people at the funeral had come to the hotel that hosted he reception. Claire ate and chatted to her friends every now and then watching the main door to see if Ricky would arrive. It seemed that every male person that walked through the doors was Ricky. But she was continually disappointed. She longed to see him because she knew that their relationship had reached an end. She struggled not to be upset, reserving her feelings for her lost friend. But she yearned inside to see Ricky for the last time. After a while it became clear that he wouldn't. She breathed a heavy sigh and immediately forgave him.

sixteen

Claire woke up early. She had gone to bed quite late the night before and even though she couldn't sleep, she was up at the crack of dawn. She sat in the kitchen and had two cups of coffee and had a cigarette. She was clueless as to what she was going to do for the day. She considered shopping, but that thought sent a stale feeling right through her body. She thought about reading her new book that she had purchased a couple of weeks ago. But "Waiting to Exhale" somehow didn't have the pulling power that it once had. She hoped to receive a call from Emma, deciding that if she didn't call, she would give her a tinkle, just to see if she fancied joining her for the day. There was no getting away from the fact that there was a distinct feeling of emptiness about her life. She could easily have been drawn to sorrow, but she maintained her strength concluding that she had cried enough the day before. But she hadn't cried for Ricky. She knew that at some point she would. It was now 9am. A letter dropped delicately through the letterbox and onto the carpet. She picked it up, sliced the seal and read.

4th May 1998
Our ref.   DPADD021.1.kk   your ref.

Dear Mr Hinds

RE: Divorce proceedings Mrs C Flower and Mr P Flower
I write to inform you that my client, Mr P Flower, after thoroughly assessing the situation has concluded not to proceed with any of the actions outlined in my previous letter and is pleased to pursue the said divorce based on arrangements already outlined.
He offers your client his deepest condolences at the passing away of her friend and hopes that her future will be a fruitful and happy one. I look forward to hearing from you in the near future to secure arrangements for the divorce settlement.

Yours sincerely

D.Noble
Partner

Claire smiled at the gesture. She had wondered what it was that had come over Paul and what it was that had made him change his mind about her relationship with Ricky. Not that it mattered now, because there was no relationship to speak of. But she would ask him all the same when next she saw him. Claire went back into the kitchen and poured herself an orange juice. There was a knock at the door. She wondered whom it could be calling her at this early hour. Her eagerness got the better of her. She hoped it would be a request for her company in some kind of activity that would help her to take her mind off things. With that it mind she hastened to the door and pulled it open without checking through the spyhole as was her wont. She stood in cold shock at the sight that beheld her at the door. It was Ricky.

"Hi," he said quietly.

"Hi," she answered nervously. She composed herself, held out a hand and pulled the door open wider to signify her permission to come in. He did so tentatively.

Ricky wondered into the living room. He was clearly tense but Claire herself was in no position to offer him any form of consolation as she felt the very same way herself. She beckoned him to sit down, which he did. She sat down on the settee opposite him, pulling back her hair to make herself look more presentable.

"You've caught me at the wrong time," she said.

Ricky said nothing. He was businesslike and obviously wanted to talk. She caught the vibe and dispensed with the small talk that she had planned to engage in.

"So what brings you here?" she asked. "I have to admit, I didn't expect to see you again."

"I couldn't have just disappeared," he said.

"I'm glad you didn't," she replied.

Ricky leaned forward in the settee, clasped his hands together and looked at her longingly.

"I'm sorry," he said.

"For what?" Claire asked somewhat cynically.

"For loving somebody else," he replied.

"Is that something you should apologise for?" she asked again with sarcasm in her voice.

"Don't make this anymore difficult than it already is," he pleaded.

Claire apologised, then listened intently.

"I'm a better man for knowing you," he said. "I guess you restored my faith in white people," he said with a coy smile. Claire was unimpressed, but Ricky was determined to make his point. "I guess I always looked at you people with a degree of scepticism. I think that a lot of people do," he continued. "I wondered at how seriously you people really see life. Figured you were all just about treating this place like it was just one big playground and that you were all just a bunch of spoilt kids, acting out your perverse fantasies on a world that was … just so short of love. I blamed you for all the evil in the world, all the hardship, all the pain. I saw you as a greedy and selfish people, barbaric in your outlook and primitive in your approach and I guess I had history to back me up.

"But Claire, you shattered the illusion and I loved you for it. I saw that you wanted to learn about me and learn from me and I was happy to play that role. I saw that you wanted to know more about me and my people than what the media or society says about us. I saw that you were able to stretch yourself far beyond the realms of the reality, which we are given to chew on on a daily basis. I found that you have an eternal soul and that you mean to stay in touch with it and I know that you thought the same of me. I loved all that about you. It was so refreshing to see more than racism, decadence and pride, which is all I've ever had from white people and when I knew that you loved me, I felt that my life was complete. I never saw you as a prize, you know in the same way that some black guys see their white women. I never saw you as a meal ticket and I certainly never saw you as a benefactor. I never saw you as an inferior or a superior. I just loved everything about you because you opened my eyes to a lot more about this world than I had ever previously imagined. It wasn't about your looks, your body, your colour, your money. It was about you, and it was such a shock to me because you made me realise that I could fall in love with someone outside of my race and perhaps most of all, someone that was white. I didn't have to lose myself, I didn't have to sell out, I didn't have to change, I just had to be happy and that was a feeling that I had never known before. You took me to a different space and a different time."

"So what went wrong?" Claire asked gently. "Did the novelty cease?"

"No," said Ricky cautiously. "You just made me see all the right things in the woman that I truly want to be with."

"Glad to have been of help," said Claire, breaking into a flush of weeping.

"So am I," said Ricky. "And you should be too. I'm a better person for having known you Claire. You've bought me to a stage where I can't even lie anymore. I had to come and see you today. You deserve honesty. Please, Claire. It's the very best that I can do."

"And what about me?" Claire imposed though broken. "I lose. I did my best with you; I tried so hard to be sensitive to everything - all your hang ups, all your anxieties. But I'm the one that ends up losing."

"And you were sensitive to the end. You gave Shaniqua your blessing. Claire face it. All those things that I adore about you. It's the right stuff. My failing was that I saw those things in you before I saw them in Shaniqua. You know it's a failing that many of my people have. I have no qualms, no hang ups about your colour. But I am one of those people that needs to be with his own. For some reason, those good, loving qualities are so hard to see in black women and many of us think that they don't exist so we date white women. Meanwhile, many of our women are suffering. Some of them, they can't exist in a white world alone, they feel no strength from white society, no love, no comfort, no support. They need the love of a black man to see them through. They know nothing else and meanwhile we just let them down all the time. Someone has to give. At some point someone has to say 'hey, my people need me' and admit that we need them.

"I don't want to save the race but I need someone with whom I can feel some kind of affinity. What makes black people the way we are is oppression, struggle, and hard times. The good points and the bad, our pysche, our mentality, our outlook is developed by inordinate amount of suffering that we have experienced right throughout history. I need to be with someone with whom I can share my struggle and not someone who will simply help me to see the back of it and ultimately help me to believe that it's not there. I strive for love Claire. I strive to be loved, but I have to achieve it honestly and I am just not at a point where I can maintain a lifestyle that doesn't help me to grow in the context of my identity."

"So it is about identity?" challenged Claire.

"No. It's about achieving freedom," replied Ricky. "Culture and identity are assured traits that I have. I did my homework, regardless of the nationality of my partner, I know my history. I will forever face racism and discrimination whilst western society continues to believe in its false notion of superiority. That is what has grounded me. But I must be free. Free to chose my way of life, free to choose my own path and free to love whom I will for whatever reasons I feel are right. Though I will not bow to hatred. It sounds selfish I know, but those are the issues that have faced us all. Amanda, Emma, Ingin. What I feel so bad about is that you taught me these things Claire. You English people can be so reserved, but damn, there is something about you that just doesn't seem to give a fuck. Many of my people won't eat foreign foods; many of us won't dance when we go out. The black man's greatest gift to England has been expression. Your gift to us is the freedom to do it."

"But we enslaved you," said Claire with confusion.

"And you taught us democracy," Ricky replied. "You all seem to take it to some crazy extremes sometimes, but hell, it's in you. These are qualities that you Claire, have bought to my life in such a controlled and thoughtful way and I do thank you."

Claire rose to her feet. Ricky's words had been encouraging. Her heart told her not grieve and not to bear a grudge. She smiled. Ricky rose to his feet also. She put her arms around him and looked deeply into his eyes.

"And you taught me so much, my love," she said, her tone changed. "You showed me a higher plane of existence that is not a fleeting dream but is so within my grasp. A style of life that has existed since and even before creation. That so many of my people have mistaken as being unsophisticated and primitive but is simplicity itself because it bases itself upon truth, reality and love. You are the salt of the earth. And unlike most of my people I will give you homage whenever I recognise the heavenly host that resides within you. My freedom makes me not afraid of you, but loves you. Go to your woman and stay amongst the lofty peaks, whose refuge I shall continue to seek. And in the days of your bliss in the heavenly rhapsody that she will bring to you, remember me."

The hug was strong. There were no more words. Ricky approached the door and opened it. He gave her one last look and could not help himself for kissing her lips. She pulled him to and caressed her cheek against his. Then Claire let him go.

"Goodbye my love," she whispered discreetly and in an instant, he was gone. She moved over to the living room window and, drawing back the curtain, watched him as he jumped into his XR2. How debilitating, she thought. Those of her friends that never got to know him, in future conversations would refer to him simply as 'The Black Guy'.

epilogue

Nearly a year later Shaniqua sat up in the hospital bed that was situated in the centre of the delivery room. At 4am in the morning she was weary. The effects of the epidural that had been administered to her were just taking effect. She was beginning to feel high. Ricky sat by the bed, worried. Shaniqua was about to deliver their second child. She was meeting the challenge like a trooper. He was a nervous wreck. He rued the fact that this was their second child but his first appearance at the birth. He held on to Shaniqua's hand tighter. She turned her head slowly and smiled half-closed eyes at him. Their contemplation was broken by the sudden brash appearance of a young nurse who was clearly stressed.

"Does anyone speak French?" she asked hastily.

Shaniqua looked, lifted a tired finger and said softly "I do, a little."

The nurse approached her in a hurried but contrite manner.

"You couldn't help me could you?" she asked. "I have a Tunisian woman next door who'll deliver soon. Her husband just came and dumped her. He said would be back when the child was delivered. She can't speak a word of English and she's in an awful lot of pain. I just want to convince her to take an epidural. I could just wheel her in?"

"Sure," said Shaniqua with a compassionate nod of her head.

In seconds the woman was bought into the room. The nurse positioned her bed next to Shaniqua's so that they could talk. The woman looked afraid, but a loving smile and an outstretched hand from Shaniqua clearly calmed her. They exchanged a few words in French before the woman smiled and nodded her head at the nurse.

"Oh thank you so much," said the nurse excitedly.

"My pleasure," said Shaniqua

The nurse approached the back of the bed and wheeled the woman out again who threw Shaniqua a smile before she left the room.

"What did you say to her?" Asked Ricky curiously.

"Not much. I told her to look at me and see how relaxed I was."

Ricky smiled.

"Well, if nothing else, that course you're doing has come in handy already," he said.

Shaniqua wore a worried expression. She stretched out her hand and touched Ricky's.

"Babes," she said. "How am I going to get a degree in French and raise two children?"

Ricky released a breath of tired air.

"Baby, we discussed this already," he said. "The studio is paying me five hundred pounds a lick for the remixes that I'm doing and I already spoke to the manager. He's cool about me having a child around. Tanika'll be at the nursery and there's always your mum and mine. It'll be OK."

"I know," said Shaniqua. "But I just worry y'know?"

"Sure, but trust me. We'll make it. Handling pressure is what we're about. Now quit procrastinating and let's have this boy." Ricky stated.

"Girl," said Shaniqua assuredly.

Shaniqua stopped short and grabbed her stomach.

"The contractions are stronger! Oh God!" she bawled. "I think it's coming."

"Hold on," said Ricky, before shooting out of the room to fetch the doctor who had just left to see another patient. In seconds he had reappeared with the doctor and the nurse in tow. He resumed his seat and grabbed Shaniqua's hand who was by now screaming frantically. The Doctor and nurse prepared themselves hurriedly and positioned Shaniqua to deliver. They ordered her to push and for Ricky to hold her tightly. Shaniqua propelled her diaphragm northward to release the child. The sweat and pain on her face now vivid.

"It's OK baby," encouraged Ricky, whose heart was beating ten to the dozen.

Shaniqua focused harder at the task in hand, calling his name. He held her tighter.

"I can see the head. That's it, just a little more," said the doctor.

"Go on baby, one last push for me," encouraged Ricky.

Shaniqua let out her loudest and longest grunt of exertion as she raised her energy level. "That's it!" shouted the doctor, who reaching forward between her legs began to release the emerging child. In seconds the room was awash with the sound of a crying child. Shaniqua breathed frantically.

"It's a girl," said the nurse, who began immediately to clean the faeces that the child had emitted.

Shaniqua turned to Ricky and smiled. He was ecstatic and hugged her tightly, before the nurse who had cut the umbilical chord and wiped the baby clean, placed her in her mother's arms.

"Told you," said Shaniqua between breaths.

Ricky said nothing but wore a proud smile as he graciously beheld his new offspring.

"You gonna make this call?" asked Shaniqua remembering something. "She said she wanted to know the minute she was delivered."

Ricky jumped to his feet.

"Sure," he said counting his loose change and heading for the door.

"Ask her if she got the things," called Shaniqua to him just as he left the room.

Ricky raced down the hospital corridor and stopped at a payphone. Eagerly he placed a large number of coins in it, pulled out a piece of paper with a phone number scribbled on it, pressed an inordinate number of digits and waited.

"The Renaissance Hotel," came a distinctly American voice eventually.

"Room 356 please," Ricky asked.

"Thank you," came the reply.

Ricky waited some more. In the swanky Manhattan hotel room, Claire answered the phone.

"It's a girl," said Ricky excitedly.

"Oh brilliant!" said Claire, her anxiety clearly removed. "God. I've been pacing around this bloody room … you just ask her what took her so long. How heavy?"

"Forgot to ask."

"Typical man."

"She wants to know if you got the stuff."

"Oh for Christ's sake. Will you please just ask that crazy woman of yours how the hell I was supposed to know she was going to have a girl?"

"Because she told you she would."

"Well I'm going to do the last of my shopping tomorrow. Crazy prices believe me, and I'm just going to go wild on some of the most amazing kiddies designs that I've ever seen."

"Don't overdo it."

"Now that's my perogative. The money that she gave me will barely get a pair of booties. I'm rich, you're not. Now get off my case. Give her a big kiss for me and tell her congratulations and tell her when I get back, I'll be readily available for baby sitting."

"Will do. See you soon."

"Bye."

Claire replaced the receiver and lit a cigarette. She walked over to the large window overlooking the brilliant New York skyline. She took a puff and blew it in the air. She viewed the cigarette and stubbed it out, reminding herself that she wouldn't be able to smoke around a baby. She took a deep breath, released a huge breath and smiled, as an almost eerie image of a smiling Amanda, holding her little one, appeared across the sky.

BRINGING US CLOSER TOGETHER

SINCERITY *'PLUS'*

Networking, Social Events, Dating, Bi-Monthly Newsletter, Black Business Directory, International Contacts, Community Development etc....

Mission Statement: "All we have to do is look around us, we can clearly see what is wrong. In our strive for self-fulfilment we all come across various problems of both personal and cultural nature and the fact remains now as it did centuries ago that we are nothing as individuals, but we are everything as people, working to achieve a common goal." Happiness !!!!!!!!!!!!!! this is our aim.

The Business Exchange
43 Temple Row
Birmingham
B2 5LJ
Tel: 0121 643 8899
Fax: 0121 631 2167
E-Mail: sincerityplus@hotmail.com
Web Site: www.sincerityplus.com